SCREAMING STEEL

Chen Shao lifted the compact electronic binoculars to his eyes and trained them on the shadowy form of a *Vindicator* that seemed to be struggling to reach his position. In the late evening dusk, it was almost impossible to see the dark gray 'Mech, but low-light binoculars lit up the gloom. The thermographic viewing circuits built into the binoculars flared brightly, telling him that the old forty-five-ton BattleMech was running close to redline. It was part of Shao's operational plan to stop the old-design 'Mech before it sighted the lights of Touchstone spaceport.

Shao swung a boom microphone up in front of his lips. "Hit him."

A pair of glowing rockets leapt out of a low cluster of bushes, arcing toward the 'Mech's angular chest. The *Vindicator* pilot saw the small, fiery wasps arrowing toward his machine and tried to wrench its torso around to face his attacker. At the same time, he kicked the gangly 'Mech into a lunging run. The combination of motions was disastrous. The *Vindicator* stumbled, then reeled. The scream of a gyro pushed beyond its limitations cut across the muddy field. . . .

BATTLETECH®

DAGGER POINT

Thomas S. Gressman

A ROC BOOK

ROC
Published by New American Library, a division of
Penguin Putnam Inc., 375 Hudson Street,
New York, New York 10014, U.S.A.
Penguin Books Ltd, 27 Wrights Lane,
London W8 5TZ, England
Penguin Books Australia Ltd, Ringwood,
Victoria, Australia
Penguin Books Canada Ltd, 10 Alcorn Avenue,
Toronto, Ontario, Canada M4V 3B2
Penguin Books (N.Z.) Ltd, 182–190 Wairau Road,
Auckland 10, New Zealand

Penguin Books Ltd, Registered Offices:
Harmondsworth, Middlesex, England

First published by Roc, an imprint of New American Library,
a division of Penguin Putnam Inc.

First Printing, April 2000
10 9 8 7 6 5 4 3 2 1

Series Editor: Donna Ippolito
Mechanical Drawings: Duane Loose and the FASA art department
Cover art by Peter Peebles

 REGISTERED TRADEMARK—MARCA REGISTRADA

PUBLISHER'S NOTE
This is a work of fiction. Names, characters, places, and incidents either are
the product of the author's imagination or are used fictitiously, and any
resemblance to actual persons, living or dead, business establishments,
events, or locales is entirely coincidental.

To Erin Chapman and Wesley James Chapman.
It was my privilege to know Donn Wes.
He was my friend, and it is to his life
and his memory that this book is dedicated.

ACKNOWLEDGMENTS

The author extends his thanks to all those who have contributed their time, effort, and expertise toward the creation of this novel. A grateful nod to those unnamed authorities who contributed their knowledge in the area of low-intensity warfare, as though there could be such a thing. Thanks to Donna Ippolito for all her efforts. Likewise, thanks to Brenda for putting up with my choice of professions.

And as always, thank You, Lord.

Detail of the Inner Sphere
Circa 3062

Coreward
Anti-spinward — Spinward
Rimward

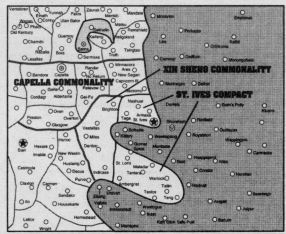

Ventabren Elnath Yunnah Palos Zaurak Menkib Mandate Moravian Smolensk
Wazan Corey Ulan Bator Matsu Perkasie
Phalo Bakhtin Remshield Lée Kathil
Old Kentucky Quemoy Kaifeng Heligoland Orbisonia Moriongahela
Chamdo Sarna Tsingtao Carmen Daïfzin
Racalla Bora Sarmaxa Truth
Lesalles Randar Minnacora XIN SHENG COMMONALITY
Bandora Capella Ares New Sagan
CAPELLA COMMONALITY No Return Capricorn III Monhegan Bethel
Cordiag Gellar Aldertaine Relevow Necromo **ST. IVES COMPACT**
Gei-Fu Nashuar Daniels Sonn's Polly
Preston Ovan Overton Brighton Taga St. Ives Shoreham Redfield Quittacas Kluane
Glasgow Vestallas Armaxis Weetabgdog Royalston Wappingers
Harloc Milos Soltatis Carmack
Sian Hexare Denbar Xittery Mandassa Happsproing Altes
Imalda New Westin Quintel Spica Corella Neretian
Castrovia Hustaing St. Loris Maladar Bold
Claxton Decus Purvo Indicass Tantara Warlock Hadnall Boonleigh
Carmen Ambergrist Textos Tallin Teng
Ito Sendalor Urzavan Wastogue Avigait Jaipur
Housekarle Zisling Ixast Bacum
Latice Homestead Immenstadt Kaln Siän Safe Port
Wright Manapire

ST. IVES COMPACT
and Surrounding Area

© 3062 COMSTAR CARTOGRAPHIC CORPS

LEGEND

8 PARSECS

MAXIMUM JUMP APPROXIMATELY 30 LIGHT YEARS
FOR NAVIGATIONAL PURPOSES USE 9 PARSECS = 29.34 L.Y.

1

Eridani Light Horse Command Center
Fort Winston, Dieron
Al Na'ir Prefecture
Draconis Combine
15 July 3061

"**E**xcuse me, gentlemen, but may I assume that this is not merely a social visit?" said Lieutenant General Edwin Amis. It was not every day such men came calling on the Eridani Light Horse—or on anybody else, for that matter.

"As a matter of fact, General," returned Victor Davion, with the briefest flash of amusement, "it's not."

Amis caught the look, but he knew Davion wasn't one to take offense at a busy commander's bluntness. Even less so now that he'd lost his own throne.

Victor glanced around the office admiringly. "It

looks like the Light Horse is just about settled in here," he said, sitting back comfortably in the padded chair facing Amis's desk.

"That's right, sir." Amis couldn't resist a smile of satisfaction. He liked the new Light Horse base here on Dieron, and was proud to command a fort named for Ariana Winston. "Things are definitely coming along." He kept his tone casual, but couldn't help wondering what the hell was going on. His two visitors had just arrived from Luthien on their way to the Second Star League Conference on Tharkad. Did they really detour all the way to Dieron to sit and make polite chatter?

Something obviously was up, but the imperturbable gaze of Theodore Kurita, Amis's other visitor, gave nothing away. It was Theodore, ruler of the Draconis Combine, who had offered the Light Horse the location for their new base. "It seems most fitting that a unit with such strong links to the old Star League should occupy one of the few original Star League bases to survive to see the League reborn," he said.

Davion nodded agreement. "Being posted here at the center of the Inner Sphere, the Light Horse can much more easily deploy wherever needed." He paused, glanced briefly at Theodore, then back to Amis. "And that, General Amis, brings me to the purpose of our visit—to discuss the current status of your brigade."

Amis figured there was more, but decided to let things take their course. "Well, sir, as of right now, we've got four regiments under arms. Two of those, the Twenty-first Striker and the One Fifty-first Light

Horse, are at pretty close to full strength. At most, down a company or two each. The Seventy-first Light Horse are a bit short-handed. The Nineteenth is the worst off. They're down a full battalion."

Davion had been listening intently. "You took heavy casualties on Huntress," he said. As second in command of the allied campaign to defeat the Clans, he had witnessed first-hand the price of annihilating Clan Smoke Jaguar.

Amis nodded sadly. The Light Horse had buried General Ariana Winston in the soil of Huntress, alongside the other Light Horsemen who'd died in the bitter fighting. "That's right, sir. We lost about half of our overall strength. We've been able to make up most of that with new recruits who graduated from the training program while we were gone. And, thanks to your generous offer of first salvage, sir, most of our losses in 'Mechs were offset by captured Clan equipment."

Amis fished a thin, black cigar out of his breast pocket. "May I?" he asked as a courtesy. The brigade already owed plenty to both of his visitors, not the least of which was respect.

He cut and lit the cigar. "I've shuffled our more experienced troopers around a bit, moving them into command slots to preserve the tactical and strategic integrity of the outfit." He blew a thin stream of blue smoke into the air. "I've given command of my old regiment to Eveline Eicher, one of Colonel Barclay's people, and promoted her to Colonel. She's got the Twenty-first now. I've given the reins of the Nineteenth to Paul Calvin, and bumped him up to Colonel, too.

"The only real problem is that the Light Horse is a combined arms brigade. Our 'Mech, fighter, and infantry arms are pretty much intact. But we lost almost all of our AFVs and most of our arty on Huntress. We have yet to make them up out of the refit and replacement pools."

"How bad off are you?" Theodore asked. Neither he nor Davion needed any explanation of the military slang for armored fighting vehicles and artillery.

Amis gave a slight shrug. "Not so good, as far as the vehicles go." He looked over at Gregory Ostroff, the Light Horse Training Commandant, who had been standing in a stiff, formal "at ease" posture slightly behind the seated group.

"You tell 'em, Greg," Amis said, beckoning the major forward.

Ostroff approached, but maintained his rigid military bearing. "We're at about forty percent of our normal complement, sirs. Our artillery arm is actually in better shape, about sixty percent. The problem is that we lost all of our heavy guns on Huntress. Seems like the Clanners hate the idea of long-range artillery. Some of our cannon-cockers who were captured and later released told me that the Jags would turn their beam lasers and PPCs on the gun tubes and melt them to slag. We've had to replace almost all of our Long Toms with Snipers and Thumpers."

"Don't forget the Pathfinders," Amis said, grinning at Ostroff around his cigar.

"How can I, sir?" Ostroff's reply carried with it a note of formal stiffness. "Neither you nor Colonel Antonescu will allow me to forget them."

"Pathfinders?" Theodore asked.

Amis turned to him. "I wasn't aware of their existence either until we got back from Huntress, Coordinator. It seems that General Winston was so impressed
with your Draconis Elite Strike Teams and the Rabid
Fox commandoes that she sent a coded message to
the Light Horse before we jumped out for Clan space.
Her instructions were that Major Ostroff should
begin to recruit, train, and equip a small body of
special-operations troops. The company is now
attached to my Command Company."

Ostroff frowned slightly. "Yes, and Colonel Antonescu isn't very pleased about it."

Amis looked from Ostroff back to his two visitors.
"Colonel Antonescu, and a few others in the Light
Horse, feel that the inclusion of such special-purpose
troopers in our TO&E 'dilutes the brigade's adherence to the lofty ideals of the Star League and our
hard-won traditions of fair and honorable combat'."
He made it clear that he was quoting someone else's
speech, learned by rote from many hearings.

"You know that I tend to agree with him, sir,"
Ostroff said.

"I know that, Greg, but the face of warfare is
changing. The days of full-blown, stand-up and slug-
it-out fights are going the way of the dinosaur. I'm
hoping that, with the rebirth of the Star League, most
military actions are going to be low-intensity con-
flicts. If that happens, then the Pathfinders may serve
us a lot better than the average line-of-battle 'Mech
jockey."

"If you say so, sir." Ostroff declined to continue
what had become a long-standing argument.

"Greg, I appreciate your assistance," Amis said,

guessing that his visitors would never get to the point until they had more privacy. "That will be all for now. You're dismissed, Major."

Amis puffed on his cigar as he waited for Ostroff to shut the door behind him. Then he sat up straight and looked both men squarely in the eye.

"Now, gentlemen," he said, "you didn't come all the way to Dieron just to check on my TO&E."

"No, General," Davion said, "that's not the sole reason we're here. There is more to it than that. We came to talk about what's been going on in the St. Ives Compact. Sun-Tzu has sent Star League Defense Force troops as 'peace-keepers' into the region, but it's pure sham. He's basically using the SLDF to reclaim the Compact worlds for the Capellan Confederation."

Victor leaned forward in his chair and met Amis's eyes. "We've got to stop him, and that's why we're here. Theodore-*san* and I have some ideas on how to do that, and we need your help."

Amis was speechless, but for only an instant. "Sir, excuse me, but are you aware of what you're saying?" Amis stared at Victor Davion in shock. "You're asking the Eridani Light Horse, a Star League unit, to take up arms against the lawful First Lord of the Star League."

Theodore answered instead. "Sun-Tzu Liao will not be First Lord by the time you go into action."

"That's a pretty thin line to argue on," Amis shot back.

"*Hai*, it is," Theodore agreed. "But then, so are Sun-Tzu's reasons for going into the Compact in the first place. He claims that its worlds have become

increasingly unstable and that its citizens are dissatis-
fied under the rule of his aunt Candace. He says that
her armed forces were on the brink of mutiny, and
that only the arrival of SLDF 'peace-keepers' into the
Compact kept open rebellion from breaking out. He
pretends he's trying to prevent bringing down the
Star League."

"Isn't that what you're asking me to do, Coordinator?" Amis asked.

"No, General. I'm asking you to protect and defend the League as you swore to do. It's taken three
hundred years to put the Star League back together.
Do you want to see history repeat itself and let another power-mad dictator destroy it again?"

"That's not what I want, Coordinator, but the brigade is one of the core units of the SLDF. What you
suggest would bring us dishonor."

The room had become absolutely quiet, the only
sounds coming from the busy grounds around the
command center. Amis thought there was really
nothing more he could say. The traditions of the
Light Horse were known far and wide across the
Inner Sphere. The restoration of the Star League had
been their beacon for three centuries.

Theodore nodded slowly. "Once, General, I faced
a similar choice, a time in my life I shall never forget.
I was torn between a son's duty to his father and my
duty to protect the Combine. Which was the greater
obligation? It was only in remembering the teachings
of my *sensei* that the way became clear. Duty is a
curious river, Tetsuhara-*sensei* used to say, it flows
uphill as well as down."

Theodore paused as though waiting for Amis to

speak. Finally he broke the silence again. "As First Lord of the Star League, Sun-Tzu's duty is to preserve it for the good of the many, not to abuse his position to plot and scheme to usurp that power. He himself fomented the unrest he says he is trying to calm—through staged incidents, carefully worded and inflammatory speeches, and thinly veiled threats. Despite all of his high-sounding rhetoric, Sun-Tzu's only goal has been to reclaim the St. Ives worlds the Capellans lost thirty years ago. And he's succeeding, at the cost of the lives and freedom of those living in the Compact."

Silence lay heavy in the room once more. None of this was news to Amis. It was true he'd been preoccupied with internal Light Horse matters since returning from Clan space, but not so much that he'd lost all his sense. He didn't like the fact that there were so many changes in the Inner Sphere while its best warriors were off fighting and dying in Clan space—too far away to know what was happening back home, much less do anything about it.

"If you want out, General," Victor said, "we'll understand."

"Now, hold on, dammit!" Amis snapped. "I didn't say I wanted out. I just said it was a thin line to walk." He stood up so quickly he almost knocked over his chair. To buy some time to sort out his thoughts, he walked over to the window and stared out at the grounds below. Which was his highest duty—to the First Lord or to the Star League? Seeing his people going to and fro as they worked to make a home on a world populated by their one-time enemy seemed to underline what Theodore had been saying.

The Star League didn't stand for anything if it didn't stand for unity. First Lord or no, Sun-Tzu's actions were a threat to that unity.

He turned back toward Theodore and Victor, his mind made up.

"So what'll it be, General?" asked Victor.

Amis looked at Theodore. "Your *sensei* was a wise man, Coordinator. Duty does sometimes flow uphill as well as down. My Light Horse is ready whenever you are."

Victor stood quickly, grinning from ear to ear. He thrust out his hand to shake Amis's. "You won't regret this, General, I promise you. If you meant what you just said, I need you to move to Kittery now. From there, two of your regiments will be sent on to your objective. The others will remain on Kittery as a strategic reserve."

Amis returned the handshake, a bit startled by the speed at which events were moving. "And where exactly will my two regiments be going, sir?"

Victor's blue eyes again briefly flashed amusement. "The objective is Milos, General, a little backwater world in the St. Ives Compact that could turn out to be a lot more important than it seems." He leaned forward to place a notebook computer on Amis's desk. He tapped its power stud, and a map of the St. Ives compact bled onto the screen. One planet was highlighted in gold; several others glowed a bright scarlet.

"As you can see, Milos is only two jumps or less from such vital Capellan worlds as Relevow, Hustaing, and Harloc. In fact, Milos could easily serve as a staging area for an assault on Capella or even the

Confederation capital on Sian. In effect, dropping the Eridani Light Horse into Milos will be like pointing a dagger at Sun-Tzu's throat."

Amis whistled. "That ought to slow him down some," he said, then couldn't help a sideways glance at Theodore Kurita.

"Is there a problem, General?"

"Well, yessir, there is, begging your pardon," Amis said slowly. "I mean no offense, Coordinator, but you know that the Light Horse has sort of a history with the Draconis Combine."

"Yes, General," Theodore replied darkly. "I am aware that your brigade still holds a grudge against the Combine for the massacre of your dependents, but that was long ago."

"It was," Amis said. "That's one of the problems with traditions, though. They help you remember who you are and where you came from, but they can also keep old wounds from closing. If I try to move the entire brigade off planet, I'm gonna have trouble, especially with the Fiftieth Heavy Cavalry and Eighth Recon battalions. They've got the greatest sense of responsibility to our civilians—to any civilians, come to that."

"Precisely, General. That is one of the reasons we chose your brigade for this mission. You have just that tradition of protecting innocents and non-combatants." Victor recovered the notebook computer and began tapping commands into its keyboard. He beckoned Theodore in close for a whispered consultation before continuing.

"Very well, General, how about this? If you want to leave one of your regiments here to protect your civilians, that should pose no real problem to the operation."

"That might work," Amis said, thinking aloud. "With all the new replacements she's got, Sandy Barclay's Seventy-first Light Horse is still too green for something like this. They can stay here on Dieron. The One Fifty-first Light Horse and the Nineteenth Cavalry go with me to Milos, and the Twenty-first Striker stays on Kittery. Though Major Fairfax and Captain Ribic aren't going to be pleased about having to leave our civvies behind. Yeah, that's it. Now, you were saying, sir?"

"You will receive the balance of your strategic and intelligence briefing once you get to Kittery," Victor said. "By the time you move on Milos, Sun-Tzu will no longer be First Lord. The new First Lord will almost certainly want to take steps to redress the St. Ives situation, so you will not be acting against the will of the Star League."

"And what if the new First Lord doesn't want to redress the situation?" Amis asked thoughtfully.

Victor and Theodore exchanged an odd look, then Victor said, "Oh, I think we can guarantee that the new First Lord will want to take those steps, can't we, Theodore-*san*?"

2

The heavy cloud cover looked low enough for *Sang-shao* Samuel Christobal of McCarron's Armored Cavalry to reach up and brush his fingers across its lead-colored underside. Until just a few days ago the skies over Touchstone, Milos's planetary capital and primary spaceport, had been a clear, high, blue vault, brushed with thin white clouds. Then, just as his regiment received its orders to ship out for a new assignment—a combat assignment—the weather closed in.

Across the black, rainswept macadam of the spaceport, Christobal watched the gray- and green-mottled shape of an eighty-five-ton *Stalker* BattleMech line itself up with the *Overlord*'s gaping 'Mech bay door, then maneuver its hulk up the ramp. He and his regiment were loading up their transport DropShips in preparation for pulling out of Milos. Christobal still did not know their precise destination, but that was no surprise in the security-conscious Capellan Confederation Armed Forces. More than likely they would head to St. Loris to link up with the rest of his regiment.

Sun-Tzu Liao, Chancellor of the Capellan Confederation was withdrawing the Star League peace-keepers from the Xin Sheng Commonality and replacing them with regular Capellan forces. That was not yet public knowledge, and Christobal thought probably the Chancellor would announce the troop movements at the Second Whitting Conference, which would begin in a few days.

Christobal's regiment had been sent to Milos as part of Sun-Tzu's bid to reclaim the region now known as the St. Ives Compact, which had seceded from the Confederation some years ago. The Chancellor had sent troops into the Compact, under the aegis of Star League Defense Force peace-keepers. Ostensibly, they were to quell civil unrest, which his own agents had fomented. On some worlds, Milos included, the inhabitants had welcomed the "peace-keepers." On others the people resisted the occupation of their homeworlds. In one instance, the rebels on Wei had used a horrific nerve gas against the Nightriders, another of McCarron's units. A full battalion of elite troops died without a single shot being fired.

Having pacified most of the occupied worlds, the Chancellor named the region the Xin Sheng Commonality, after his reform program by that name. Christobal's new rank, *Sang-shao*, was also the result of the Capellanization process. The title was equivalent to Colonel.

He had also been hearing that many of the mainline combat units currently occupying pacified worlds were being rotated to the front where the fighting against the St. Ives forces was beginning to bog down. With the exception of a few scattered guerrilla raids, Milos was one of those peaceful worlds, so Christobal surmised that he and his men were being sent to where the "real war" was. He relished the idea of seeing combat once again, where a good commander acted, rather than reacted to what he viewed as criminal attacks staged by partisans and guerrillas.

With a shrug, he turned his attention back to the loading of his regiment's 'Mechs. The *Stalker* was almost halfway up the ramp when a dull, yellow-white flash lit up the clumsy-looking machine's right side. A second stroboscopic flare blossomed against the *Stalker*'s armor even as the first faded. A pair of odd, flat bangs followed a few seconds later, carried across the kilometer's distance by the rain- and snow-laden wind.

"Dammit all!" he spat, recognizing the sound of detonating anti-armor missiles. He fumbled beneath the voluminous folds of his marginally effective poncho, finally extracting a hand-held personal communicator from the nylon pouch at his left hip.

"Comm center, this is Christobal. What the hell is going on out there?"

Before the technician manning the communications

center could reply, the hollow rattle of heavy machine-gun fire echoed faintly through the dripping air. The deeper bark of an autocannon spoke in reply. From the tiny parking area beneath the spaceport's observation deck, a pair of Blizzard hover transports streaked off across the tarmac. Their passage blew the puddles of standing rain and snow-melt into a fine mist, while the piercing keen of their lift fans set Christobal's teeth on edge. The shriek blanketed the comm center's reply.

"Say again, comm center!" Christobal shouted.

"I say again. *Sao-wei* Fuller reports guerrilla activity along the eastern perimeter," the tech repeated. "He says it looks like a reinforced infantry platoon. He doesn't think there are any 'Mechs in the area, but he can't be sure. So far all they've done is fire a few shoulder-launched missiles and rake the compound with small-arms fire. *Sang-wei* Arai has already scrambled our own infantry to try to track them down. He wants to know if he should send in BattleMechs as well."

"No!" Christobal bellowed into the communicator, his voice cracking with anger. "We don't know if the guerrillas are just trying to draw us out or not. God only knows what they've got hidden out there. Tell Arai that he is to move his company up to the perimeter fence, and no further. Tell him I'm on my way out there. I'll decide what to do when I can see for myself what's going on."

With a frustrated snarl, Christobal jerked the cumbersome poncho over his head and threw it to the ground.

He'd rather be wet than wear that damn canvas

strait-jacket one minute longer. Yelling for his driver, Christobal ran to his hover jeep and vaulted into the front passenger seat. At least this would give him some cover from the rain.

A few minutes later, the jeep skidded to a stop in the lee of the *Overlord*'s armored hull. A pair of MAC infantrymen hunkered there, waiting for him, their weapons held at the low-ready, pointing off in the direction of the enemy. Christobal yanked his side-arm from its holster and leapt from the jeep. A few long strides and he was alongside the infantrymen.

"Where is *Sang-wei* Arai?" he snapped.

"In his 'Mech, sir." One of the troopers pointed across the tarmac at a slab-torsoed *Cataphract*, which was standing brazenly out in the open, as though daring the partisans to take a shot at it. The seventy-ton war machine's armor was thick enough to withstand a first strike from nearly any BattleMech ever built, and could slough off small-arms fire as easily as it did the steadily falling rain.

Taking up his comm unit once again, Christobal adjusted the frequency and called, "Arai?"

"Yessir?"

"What is the situation here?"

"Can't say for certain, sir. Looks like the guerrillas were following their usual pattern: sneak up to the fence, fire off a few rounds, and pull out before we can mount a defense." Contempt for the guerrillas' hit-and-run tactics was plain in Arai's voice. "Some of my foot-sloggers think they located their positions, though. They found a few spots where it looks like someone touched off a missile launcher, and the back-blast scorched the ground a bit. It's too hard to tell, sir. The rain is wiping out tracks almost as soon as they're made. What do you want me to tell them, sir?"

Before Christobal could reply, a deep, whining roar sounded out of the mist. Shards of reinforced steel flew off the *Cataphract*'s shoulder as tracer rounds smashed into the big machine's heavy armor, followed by another missile volley streaking toward the *Cataphract*. Instead of impacting with the 'Mech, the projectiles burst, spewing gouts of burning petrochemicals. Fortunately, most of the Inferno fuel missed Arai's machine, falling instead on the ferrocrete landing stage. Some of the napalm spattered on the *Cataphract*'s armor. Christobal did not have to imagine the sudden wave of heat that flooded into the 'Mech's interior. Inferno rounds were not intended to destroy a 'Mech, but to cause it to overheat and shut down. They had the side effect of often killing the pilot by roasting him in his cockpit.

To Christobal, it seemed that Arai failed to notice the flames and heat. Instead, the heavy 'Mech's torso rotated a few degrees to the left. A tongue of flame a meter long leapt from the machine's side. As Arai unleashed the Mydron dual-purpose autocannon mounted just above the *Cataphract*'s right hip, Christobal briefly glimpsed the shape of an *Enforcer* bearing the crest of the Second Blackwind Lancers through the falling rain. Arai's burst of cannon-fire laced the gangly 'Mech's torso and arms. Then a gust of wind drove the cold rain into Christobal's face. By the time his vision cleared, the enemy machine had vanished.

Other McCarron's Armored Cavalry 'Mechs were

beginning to join in the fray. At the same moment, the hail of fire coming from outside the spaceport dramatically slackened and stopped.

"*Sang-shao*, this is Arai," came the MechWarrior's voice over Christobal's communicator. "They've pulled out, sir, this time for real, I think. But you never can tell with these guerrillas. What do you want me to do, sir?"

Christobal spat an unprintable curse on the guerrillas before he remembered that his men were watching.

"Okay, *Sang-wei* send out a patrol. A couple of medium lances should do it. Don't let them go too far from home. I don't want the guerrillas to get a chance to pick off an isolated patrol."

Switching channels, Christobal passed fresh orders to the communications center.

"Let's double the number of pickets," he instructed the officer of the day. "And see if we can scrounge up any more remote sensors. It seems that the bad guys are down to harassment attacks, but, even at that, they can still hurt us.

"The guerrillas are going to be someone else's problem soon, and I'd rather not lose any of our own people to them if we can avoid it."

3

The doors to the Touchstone spaceport's passenger lounge swung silently open, admitting a small knot of uniformed men and women. From his place near the large windows overlooking the tarmac, Samuel Christobal watched the new arrivals strolling across the empty lounge.

In the lead was a man so nondescript that he seemed terribly familiar although Christobal was convinced he had never seen the man before. Christobal had often heard of the legendary "gray man," a person so characterless he could not be picked out of a group of people, though the one making the choice had spent several hours alone in that person's company. Now here before him was the embodiment of that legend.

The man was a trifle below average height. His short black hair framed the strong oriental features common to the upper social classes of the Capellan Confederation. He was clad in the dark gray-green combat fatigues of the CCAF. His rank insignia proclaimed the newcomer to be a *Zhong-shao*. Technically, Christobal outranked the man stalking purposefully across the lounge, but he knew that the technicality would not stand up long.

Pinned to the Capellan officer's left breast pocket was a tiny silver skull. The small device, so easy to miss, proclaimed him as a member of the elite Death Commandos. Among the finest warriors in the Confederation, they were certainly the most loyal. Before entering active duty, each Commando swore a "blood oath" of personal fealty to the Chancellor. The price of breaking that oath was death at the hands of his own comrades. In addition to the military skills common to the rest of the military, the Death Commandos were given training in espionage, intelligence-gathering and analysis, sabotage, and other less pleasant subjects. Many were highly skilled MechWarriors or aerospace or starship pilots. Christobal knew without being told that this was his replacement officer.

Behind this "gray man" walked a woman with blue eyes and shoulder-length, dark blonde hair that should have made her attractive, but for some reason did not. Of the small group that trailed the Death Commando officer across the lounge, she was the only one not wearing the uniform of the CCAF. A baggy off-tan work shirt showed beneath a standard Capellan fatigue jacket. A pair of obviously foreign-made black denim trousers were tucked into a pair of Lyran-issue black combat boots. The open display of the contraband denims spoke more about her than the company she kept. She had absolutely no fear that her possession of goods specifically forbidden by Capellan law would cause her even the slightest bit of trouble. A cotton scarf printed in jungle camouflage colors was wrapped around her throat. She clutched a heavy, black metal case in her right hand.

The woman caught Christobal's stare and returned it with the unblinking intensity of a doll's lifeless gaze. It was then that he realized what marred her moderate good looks. She had the emptiest eyes he had ever seen.

"*Sang-shuo* Christobal? I am *Zhong-shao* Chen Shao, commanding the 116th Home Guard Regiment. I am your relief officer, sir." The Death Commando performed a short, crisp bow.

Christobal started. He had been so absorbed in the woman's appearance that he hadn't noticed Shao stepping up to where he sat.

"Ah, er, yes," he managed at last, surging hastily to his feet.

"*Sang-shao* Samuel Christobal, MacCarron's Armored Cavalry," he blurted, trying desperately to recover his manners and composure. "Welcome to Milos, *Zhong-shao*."

A flicker of pleasure crossed Shao's eyes. It seemed to Christobal that the man had intended for his sudden appearance to disconcert him all along.

"May I present my adjutant? This is *Sao-wei* Claus Basara." A sandy-haired young man stepped forward, bowed, and extended his right hand toward Christobal, who took it out of courtesy and of a need for a gesture upon which to rebuild his poise. Like Shao, the *Sao-wei* was clad in the uniform of the CCAF. Unlike his commander, Basara did not wear the emblem of the Death Commandos.

"Glad to make your acquaintance, *Sang-shao*," Basara said with a wide grin. "Don't let the *Zhong-shao* frighten you too much. Sometimes I think he likes playing on the reputation of the Death Commandos just to put a scare into folks."

Shao groaned softly and rolled his eyes. In that simple gesture of long-suffering frustration with a subordinate's non-military antics, he was transformed from an object of uneasy fear to just a regular person. The woman did not seem capable of any such humanizing actions. She gave Basara and Christobal both an icy glare.

"My forces are on their way in, even as we speak," Shao said, forcing Christobal's attention back to the business at hand. "We're just Home Guard, so we don't have any major needs. I've got a single battalion of BattleMechs, one tank, and one jump infantry battalion. I assume the local garrison post will be big enough to house us?"

"Yes, sir." Christobal nodded. He was glad to have routine things like troop strength and the size of the billet needed to distract him from the nature of the man standing before him. "The garrison is on the north edge of the spaceport. It's big enough to house a brigade, so it should be more than adequate for your needs."

"Thank you, *Sang-shao*." Shao paused and smiled broadly, revealing small, even teeth. "Listen, *Sang-shao*. It's true that I'm a Death Commando, but I'm not going to eat you alive. Most of the veteran 'Mech commanders are needed at the front. When Milos was declared secure, they wanted someone to take command of the 116th, and I got picked. My specialty is working with local forces, training planetary militias, that sort of thing."

"Okay," Christobal said with a short, self-conscious chuckle. "Well, then, *Zhong-shao*, I formally pass command of the Milos garrison to you and to the 116th Home Guard Regiment. Do you want me to stay on awhile, until your troops arrive?"

"No, *Sang-shao*. That shouldn't be necessary." Shao smiled again. "Go ahead and join your troops. I only wish that I were coming with you, rather than being stuck here on this forsaken rock."

Christobal pulled himself to attention and returned Shao's salute.

"Thank you, *Zhong-shao*. Enjoy your stay on Milos."

"Thank you, *Sang-shao*. Good luck, and victory."

Without another word, Christobal turned away from his relief officer and walked quietly out of the lounge. As the doors were swinging closed behind him, he contemplated Chen Shao's friendliness, a trait he found surprising in a fearsome Death Commando. It was then that Samuel Christobal realized that no matter how broad Shao's smiles were, they never touched his eyes.

*   *   *

"Fool!" Basara spat the word as the lounge doors drifted shut behind the withdrawing Armored Cavalry officer.

"Yes, but a necessary fool, Claus," Shao agreed. In the handful of seconds required for the lounge doors to close in Christobal's wake, the false front of good-natured camaraderie had evaporated from both men like coolant in an over-taxed heat sink. "Now we must set about our assignment. What does the Maskirovka have to report about the dissidents of Milos?"

For a moment, Basara cocked his head to one side, as though listening to a voice that only he could hear. Shao knew that Basara had a eidetic memory. As an operative of the Cultural Monitoring Section of the Capellan Confederation's intelligence service, he had been extensively briefed on the political, social, and cultural climate on Milos. The cocked-head posture was an affectation.

"There are surprisingly few dissidents to be found, *Zhong-shao*," Basara said at last. "Perhaps the most vocal is Doctor Rawley Markotan, of the University of Touchstone. He seems to fancy himself one of the more advanced thinkers on the planet, if not in the entire Xin Sheng Commonality. Ever since the Chancellor began his 'new Capellan effort' program, Doctor Markotan has been speaking out against the Confederation. Even before the campaign to reclaim our occupied territories in St. Ives began, he was railing against what he called 'the militarization of the border.' As the campaign to reclaim our rebellious worlds began to see success, he reduced the number of his speeches while increasing the intensity of his rhetoric. Now that Milos is back in our hands, Markotan has all but ceased to speak in public. When he does, his words drip with venom aimed at the Confederation in general and at the Chancellor in particular. All gentle efforts to persuade him to amend his views have failed. In addition, there are rumors, fairly well-substantiated rumors, of the doctor giving aid and comfort to anti-Capellan partisans."

Shao sat down in the chair recently vacated by Christobal, leaned back, steepled his fingers, and closed his eyes. For several minutes he remained there, immobile.

"Nessa?" He said quietly, without opening his eyes.

The blond-haired, empty-eyed woman turned to look at the Death Commando leader but did not speak. For a moment, the cold stare appeared to soften. He seemed to sense her gaze and continued.

"I think that Doctor Rawley Markotan presents a clear and present danger to the Capellan state, one worthy of your special talents. We have an opportunity here to set an example for any who might take courage from his reckless and traitorous attitude."

"Yes," the woman answered softly. Without another word or sign passing between them, she nodded in Shao's direction, hefted her heavy metal case, and slipped noiselessly from the lounge.

"Uufffh." Basara shivered as the doors closed behind her. "*Zhong-shao*, I am not ashamed to admit it. That woman frightens me."

"Claus," Shao said in a reproving tone. "You have absolutely no reason to be frightened of Nessa Ament. She is no danger to you, or to me, or to any other loyal citizen of the Capellan Confederation."

Shao sat up and opened his eyes, gazing intently into his subordinate's face.

"Only those who would work against our lawful master, Sun-Tzu Liao, and against his wise policies, it is they who should be afraid."

4

Touchstone, Milos
Xin Sheng Commonality
Capellan Confederation
03 September 3061

Gray mist rose from the carefully groomed lawn like steam off a boiling pot. The rain that had fallen on Touchstone for most of the day had tapered off into a thin, ugly drizzle that lasted until well after sunset. By midnight, even that had ceased. In its place rose fog, a clammy haze that seemed to penetrate through clothing and flesh alike, to chill the bones and the soul.

Nessa Ament noticed neither the wet nor the cold. She sat quiet and still in the deep black shadow of an ivy-wreathed, brick archway that separated the grounds of Touchstone University from the rest of the city. The mist settled on the shoulders of the black, hooded sweat suit for which she had exchanged her uniform jacket and jeans. It plastered her hair flat against her skull and collected on her face and gloved hands. Had there been anyone to see, they might have thought Ament no more than a figment of the imagination; a thin, hungry ghost, born of wet and fog, and the uneasiness that night often brings.

Typical, she told the night fog. Those who inhabit the halls of academia shut themselves away from the public their schools are meant to serve. They hide behind brick and mortar and ivy vines pretending among themselves that the real world doesn't exist, or, if it does exist, then it only does so to support and to serve the so-called great thinkers who inhabit the ivory towers. Well, tonight the real world comes calling, she promised silently.

Rising sinuously, she slipped from her nest in the leaves and walked swiftly across the fog-shrouded lawn. The Lyran-issue boots she wore left little impression in the soft earth. The house she had been patiently watching ever since she'd followed Doctor Rawley Markotan home had been dark for hours. In some remote part of her mind she thought that the large white-painted dwelling looked like it might house a happy family. She aborted the thought before it was half-birthed. The man who lived in the big, white house was an enemy of the Capellan state. He had been warned several times by the provisional government to cease making inflammatory, seditious, treasonous speeches. Yet he persisted. Since he had refused to be convinced, he would have to be silenced.

Ament circled the house once, carefully observing every window, every door, every crack in the paint covering the real wood siding. In the backyard, she took a small electronic device out of a black nylon bag she had slung over her shoulder, tapped a control stud, and set it on a window ledge. The eight-centimeter-high box contained a small, powerful electronic jammer. The jammer's circuits sent out a powerful but short-ranged cloud of electronic white noise sufficient to prevent any radio-based communication.

The back door was locked. No doubt Doctor Markotan thought it was secure, but the cheap bolt would not impede thieves, let alone a trained and determined predator. Ament extracted a blackened steel pry bar from the black bag. With a snap, she pried the door from its jamb and held her breath. No sound came from within the house. If the house had an alarm system, it was of the "silent" variety. Ament hoped that the alarm, if there was one, was connected to the wireless phone system, which was being rendered useless by the jammer.

After a rapid search of the ground floor, Ament found the system's master control panel in the dining room. The red "trouble" light remained dark.

Never one to question a gift, Ament reached back under her sweatshirt and drew a long, heavy-bladed knife from where it hung, hilt down, across her back. Mounting the stairs to the second floor, she went to work.

Now that's odd, Julia Pareme thought. Doctor M. never left this door unlocked. She elbowed the back door open and passed inside, balancing two large bags of groceries and fumbling to return her keys to her purse. In the five years she had been house-keeper, she had never known the Doctor or his wife to go to bed without locking up.

Another discrepancy struck Pareme as she set the bags down on the kitchen table. None of the Marko-tan family had yet risen and it was long past their accustomed hour. Surely Liza had to be up by now, if for no other reason than to feed the baby.

Well, wake-up alarms mustn't have gone off, the housekeeper surmised. Perhaps she'd better go wake them.

Trying to move quietly, Pareme climbed the stairs. Near the top, she noticed a brown-orange smudge on the white oak banister. A faint chill ran up her spine. Something was wrong. A faint, coppery smell rose from the smeared spot.

Careless of any noise now, Julia Pareme rushed the length of the upstairs hall. Without knocking, she flung open the door to the master bedroom.

The first thing she saw was the bed. The white coverlet was now stained a deep red-brown. Liza Markotan lay face down, halfway between the door and the bed. Her nightgown hung in bloody tatters, the flesh of her back covered by deep stab wounds.

Doctor M. lay in the bed, his throat a scarlet mass of shredded tissue.

Stunned, Julia turned toward the crib. Lying be-neath the blue flannel blanket that she had given him was the body of Jeremy Markotan. On the tiny pillow lay his head, which had been cleanly severed from his body.

Just above Jeremy's crib, smeared in blood across the wall in crude letters was the word REVENGE.

Julia Pareme turned away and closed the door behind her. She managed to get downstairs and summon the police before she fainted.

"That's all from the scene of this grisly triple homicide. I'm Albert Rush. Now, back to the newsroom. Jake?"

Cheng Shao stabbed the power stud on the holovid's remote hard enough to cause the black plastic device to slide in his hand. The reporter had managed to slip past the policemen and capture the murder scene in all its savagery before being hustled back out into the street. The man was a veteran newsman, yet the sight of the shambles that was the Markotan family's bedroom had left Rush with a greenish cast to his blandly handsome features. Shao imagined that the sight of the little family slaughtered in their beds had produced the same effect in every home on Milos.

The gory scene affected Shao not at all. In his career as a Death Commando, he had seen and inflicted worse, but that had been against warriors, political dissidents, and traitors, not a helpless infant. He felt a fresh wave of anger bubble up in his gut. The annoyance was not because of the murders themselves. He had ordered the killings. His ire was roused by the public and sensational way in which they had been carried out.

From the small bathroom in his quarters, the sound of running water tapered off, followed a few moments later by the pad of soft footfalls crossing the carpeted floor. Shao didn't turn as a long, slim hand dropped lightly onto his shoulder.

"Have you seen this?" he asked, with an edge to his voice. "We wanted to make an example of Markotan. Now, the press is going to make him a martyr."

His words prompted no reply. With a hiss of frustration, he punched a series of commands into the desktop vidphone, carefully blocking out the tiny camera's video feed.

"Basara," came the response, once the link was established.

"Claus, have you seen the news?"

"Yes, sir. In fact I was about to call you. I take it that this killing was ordered?"

"Yes," Shao answered. "How can we turn this around? How can we turn this so it will come out to our advantage?"

"We use the oldest dodge in the book," Basara replied unhesitatingly. Shao got the impression that the leader of his Maskirovka team had been considering that question from the moment he saw the news report. "We let it leak out that Markotan was actually one of our people playing a double game with the pro-St. Ives independence, pro-Davion rebels. We hint that he was about to hand over the leaders of the local resistance cells, that the rebels found out and killed him for it. The 'Revenge' painted on the wall fits in with our story."

"All right, Claus, set things in motion," Shao ordered. "Report back to me when the news outlets agree to run our side of the story." His tone left little room for doubt that the Maskirovka officer could convince the news media to see the official version of the murders as the real sequence of events.

As he shut down the vidphone, Shao turned at last to look at the woman standing behind him.

Clad only in a large towel, Nessa Ament seemed thinner than when she wore her usual mismatched combination of civilian clothes and military uniform. Shao glanced at the long, jagged scar that ran across her throat and almost to the point of her right shoulder. He had seen the scar many times, yet the line of thick, twisted tissue never ceased to fascinate him. When he had first seen the scar, he had assumed that it had been inflicted in some desperate battle against an enemy of the Capellan state. How prosaic it seemed to him when he learned that the disfigurement was the result of a ground car wreck when she was a child.

Ament caught him gazing at the mark and swiftly turned away. She was irrationally sensitive about the scar. She snatched up a gray cotton scarf from the still-unmade bunk and knotted it around her throat. Even in the hottest weather, she wore a scarf or her high-collared uniform jacket.

"Nessa," Shao said flatly. "I had hoped that you would be a little more circumspect in carrying out your assignment."

"I was circumspect," she said quietly. "No one saw me enter the traitor's house. No one saw me leave. I completed my assignment quickly."

"Quickly, but not cleanly," Shao said sharply. "It was to be a simple assassination of an enemy of the state, not a blood bath. In killing the whole family, including the infant, in so spectacular a fashion, you have placed our entire operation at risk. If the populace learns that we, their supposed saviors, were responsible for the butchering of an entire family, we will lose their support, and the Chancellor will lose the support of the Star League Council. If that happens, we will be driven off this miserable little planet, and the Confederation will be forced to withdraw its claims to the Xin Sheng Commonality, possibly forever."

"Cheng, you were always a bit overdramatic." Nessa smiled faintly. "Come, let's speak no more of this, at least for an hour or two."

For an hour or two, neither Cheng Shao nor Nessa Ament spoke of anything of consequence.

Several hours later, another occupant of Milos had something to say about the slaughter of the Markotan family and the spin the media was putting on the story. Most of what he had to say was unprintable.

"For the love of God!" he cursed. "What do those bloody-damn fools take us for? How can they say it was the resistance that killed Markotan? How can they expect anyone to believe he was a double agent?"

Captain Dana Messner, late of Bravo Company, First Battalion of the Blackwind Lancers, snapped off the portable vid-set with another hissed profanity. For weeks, he and the survivors of his company had been hiding in the rough hills east of Touchstone, waging a guerrilla war against the Capellan forces occupying the planet. When the Lancers had pulled out, under pressure from the Capellan-backed "peace-keepers" of the Star League Defense Force, Messner's shot-up company had been cut off from the spaceport. Major Nicole Allings, his battalion commander, would have re-routed one of the Lancers' surviving DropShips to evacuate his battered troops, but Messner had decided to remain behind. Had the Major sent in the DropShip, it was likely that not only would Bravo Company have been lost, but also the valuable DropShip and the 'Mechs and warriors already aboard her. It had been one of the hardest decisions of Messner's career.

Ever since the Lancers bugged out, he and his men had managed to survive for nearly a year on an enemy-held planet, and waged a moderately successful guerrilla campaign to boot. In all modesty, Messner had to admit that the feat was nothing short of miraculous. Unfortunately, the campaign had cost all but a handful of his original command. He had put together a small band of partisans to help them in their resistance, but it wasn't enough to challenge the strength of the BattleMech garrison. Instead, the guerrillas contented themselves with ambushing small patrols, sniping at officers, and occasionally raiding the mercenaries-turned-house troops for supplies. The one time they did engage in a direct 'Mech-to-'Mech battle, the weight of superior numbers told against the partisans. Since then, they'd been hiding in the narrow, rocky valleys in the hills east of Touchstone, emerging occasionally to strike at small, lightly defended targets. Now that the MAC troops were being replaced by home guard units, it might be time to step up their operations.

A hollow metallic clatter rang across the narrow valley. Messner twisted in his seat, dropping his hand to the butt of the heavy Sunbeam laser pistol riding high on his right hip. Heat touched his cheeks as he realized with embarrassment that the noise had been caused by a technical crew dropping a sheet of armor plate. His nerves, wound tightly by the stresses of guerrilla warfare, had been drawn out a few more notches by the news report's accusation against his warriors.

For a few moments, he watched the technicians as they scrambled along the steel gantry facing the shot-up *Enforcer*. The medium 'Mech had taken damage when he and his troops launched a hit-and-run raid on the Touchstone spaceport a few nights before. The technicians were finishing up the repairs. The job should have taken only a few hours, but Messner's band of partisans lacked a great many things, including trained and qualified 'Mech technicians. Still, there was something comforting about watching the techs poking around the innards of the fifty-ton metal giant. The sight leant an air of normalcy to their situation.

Messner was a soldier, trained to fight an enemy openly, with a clearly defined strategy. He was used to making war on other warriors. But he had been forced into another role for which he had never been trained, that of guerrilla. He was rapidly learning that guerrilla warfare had a completely different set of rules. As a front-line soldier, he was used to violent death. Like most MechWarriors, he took great precautions to avoid inflicting casualties on civilians. But, as the news reports on the Markotan murders clearly demonstrated, noncombatants, no matter how innocent or defenseless, were fair game. This new style of warfare, and its bloody aftermath, left him feeling slightly sick.

5

"**T**en-hut!"

In response to Regimental Sergeant Major Steven Young's bark, the regimental commanders of the Eridani Light Horse shot to their feet. As he entered the room, General Edwin Amis waved them back to their seats. A tall, gray-haired man wearing the sunburst insignia of a FedCom Leftenant General entered the briefing room on Amis's heels.

The Light Horse's three regimental commanders and their aides settled back into their seats. Colonel Charles Antonescu leaned forward, staring at Amis with a hint of disgust. Amis had been the most senior of the Light Horse's three colonels when General Winston was killed on Huntress. Prince Victor Steiner-Davion had promoted Amis in the field to the rank of Lieutenant General.

Across the wide, wood-veneered table from Amis were the two remaining regimental commanders, Colonels Paul Calvin and Eveline Eicher, recently promoted following the Light Horse's return from Clan space. Eicher took over the Twenty-first Striker Regiment from Amis when he was promoted. Calvin, however, had a more prestigious and more difficult slot to fill. He was the first commanding officer of the Nineteenth Cavalry Regiment in nearly three hundred years. The Nineteenth had been wiped out during the bloody fighting attending the fall of the original Star League. Only with the birth of the new Star League did the tradition-bound Eridani Light Horse feel justified in reactivating that regiment.

"Okay, folks, here it is," Amis began with his usual lack of preamble. "You all know that Sunny-boy has gotten to feeling pretty spunky about himself, being First Lord and all. Well, moving into the St. Ives Compact was a big mistake, First Lord or no." Crooking his right thumb at the FedCom officer, he continued, "This is Leftenant General Arden Sortek, now serving on the Star League advisory council. He is going to be in overall command of the upcoming operation to kick Sun-Tzu out of the Compact. General?"

"Thank you, General," Sortek said softly as Amis took his seat. "Ladies and gentlemen, the Eridani Light Horse is being called upon as part of the Star League Defense Force to assist in a peace-making operation in the St. Ives Compact. Notice, I said peace-making, not peace-keeping. Sun-Tzu has abused his authority as First Lord by invading the St. Ives Compact. Our job will be to push him back across the 3030 borderline.

"Your mission will be strategic. Two regiments of the Eridani Light Horse are to launch an assault on the planet Milos. The other regiment will be held here as a strategic reserve."

As he spoke, a holographic map of the Inner Sphere sizzled into existence about five centimeters above the top of the briefing-room table. Milos was highlighted in gold. The worlds that could be threatened by a force stationed there were limned in scarlet.

"Our intelligence reports indicate that Sun-Tzu is running short of native Capellan front-line troops. Almost as soon as a world is declared secure, he rotates out his own units and brings in forces borrowed from the Magistracy of Canopus. But things seem to be bogging down, and Sun-Tzu is being forced to draw more heavily from the Magistracy.

"Our sources tell us that more and more of the 'pacified' worlds are being garrisoned, not by front-line 'Mech forces, but by home guard units trained and reinforced by Capellan 'advisors.' We believe that some of these advisors are bringing with them small detachments of low-readiness-level Capellan troops to act as training cadres. Some unconfirmed reports also seem to indicate that these advisors either are, or are being accompanied by, Death Commandos or Maskirovka agents, or both."

Sortek paused briefly to allow those Light Horse officers who were taking notes to catch up.

"We unfortunately do not have any on-site intelligence regarding the garrison at Milos. Frankly, the place has always been such a backwater that we never thought to place any humint assets there. We've been relying on electronic intelligence assets, and now even those are down. You will have to assume that you'll be making a combat drop against a hostile force."

"General," Amis interrupted. He'd been scanning the intelligence reports Sortek's staff had issued. "I see from these reports that the residents of Milos seemed to have embraced the Liaoist invaders with open arms. Your analysts suggest that many of the citizens have banded together into loose, unofficial militia companies. These documents also indicate that one of the militia companies has already injected itself into a raid being staged on that planet by 'unspecified St. Ives forces.' May we assume then that these hostile units will include irregular forces? Possibly even armed civilians determined to resist our efforts?"

"Yes, General," Sortek said. "That is our assessment."

"Oh, brother!" Amis snorted, looking pointedly across the table at Antonescu. "Looks like I was right about the Pathfinders," he said quietly. "Just wish I hadn't been right so soon."

Antonescu ignored his commander's attempted jibe. The Pathfinders had been a sore point between them ever since they'd learned of the unit's formation. Never mind that the original idea for the special-purpose troops had been General Winston's.

"General," he said, allowing his broad Gallic accent free rein, giving his words an air of superiority and contempt. "You are aware that the Eridani Light Horse has a long-standing tradition of protecting the weak and helpless, *non*? A tradition that goes all the way back to the original Star League? I can almost guarantee that our troopers, especially those of the Fiftieth Heavy Cavalry and the Eighth Recon Battalions, will not fire on civilians."

"I'm not suggesting that they do that, Colonel." Sortek put just enough emphasis on the last word to remind Antonescu that he was addressing a superior officer. "These are not civilians, they are partisans and guerrillas, as will become painfully obvious should you happen to run across them. What few reports have trickled back across the border suggest that some, if not most, of these guerrilla bands are little better than terrorists. There are low-confidence reports that suggest that a few of these 'militias' have been murdering people in their beds. Had you bothered to study those reports a little more carefully, you might have noticed that information."

"I saw the reports, General," Antonescu replied condescendingly. "As you said, they are low-confidence, *non*? Graded F-3, I believe? No way of confirming the report, but possibly true? I merely wish to remind you that you may neither ask nor expect Light Horse troops to fire upon civilians without very strong provocation."

"As much as I hate to say this," Amis said with a smile, cutting his subordinate off with a curt wave of his hand, "I have to agree with Charles. Unless they are fired upon first, most of our troopers simply will not fire upon civilians, whether the civvies are armed or not."

Sortek breathed deeply and sighed.

"All right, General. I can't order you to violate conscience or break with your traditions. But when the guerrillas start sniping at your bivouacs or stuffing home-made bombs into your 'Mechs' knee joints, I think you'll see things differently.

"I realize that the Light Horse just came off a long and hard-fought campaign," Sortek continued. "I also realize that you lost your commanding general during that bloody operation and have had little time to grieve, rest, and refit. I wish there was someone else I could send, but most of our available units are tied up in other operations, too far from the theater of combat to get there in time, or are maintaining a loyalty to Sun-Tzu. . . ."

"Yeah, I wanted to ask you about that, General," Amis interrupted. "Technically, we're Star League troops. Now personally, I think Sunny-boy is a prize jackass. But we can't haul off and launch an offensive against him just because he did something we didn't like. He's still the First Lord, which makes him our boss. Making any kind of military move against him or the Star League peace-keepers he's got stationed around the Compact is an act of treason and/or open rebellion against a lawful authority."

Amis leaned back in his chair, lit one of his long black cigars, and smiled encouragingly. "How do you propose to get around that little obstacle?"

"That shouldn't be too much of a problem, General," Sortek answered with a trace of a smile. "Remember, the Council will be meeting soon. After that, I have a feeling that our friend Sun-Tzu Liao won't be in much of a position to protest."

6

Eridani Light Horse Operations Center
CanFu City Spaceport Kittery,
Capellan March
Federated Commonwealth
01 October 3061

General Amis shook his head at Sortek's veiled suggestion that, after the upcoming Star League Council meeting, Sun-Tzu Liao would not be in a position to oppose the Light Horse's attack on Milos.

"God above, but I hate politics," he snorted. "All this smoke-filled back room stuff makes me wish I was back on the line as a lance commander."

"Well, General, if that's what you really want . . ." Sortek gave a brief, toothy grin. "No, on second thought, I think we'll leave you right where you are. Make it easier to keep an eye on you."

Then his tone changed quickly. "General Amis,

you've got to plan this mission well. I wish I could give you more time, but we're up against a tight schedule. If we don't stop Sun-Tzu soon, there won't be anything of the St. Ives Compact left to save."

"We'll do our jobs, sir," Amis replied.

"Good. Then I'll leave you to it." Sortek gathered up his papers, saluted sharply at the assembled Light Horse officers, and left the briefing room.

For a few minutes, Amis sat silently in his chair, puffing thoughtfully on his cigar. His eyes seemed to be fixed on something that none of the other Light Horse officers could see. Then, with no indication of what was coming, his expression changed and he began to speak.

"All right, here's the way I want to play this. Charles, I want you to prep your regiment for this operation. The 151st is pretty much intact. Of the three regiments that fought on Huntress, the Dark Horses are closest to their pre-Huntress strength. Most of its officers and non-coms are vets."

"*Oui*, General," Antonescu agreed as Amis turned to his other veteran regimental commander.

"Evie, you're gonna have to stay here." He raised a hand to ward off the protests he knew would be launched in the wake of his decision. "Colonel Eicher, the Twenty-first is going to stay here and form our strategic reserve. If we run into trouble, you're only one jump away. I know you aren't happy about it, but then neither was Sandy when I left her behind on Dieron.

"Paul, I'm sorry, but that kind of leaves you for the high-jump. I know that the Nineteenth Cavalry is mostly untried, but your regiment is the closest to full strength after the 151st. So you and your boys are coming along on this little jaunt."

Calvin gave a jerky nod. "Got it, boss."

"Now here's what I want from you. Charles, Paul, I want you to put together an operational plan for the approach and drop onto Milos. Take whatever figures Sortek gave us and add fifty percent. Bloody intelligence officers never seem to give us the straight skinny on anything.

"Evie, I want you to write up a training program. I want your battalions as close to combat readiness as you can get them. See if you can tap into the AFFC's office of civilian affairs. Pull up everything you can about dealing with civilians, especially civilian resistance forces. Share whatever you get with Charles and Paul. Seems like we're all going to have to deal with partisans, but they're gonna step in it a lot sooner than you will.

"We'll meet back here at 0900 tomorrow and go over what you've got. Any questions? All right, dismissed."

Amis leaned back in his seat and watched his regimental commanders file out of the room. For a few moments he sat there, his eyes open, but focused on nothing in particular. Had anyone looked into the briefing room at that moment, they might have gotten the impression that Amis was merely daydreaming in his chair. But there was a great deal of thought going on behind the bright blue eyes. Amis's sharp mind was sorting through stacks of data as quickly as a BattleMech's on-board computer.

Arriving at a conclusion, he levered himself out of his chair and straightened his uniform jacket. He

picked up the small data unit he'd been using to
take notes and made his way out of the headquarters
building. Turning up his collar against the cold wind
that swept across the tarmac of the Can Fu City
spaceport, Amis angled toward a large, squat structure on the north edge of the facility's military quarter. Here and there, ground cars and hover jeeps
darted across the pavement, their crews off on mis-
sions of their own. Most of the vehicles were painted
the standard drab green. Some bore the sunburst-
and-fist insignia of the Armed Forces of the Federated Commonwealth. Others were decorated with the
crest of one of a half-dozen mercenary companies
currently stationed on Kittery. A few even carried
the Cameron Star of the Star League Defense Force.

Perhaps the most unusual sight on the base was
that of the several score OmniMechs billeted close to
the center of the installation, well away from prying
or curious eyes. There was nothing unusual about
OmniMechs, in and of themselves; several of the warriors under his command had gladly accepted Victor
Steiner-Davion's offer to re-equip themselves from
the spoils of Huntress. What made these machines
and the warriors who piloted them so remarkable
was the fact that they belonged to Clan Nova Cat. In
the war of annihilation against the Smoke Jaguars,
the Nova Cats, led and influenced by the mystics
among their leaders, had given their allegiance to the
Star League.

The Nova Cats had sent their Tau Galaxy to Kittery
to form a strategic reserve.

As the commanding general of a reinforced brigade of SLDF troops, Amis could have requested a

jeep and driver of his own. But he was still, in his own mind at least, a soldier. Even his uniform jacket proclaimed him as such. Though he no longer showed up for staff meetings dressed in the same combat fatigues he'd been wearing on the previous day's field exercise, his uniform was surprisingly devoid of the awards, medals, and decorations to which he was entitled. Aside from the single silver star of a Lieutenant General, which he still wore with a bit of self-consciousness, and the gold and black crest of the Eridani Light Horse, the only bit of color on his drab green uniform was the narrow silver bar of an expert infantryman's badge. Few Light Horsemen were entitled to that particular decoration. Amis had earned the bar during his first term with the Light Horse, and wore it with pride, not as a mark of superiority, but as a reminder that he had not started out as a MechWarrior.

Amis was forced to dodge a hover jeep as the vehicle careened around the corner of a hardened 'Mech hangar. He bellowed a vitriolic curse after the driver, then stifled a laugh. Maybe he hadn't come so far from the ranks after all.

He shoved open a side door to the huge, reinforced concrete structure. Inside the vast, echoing hangar stood the BattleMechs of his command company in two silent rows. As he walked the length of the bay, he studied the silent steel monsters flanking him on either side. Standing near the center of the hangar stood his brand-new CP-11-A *Cyclops*.

Edwin Amis did not believe in omens. He considered himself to be a practical man, not given to flights of fancy. Still, the very sight of the ninety-ton assault 'Mech sent a shiver along his spine. Ariana Winston had been piloting such a 'Mech when she'd been killed on Huntress. The only difference between Winston's command 'Mech and his own lay in his machine's lack of the second cockpit that Winston had had installed in hers. That auxiliary position had been occupied by Warrant Officer Kip Douglass, a skilled Communications and Sensor Operator. Douglass died as he had served, following his general into death.

Some may have found it strange that none of the warriors of the Light Horse Command Company were piloting captured Smoke Jaguar OmniMechs. Amis had discarded the idea almost out of hand. Though the adaptable war machines fielded by the Clans were in many ways superior to those being produced by the Inner Sphere, Amis thought it far more fitting that the Command Company at least stick with "home grown models." It was perhaps merely a symbolic gesture, since many of the machines destroyed on Huntress had been replaced by Clan equipment. But to Amis and his immediate subordinates, the Command Company's use of Inner Sphere designs was still another link to the past they were loathe to give up.

Veteran Light Horsemen had been shuffled from one command to another. Some were promoted several grades and given command of lances, or even companies, to prevent entire units from being too green.

It wasn't not having the manpower that caused Amis a pang of disquiet. It was the equipment losses the Light Horse had taken during the long, bloody fighting on Huntress. Most of the brigade's artillery assets had been captured and destroyed by the Smoke Jaguars. The artillery was an integral part of the Light Horse's philosophy of combined-arms tactics. To a degree, the losses had been made up by the SLDF. But most of the replacement equipment was lighter Sniper and Thumper cannons or even tracked LRM carriers.

Amis added a note to his already overflowing mental "in-basket" to speak with his planning staff and have them work up new operational procedures based on the lighter and shorter-range replacement assets.

His stroll had taken Amis the length of the 'Mech hangar, and left him standing in front of the box-like shape of his *Cyclops*. With a weary sigh, he dropped onto the 'Mech's claw-like left foot and leaned back against the cool metal of its leg. A faint grin creased his lips and a low snorting laugh escaped his throat. Like it or not, he was no longer a regimental commander, but was now responsible for a brigade of four regiments. He made a silent promise to his troopers and to the shades of every Light Horseman who had gone before him that he would not let any of them down.

Whine, thump. Whine, thump. The sound of straining actuators and overtaxed myomers carried clearly through the damp, chilly air.

Chen Shao lifted the compact electronic binoculars to his eyes and trained them on the shadowy form of a *Vindicator* that seemed to be struggling to reach his position. In the late evening dusk, it was almost impossible to see the dark gray 'Mech, but low-light binoculars lit up the gloom, even if they rendered the scene before him in ghostly shades of green and black. The thermographic viewing circuits built into the binoculars flared brightly, telling him that the old forty-five-ton BattleMech was running close to redline. It was part of Shao's operational plan to stop the old-design 'Mech before it sighted the lights of Touchstone spaceport, ten kilometers to the west of his position.

Letting the binoculars dangle from their nylon neck strap, Shao swung a boom microphone up in front of his lips. "Hit him."

A pair of glowing rockets leapt out of a low cluster of bushes, arcing toward the 'Mech's angular chest. The *Vindicator* pilot saw the small, fiery wasps arrowing toward his machine and tried to wrench its torso around to face his attacker. At the same time, he kicked the gangly 'Mech into a lunging run. The combination of motions was disastrous. The *Vindicator* stumbled, then reeled. Shao imagined the pilot fighting the controls of his suddenly clumsy war machine, struggling to keep its balance. The scream of a gyro pushed beyond its design limitations cut across the muddy field.

The missiles impacted on the *Vindicator*'s chest and detonated with a pair of barely audible puffs. Bright red paint sprayed across the 'Mech's torso and arms as the pilot finally regained his equilibrium.

Shao tapped a stud on the communicator attached to his web belt. Static hissed in his ear as the unit switched channels.

"Traud, we just notified your next of kin," he said

harshly, checking the militia trainee's name on a portable data reader. "I've told you, and I know *Sao-wei* Hribal has told you, at least a dozen times. Check your sensors, especially when operating at night. That's what they're there for. You can't just look around with your eyes. You have to trust your electronics.

"And we told you to watch your heat levels. You cannot run a BattleMech full out, blazing away with all your weapons. We warned you about the amount of heat that PPC puts out. If those had been inferno rockets, you'd be roasting to death right now, instead of sitting there listening to me chew you out.

"Because you refused to listen to our instructions, you allowed the enemy to destroy a valuable machine, perhaps costing us the entire campaign. And you got yourself killed in the process.

"Now, get your feet back under you, and take that 'Mech back to the barn."

Shao closed the communications link without giving the trainee pilot time to respond.

Looking down at the data unit, he considered the results of the tests he and his staff had conducted over the course of the previous three days. Of the fifteen recruits who had showed aptitude for piloting a BattleMech, only three had any real skill, mainly gained while piloting Agro- and LoaderMechs on one of the farms or processing plants surrounding Milos's capital city. The rest were just wannabes. Intrigued by the romantic nonsense that the Davion-backed entertainment/propaganda industry had pumped into the vulnerable minds of the youth of the Xin Sheng Commonality, nonsense fed by the flood of computer and holo games that had been imported from the Federated Commonwealth simulating 'Mech combat.

Shao snorted in disgust at the foolishness of the notion that playing a game might ready someone to be a warrior. Still, given all the evil that the Davions had obviously tried to work on the people of Xin Sheng, he had been pleasantly surprised at the level of cooperation and the degree of eagerness the residents of Milos had shown his training cadre. No matter where his troops went, they were embraced by the locals as liberators. That accounted for the flood of recruits when he announced the formation of the Milos Home Guard regiment. He had received enough applications to form five full battalions.

Even more surprising was the number of recruits who showed up carrying their own slightly out-of-date weapons and wearing their own, somewhat threadbare, uniforms. He surmised, and Maskirovka agent Claus Basara confirmed, that many of his recruits were the children or grandchildren of the original Milos Home Guard, which had been overrun during the invasion of 3028. Most of the original loyal Liaoist troops had simply gone underground, waiting for a time when they could rise up and strike a blow for their freedom. Now their sons and granddaughters were proudly taking up their weapons and uniforms to reform the Milos Home Guard Militia.

A few of the trainees showed real talent. Shao earmarked their files, planning to pass their names along to the CCAF training command. But before these recruits were recommended for slots in the regular Capellan forces, Shao would have Basara do an extensive background check on each of them.

For a moment he wondered if he were being a bit too suspicious, then quickly squelched the thought. He was a Death Commando, and he knew too much about the value of deception and misdirection to take anyone or anything at face value.

— 7 —

Eridani Light Horse JumpShip **Gettysburg**
Nadir Jump Point, Kittery system
Capellan March
Federated Commonwealth
20 January 3062

"**G**eneral, we're on line-up for docking now."

The shuttle pilot's voice dragged Ed Amis's attention away from his noteputer long enough for him to mutter a reply. After these months of delay, it was about time this mission finally got underway, he thought.

Amis looked up through the KR-61 shuttlecraft's thickly glazed and heavily reinforced viewscreen. Looming huge in front of the relatively tiny, delta-winged shuttle lay the *Gettysburg*, the Eridani Light Horse's command ship. The "G-burg," as she was often called, was a *Monolith* Class JumpShip. The

Monoliths were the largest of all transport-type JumpShips. Three-quarters of a kilometer long and massing almost four hundred thousand tons, they were capable of hauling up to nine DropShips and six smaller craft across vast distances through the netherworld of hyperspace.

Such vessels were absolutely essential for interstellar travel. The JumpShips, with their massive Kearny-Fuchida drives, were able to literally tear a hole in the fabric of space and hurl themselves and their passengers through the rift, emerging from the nowhere existence of hyperspace as much as thirty light years away from their starting position. One drawback to this kind of travel was that a JumpShip's K-F drives were so massive that it was impractical for a starship to land on a planet's surface. To handle that particular task, JumpShips were forced to carry smaller, intra-system craft like the KR-61.

More commonly, travel between a JumpShip and the planet's surface was accomplished by a DropShip. Ranging in size from the ponderous 52,000-ton *Mammoth* Class civilian cargo-carrier to the 1,400-ton *Avenger* Class assault ship fielded by most of the Successor States' "black-ocean" navies, DropShips were the primary means of moving men and equipment between a planet's surface and a JumpShip patiently holding station at the system zenith or nadir jump point. Unfortunately, because most commercial and military vessels arrived and departed from points in space above the "northern" or "southern" poles of a system's central star, it often took ten days or more to make the trip to the planet's surface.

Amis folded down the LCD screen of the noteputer

and watched the shuttle pilot. He knew that Warrant Officer Gehr was one of the best in the transport arm of the Eridani Light Horse, and Amis admired experts of any stripe. If Gehr was conscious of his commanding officer's interest in his performance, he showed no sign of it. He kept right at his task of guiding the shuttle into the open small-craft bay nestled into the *Gettysburg*'s starboard side, just aft of deck five.

Craning his neck, Amis peered through the shuttle's side viewscreen, catching a glimpse of a point of light a bit larger and brighter than the stars surrounding it. From the bright dot's position, Amis guessed that it had to be the *Star Lord* Class JumpShip *Forrest*. The *Circe*, an *Invader* Class ship, third in the flotilla that would carry the Eridani Light Horse to Milos, was lying a few thousand kilometers off the *Gettysburg*'s port side. Between the three JumpShips, they had enough room to carry eighteen DropShips, more than sufficient to transport the two short regiments he was taking into Milos.

For a moment, Amis felt alarmed as the KR-61 passed into the *Gettysburg*'s hangar bay. He'd been aboard shuttles before, but this was his first time on the flight deck of a small spacecraft as it docked. For a brief moment, it looked like the shuttle's right wing would slam into the JumpShip's hull, but W.O. Gehr gave the flight yoke a miniscule touch, and the narrow, delta-winged vessel drifted smoothly into the docking bay. The shuttle sank into its docking cradle with only a slight bump, hardly surprising when one considered that the craft and its parent vessel were in free-fall. Artificial gravity, apart from that generated by centrifugal force or acceleration, was still the stuff of science fiction.

Even before the locking clamps came up around the KR-61's fuselage, Amis had unbuckled his restraint harness and pushed himself out of his seat and headed aft toward the vessel's primary ingress/egress hatch. Only the small, powerful magnets built into the soles of his boots allowed him to walk at all. The footgear was commonly worn by all officers and crewmen of the Light Horse's Space Transport Division and by many of the brigade's field-grade officers. Amis wasn't really sure how the boots knew when to grip and when to release. He just knew that they worked.

As he moved along the small spaceship's narrow companionway, he felt a low, rumbling thud coming through the KR-61's hull to the soles of his feet. A few moments later, W.O. Gehr's whiskey-tenor voice sounded from the ship's intercom.

"All hands and passengers. The docking bay is now sealed, and the pressure has been equalized. You are now free to disembark." The noise had been a combination of the bay doors being closed behind the shuttle and powerful, high-speed pumps supplying a normal atmospheric pressure to the cavernous bay. The pilot continued, "And thank you for flying Light Horse Spacelines."

Amis snorted and thumbed the hatch control stud. With a high-pitched whine, the hatch slid open to reveal a small welcoming committee making its way across the hangar deck.

In the lead was a short, stocky man with a thick mane of yellow hair and a short, bushy beard to match. Displayed on the shoulder of his khaki and gray uniform was the single silver pip of a Star League Rear Admiral. No one in the Light Horse called David Natale Admiral, his official Star League Naval rank. To everyone in the brigade, he was simply "the Captain."

Behind Natale were four others. Three were wearing SLDF officer's uniforms. The fourth wore a noncom's uniform with the oddly divided patch of a master sergeant bearing a single gold star in the center. There was only one insignia like it, and it belonged to Regimental Sergeant Major Steven Young. A silver horse prancing against a black background sewn onto the left shoulder of their fatigue jackets proclaimed them to be members of Amis's command company.

"*Guten tag, herr* General," intoned a tall, muscular man, whose hair was a paler shade of blond than Captain Natale's. "Welcome aboard."

"Afternoon, Otto," Amis acknowledged his subordinate's greeting. Then, stopping in his tracks, he brought his right hand up to his brow, in the formal, palm-outward salute adopted by the Eridani Light Horse. "Captain, I formally request permission to come aboard."

"Come ahead, General," Natale replied, answering the salute. "Permission granted."

"Thank you." Amis grinned. "Nice to be aboard again, Dave."

"Good to see you too, sir. We'll be ready to jump in about fifteen minutes. We're just sealing up the sail locker now."

"Okay." Turning to the most junior of the commissioned officers present he said, "Captain Nichols—"

"Major Nichols," Natale cut him off.

"You're right, Captain. Major Nichols," Amis corrected himself, stressing the title. It was a tradition to give all ground-pounder captains a temporary, honorary promotion while aboard ship. There could be only one captain aboard any vessel, and that was David Natale. "What is the status of the brigade?"

"Sir," Nichols said, "I have two regiments, the 151st Light Horse and the Nineteenth Cavalry, stowed safely aboard the *Gettysburg, Forrest*, and *Circe*. All troopers are billeted, and their gear is stowed. The brigade is ready to jump."

"Very well, Major," Amis said. "Captain Natale, we jump whenever you're ready."

"Yessir," Natale returned with a nod. "Now, General, if you'll follow me, I'll show you to the bridge."

"Blast it, Dave, stop treating me like the bloody Star Lord," Amis growled. "I've been aboard the G-burg almost as much as you. I know my way around. And stop with all the formality, will ya? Just 'cause someone hung a gold star on my shoulder doesn't mean I'm any better than anyone else. I'm still the same guy you cleaned out at that poker game the night before we went into Huntress."

"Yessir," Natale answered. He led the way across the small-craft hangar toward the JumpShip's central core and liftshafts.

Amis brooded a bit as he fell in behind the *Gettysburg*'s captain. He knew he could not afford to be the same person he had been as colonel of the Twenty-first Striker Regiment. He was the brigade commander now, the commanding general, the "old man" of the entire Eridani Light Horse. A close, almost familial relationship between commanders and troopers under them was traditional in the Eridani Light Horse.

But, as brigade commander, Amis knew he must maintain a certain distance from the men and women under his command. He could not afford to develop close ties with them, especially when he knew he would someday order them into battle, where some of them would be killed or maimed. Detachment was a necessity in a general officer if he wished to lead combat troops and still maintain his sanity.

The lift eased to a stop, and the doors hissed open to reveal the starship's bridge crew preparing the vessel for jump. A low rumble of voices sounded across the small, claustrophobic space. Amis had been privileged to tour some of the larger WarShips of the new Star League fleet, and all but the smallest corvette or patrol ship boasted a control deck more spacious than that of a *Monolith* Class JumpShip.

"Attention! Commanding General on deck! Captain on deck!" bellowed an assistant petty officer from his post near the liftshaft.

"As you were," Natale snapped almost before the PO finished speaking. Amis knew that none of the bridge crew would stop to come to attention at the arrival of the ship's captain and the brigade commander. The shouted order and Natale's countermand were long-standing naval tradition.

"Captain," Lieutenant James Wilk, the *Gettysburg*'s first officer, said. "The solar sail is stowed, and we're sealing up the locker now. We expect to have the jump drives on line in about five minutes. The *Forrest* and *Circe* report charged, stowed, and ready for jump."

"Very well, Lieutenant." Natale responded, then launched into a long stream of commands that meant little to Amis's decidedly ground-pounding mind.

So, it looked like this was something else he was going to have to learn—starship operations. He never appreciated exactly how much there was to this job while General Winston was doing it.

Leaving Natale to oversee the final preparations for jump, Amis sauntered across the deck to gaze intently at a flat-screen projection of the Kittery system. Though he was able to read the display easily enough, he found himself wishing for the three-dimensional holotank that dominated the bridge deck of the WarShips. Unfortunately, such devices were large and expensive. Their control computers alone occupied an entire corner of the ship's main computer center.

The flat screen showed more than a dozen Jump-Ships and two WarShips lying doggo above Kittery's central star. The JumpShips were represented by tiny blue diamonds, while WarShips were indicated by wedge-shaped icons. Here and there, shuttles, DropShips, and fighters drifted across the display, portrayed as elongated Us or tiny daggers, depending on what type of craft they were. Amis gazed wistfully at the small open Vee icon representing the *Avalon* Class cruiser *Melissa* and wished that the powerful WarShip was accompanying them on their journey.

Now where did that come from? Amis asked himself. This was supposed to be a low-hazard milk-run. Why would he want a WarShip along on a job like that?

Probably because you have an old distrust of easy assignments, he answered himself. All of his uneasiness about the current operation boiled down into one thought. It all sounded too easy.

"General?" Natale called, the tone of formality still in his voice. "All stations report secured for space and ready to jump."

"All right, Captain," Amis said. "Let's get going."

"Very well, sir." Natale turned to face the bridge crew.

"All stations, prepare for jump. Navigator, lock the course into the computer."

"Course and destination plotted and laid in, sir."

"Engineer, power up the K-F drives," Natale said.

"Kearny-Fuchida drives are at full power and on line, Captain."

"General, all systems are on line and the ship is ready to jump," Natale reported, receiving a nod from his commander.

"All right, Engineer, prepare to jump," Natale said briskly. "Sound the horn."

A loud klaxon honked three times, its harsh note sounding throughout the ship.

"Engage the field initiator and jump."

"Initiator active," the *Gettysburg*'s chief engineer called out. "Jump in five . . . four . . . three . . . two . . . one . . . Jump!"

To Edwin Amis, the universe abruptly seemed to turn at right angles to itself, as a net made up of energy and quantum physics expanded around the

Gettysburg. It was as though a hole had opened in the fabric of reality, and the huge JumpShip tumbled through it. Light, color, and sound battered against his mind and senses.

Then, with shocking suddenness, like a bucket of ice water thrown into a sleeping man's face, the chaos of hyperspace vanished, leaving the passengers and crew of the *Gettysburg* to recover from the stomach-churning effects of hyperspace travel. The effects of the unnatural process of being catapulted across thirty light years of space ranged from mild nausea to debilitating muscle cramps and blinding headaches. Fortunately, Amis seemed to be immune to the worst effects of jump-sickness.

Captain Natale was the first to recover.

"General Quarters!" he bellowed. The *Gettysburg's* veteran bridge crew exploded into activity.

"Captain, all stations coming to General Quarters," the ship's executive officer called. "All airtight doors are shut and sealed. All aerospace fighters report manned and ready for launch. Damage control parties standing by."

"Very well. Sensor officer, report all contacts."

"Sir, I have eight contacts in system," the stocky woman manning the sensor panel said. "One is the *Forrest* and another the *Circe*; six are unknowns, possible hostiles."

"Let me see them."

The flatscreen display Amis had been examining just a few moments before flashed as six tiny icons were drawn across its face by the *Gettysburg's* central computer. Four were the small dagger-shaped symbols representing aerospace fighters. One was a long, narrow U, indicating that the contact had been evaluated as a DropShip or shuttlecraft.

The last icon caused Edwin Amis to feel a chill. It was the red wedge of an unknown WarShip.

8

Eridani Light Horse JumpShip **Gettysburg**
Zenith Jump Point, Milos system
Xin Sheng Commonality
Capellan Confederation
20 January 3062

"Captain, computer analysis indicates that contact Sierra-Six may be a WarShip," the sensor officer sang out. "Class unknown. Estimated mass suggests she may be a destroyer, possibly hostile."

"Dammit!" Natale said. "What's she up to?"

"Nothing at the moment, sir . . . No, belay that. She's powering up her maneuver drives and rounding on us. I think she means to close and engage."

The sensor operator's analysis contained a death sentence for the three unarmed transport JumpShips of the Eridani Light Horse. This was the great trap of JumpShip travel. A starship's engines expended their entire charge in executing a single hyperspace jump. Then the jump sail, actually a huge solar-energy collector, had to be rigged out to build up the necessary charge to power the K-F drive for another jump. The process could take as long as nine days to accomplish. To counteract this "sitting duck syndrome," many JumpShips were being retrofitted with lithium-fusion batteries, which could be used to power an emergency jump. But no captain liked to rely on L-F batteries or to place additional strain on the delicate jump drives that a double jump created, unless presented with the choice of a double jump or losing his ship to enemy action. The transports' conventional spacecraft engines were so low-powered that they could not be used to escape from the War-Ship in rational space. A JumpShip's maneuvering thrusters were designed to move the ship into position for recharging, not to run from a faster, more powerful combat ship.

The *Circe*, as an *Invader* Class vessel, carried a pair of particle projection cannons, but these weapons were short-range, suitable only for point-defense against single fighters. Against a WarShip, the *Circe* might as well throw spitballs.

"Captain, the bogie is hailing us."

Natale jerked a thumb toward the bridge's central view screen.

"Put him on."

The ship's communications officer tapped a few controls. The large gray panel lining the forward bulkhead smeared into the two-dimensional image of a cold-faced young man wearing the dark olive green uniform of a Capellan Confederation naval officer.

His almond-shaped eyes narrowed in apparent disdain for all persons not of his own perceived station.

"This is *Kong-sang-wei* Tullio Kar, of the Confederation Warship *Elias Jung*, to the intruding JumpShips now entering the Milos system. You are intruding upon a Capellan Confederation quarantine zone. You must withdraw from this system immediately or be engaged."

"*Kong-sang-wei* Kar, I am General Edwin Amis, of the Eridani Light Horse, Star League Defense Force." As commander of the Light Horse task force, it was Amis's place to speak for his troops. "My brigade was ordered here by the SLDF. We are acting directly under the orders of the SLDF and will not withdraw."

"That does not matter here, General." Kar spat. "Chancellor Sun-Tzu Liao has stated that the St. Ives conflict is strictly a Capellan problem. This is an internal matter for the Confederation. The Star League has no vital interests here. Your presence is unwanted and illegal. You must withdraw at once."

"*Kong-sang-wei* . . ." Amis began, anger creeping into his voice.

"Captain!" the sensor officer yelled. "Sensors indicate that the Capellan has switched on his fire-control sensors. I believe he is trying to lock his antiship missiles onto us!"

"*Kong-sang-wei* Kar, locking missiles onto an unarmed transport JumpShip might be considered a violation of the Ares Conventions," Amis growled.

"Then withdraw from this system before I am forced to launch those missiles."

"Captain Natale . . ." Amis glanced across the

bridge at the *Gettysburg*'s commander. Natale's face was livid, his eyes smoldering. The Capellan had threatened to attack more than an SLDF vessel going about its lawful duties. He had threatened to fire upon his ship.

"Captain Natale!"

"What?"

Amis jerked his head slightly toward the screen where Kar waited. Natale caught Amis's meaning and slashed a finger across his throat. The communications officer cut the bridge audio pickups out of the loop.

"What do you think?" Amis whispered harshly.

"What do I think? I think we don't have any choice." Natale was furious at both the situation and his inability to cope effectively with it. "We might try to launch fighters or pop our DropShips, but that destroyer out there would shoot us to pieces before we got half of them spaceborne. Even if we did get enough fighters out there to take down a destroyer, I doubt we'd be around to celebrate the victory."

"Yeah, changing face of warfare, huh?" Amis grunted. "I know Sunny ordered that no unarmed transports be destroyed, but what do you want to bet he gave one order in public and another in private?

"Lemme talk to 'im." This last was directed at the communications officer.

"All right, *Kong-sang-wei* Kar, you win. We'll jump outsystem as soon as we can. We don't carry lithium-fusion batteries, so we'll have to recharge our engines. Can you give us enough time to do so?"

"Yes, General. The Chancellor is merciful," Kar replied, smirking. "You may recharge your drives and

jump outsystem peacefully. You are granted eight
standard days. That will be more than enough time
to complete the operation."

Then Kar's voice turned harsh.

"But you may not detach DropShips or send out
covering fighter patrols. Nor may you engage in
scanning this system with either active or passive
sensors. If you attempt to do any of these things, I
will consider it a hostile action against the Capellan
Confederation and engage your little fleet with every
means at my disposal."

Amis signaled the communications officer to sever
the connection, and snarled at the dimming screen.
"All right, you Capellan buzzard, don't rub it in."

"Well, General, now what?" Natale asked wearily.

"Now we rig out the sail, recharge, and jump outsystem, just like he told us."

"Uh-huh." Natale's voice carried a note made up
of equal parts disbelief and anger.

"Listen, Dave, I'd rather have called his bluff. Hell,
a year ago I probably would have ordered you to
engage. But now? Now I've got the lives of the whole
brigade in my hands. We just can't afford to take
that kind of risk.

"You ought to know that by now. You were at
Trafalgar and Huntress. You know that a JumpShip
stands absolutely no chance against a WarShip. And
even if Kar decided to cave in on the issue of attacking the transports, I really doubt he'd have the
same reservations about running down our
DropShips. Either way, we'd be wiped out before we
could begin our mission here."

"So you just want to give in?" Natale's tone suggested that he didn't believe he was talking to the same Edwin Amis he'd known as the headstrong leader of the Twenty-first Striker Regiment.

"Well . . . sort of," Amis answered with a sly grin. "We rig out the sails and recharge just like that buzzard out there wants us to. Now, he said no scans. Would he know it if we went ahead and ran probes anyway?"

Natale's gloomy expression brightened a bit.

"Active probes, like radar? Almost certainly. But passive? No way to detect passive scans that I know of."

"Okay, Captain, get every passive scanner you've got online. I want a recording of everything from magnetic anomaly detector traces to the morning radio news. That Capellan buzzard may have run us out this time, but we're coming back, and I want every piece of intel we can get."

9

"Whip, this is Knife. I'm at the bivouac. I see four 'Mechs and about a dozen tents. The 'Mechs are all powered down, and I don't see but two or three men moving around the camp. Looks like they've all hit the sack for the night."

"All right, Knife, keep up the surveillance. Whip team is moving into position now."

Captain Dana Messner handed the field-radio handset back to his communication operator. The heavy, PRC-58 basic field communicator was clumsy and inefficient for the type of work Messner's little group of partisans had undertaken. Adding to his concern was the idea that the frequencies might have been compromised. The communicator, along with its mate, which was currently in the hands of the three-man surveillance team code-named Knife, had once belonged to the Milos garrison, and the garrison post itself was now in the hands of the Capellan invaders.

A quick glance at the faintly glowing numbers on his watch told Messner that he had just over a half hour to get his team into position. That would be no great problem. Getting them deployed quietly would be difficult. Of the twenty men under his nominal command, only six were actually soldiers, former members of the Blackwind Lancers, like himself. The rest were civilians, partisans who hated the Capellan invaders.

For some weeks, he and his band of resistance fighters had been monitoring the movement of the Capellan troops. Now that surveillance would pay off. Having gotten the timing of the enemy's patrols and training exercises down pretty well, his men were about to launch the most daring attack they had undertaken since the Capellans landed on Milos. They were going to stage a night raid against an enemy training patrol's bivouac.

"Okay, mount up." Messner passed the word. "I'll take point with Danny. Marj, you're on rearguard. The civvies go in the middle with the trucks. You all know your jobs, so let's do it right and try not to get killed. Let's go.".

Messner stripped off his field jacket and pants, shivering in the cold night air. Wasting no time, he shrugged into the bulky cooling vest that would help keep him alive and functioning in the stifling heat of a 'Mech cockpit during combat. After sealing the vest, he scrambled up the swaying chain ladder dangling from the open cockpit hatch of his somewhat abused DV-7D *Dervish*. The 'Mech's cockpit was warmer than the night air, owing to the heat produced by its fusion-powered engine. Heat was one of a MechWarrior's greatest enemies. Not only did the power plant produce waste heat, but so did the war machine's weapons systems and the myomer bundles that gave it the ability to move. Too much heat, and the 'Mech would become balky, targeting systems would grow sluggish, and the fusion plant could even shut down. Even more catastrophic was the possibility that the high heat levels might detonate the missiles in the *Dervish*'s magazines.

The thought of the missiles gave Messner a brief moment of concern. His fifty-five-ton machine usually carried a total of 240 long-range missiles and 100 rounds for the "double-barreled" Streak launchers replacing each of the DV-7D's hands. Currently the magazines held enough missiles to fire six volleys from each of its ten-tube LRM launchers, and twenty from each of the more accurate Streak SRM 2s. When those were gone, he'd be limited to the ChisComp medium lasers set into the *Dervish*'s wrists behind the launchers. All of these thoughts ran through his mind and were dismissed automatically as Messner ran his BattleMech through its start-up procedures.

Another glance at his watch—0340, twenty minutes to go. Somewhere, Messner had heard that the best time for a surprise attack was at 0400. The enemy would supposedly be at his lowest ebb physically and mentally, giving the attacker the edge. He and his partisans were about to test that theory.

He set his mechanical mount off in a rolling stride. Behind him marched Private Daniel Colonna in his battered *Enforcer*, which was followed by three all-terrain pickup trucks, their original paint jobs obscured by crude mottlings of green, gray, and black. Each carried four or five men armed with a motley assortment of civilian hunting rifles and captured military weapons. Corporal Marjorie Rhom brought up the rear of the little column. Rhom's *Anvil*, at sixty tons, was the heaviest Lancer 'Mech left on planet. It was also the only one of the three still under Messner's command that didn't have to worry about a rapidly dwindling supply of ammunition. The ANV-3M was armed exclusively with laser weapons.

Ten minutes later, his *Dervish* was standing in the shadow of a low hill overlooking the Capellan encampment. The 'Mech's light-enhancement system allowed him to see that there were only a few soldiers up and moving, most likely sentries. The four 'Mechs standing in the middle of the camp like sleepy giants were cold, their engines shut down for the night.

"All right," he whispered into his communications headset. "Let's try to do this quietly. Knuckle group, you move up to the 'Mechs and set your satchel charges. Do not ignite the fuses until I give you the word. If you get spotted by a sentry, try to take him out quietly. One loud noise and this thing will go straight to hell. Pockets, your group will grab the trucks. I hope they haven't unloaded all of their supplies for the night. Let me know when you're ready to roll, and we'll start our end of this little party.

Danny, Marj, we're cover group. If the balloon goes up, we engage, but watch your fire. We're going to have friendlies in the way, and we don't want to hit them.

"Okay, move out."

In his light-enhanced viewscreen, Messner watched as a dozen men and women crept cautiously into the enemy's camp. Occasionally one of them would drop flat onto his belly, as one of the two Capellan sentries stopped and peered around. As soon as the guard moved on, the guerrilla would be back on his feet again, moving as rapidly and as stealthily as the terrain and his brief training would permit.

Knuckle group reached the encampment first. Their goal was to stuff homemade satchel charges consisting of mining explosives into the vulnerable knee joints of the enemy's BattleMechs. The blast could ruin a 'Mech's mobility or even sever its leg.

Pocket group was the most important part of the raid. Their job was to grab the pair of two-ton trucks parked on the edge of the bivouac. Messner, based upon surveillance reports and his own experience, hoped that the so-called "prime movers" would contain the food, ammunition, and supplies his partisans desperately needed. If all went well, the truck thieves would be in the vehicles with the engines started before anyone in the camp knew they were there.

Messner stiffened as a burst of automatic weapon fire ripped through the cold night air, punctuated and terminated by a deep boom. Sounded like one of the guards had unleashed an automatic weapon at one of the intruders and gotten a blast of shotgun fire in return. Now lights were coming up, and the camp was becoming a hive of chaotic activity. More gunfire rang out from the camp. Messner, looking through the light-amplified viewscreen, could see one of his partisans standing outside a Capellan tent spraying the nylon field shelter with a submachine gun. When he finished, the tent, and anyone inside it, had been cut to ribbons.

A sharp, flat crack and brilliant white flash temporarily blanketed all other sights and sounds. One of the partisans' satchel charges had gone off. The uncontained nature of the explosion told Messner that the charge had not been shoved home into a 'Mech's knee joint, but had probably been armed and hurled as a makeshift hand grenade.

Then two of the Capellan 'Mechs blossomed white as their power plants came on line. The militia infantrymen had bought enough time for the 'Mech pilots to mount up and bring the war machines to life.

"That tears it! Marj, take out that *Vindicator*. Danny, you take the *Centurion*, but watch your ammo. Don't run yourself dry!" Messner shouted into the communicator. "And remember, we've got friendlies on the ground. Try to lure 'em out of the camp if you can."

Before either of the Lancers MechWarriors could acknowledge the order, the third Capellan 'Mech, a tall, gangly *Enforcer*, came to heat-glowing life.

"I'm on the *Enforcer*," Messner yelled, bringing the *Dervish*'s arms up into firing position. The amber targeting reticle floated across the Capellan 'Mech's boxy chest and settled into place over its center of mass. The cross hairs flashed red, and Messner squeezed the triggers, sending twin lances of amplified light to burn their invisible way into the *Enforcer*'s armored belly.

Dana Messner thumbed the targeting lock for the heavy Streak SRM launchers, but then recalled his own warning about friendly troops being in close proximity to the target. The missiles' shaped-charge warheads would punch deep holes into the *Enforcer*'s armor, but they would shower the area with shrapnel, endangering his men in the bivouac. Even as the warbling "target acquired" tone sounded in his ears, Messner cycled the weapons selector and fired another one-two punch from his medium lasers.

The Capellan seemed to finally realize where the deadly laser blasts were coming from, because he brought up his 'Mech's right arm and let loose a long, thundering burst of autocannon fire that flayed nearly a ton of armor off the *Dervish*'s left leg.

Messner stomped hard on the pedals beneath his feet, firing the *Dervish*'s jump jets. The fifty-five-ton machine soared into the night sky, ruining the Capellan MechWarrior's target lock. A second stream of tracers and a bright blue beam from the *Enforcer*'s large laser ripped through the air where the *Dervish* had been standing an instant before.

Cutting out the jets, Messner flexed the 'Mech's knees so as to take up the shock of landing. As the *Dervish*'s feet touched the ground, he once again laced the enemy's torso and arm with laser fire.

Now it was the *Enforcer*'s turn to jump away. But, in so doing, the Capellan made a critical mistake. He jumped out of the bivouac area. Now Messner could hit him with the heavy stuff. Messner cut in his 'Mech's targeting interlock circuit, settled the aiming cursor over the Capellan 'Mech, hesitated for three seconds while the Streak systems acquired the target, and squeezed the trigger.

As the *Enforcer* landed, twin blasts from Messner's lasers gouged furrows in the enemy's already weakened breast and arm. Four hyper-accurate Streak short-range missiles added their high-explosive punch to the firestorm surrounding the enemy machine. When the smoke cleared, the *Enforcer's* right arm lay on the muddy ground, its cooling jacket sizzling. Gaps had been opened in the 'Mech's chest, and a deep, ragged wound in its left thigh displayed thick, metallic gray bundles of myomer. The *Enforcer's* head split open as the enemy MechWarrior ejected from his crippled machine. The Capellan had apparently decided he'd had enough combat for one night.

In his brawl with the *Enforcer* Captain Messner had lost track of the rest of the battle, not a wise thing for a veteran commander to do.

"Lancers, call in," he snapped into the communicator, hoping the abruptness of his tone would cover his anger at himself.

"Lancer Three, clear." Marj Rhom was the first to answer. "The *Vindi's* down, missing a leg, but I think we might be able to salvage it. It looks like the ground-pounders managed to take care of the fourth 'Mech. Knee-capped it, I think."

Messner had noticed that the last Capellan 'Mech, a squat, ugly *Jenner*, had not participated in the battle.

"Lancer Two's clear, boss." An odd dryness in Danny Colonna's voice made it sound as though he might be in pain. "Sorry I couldn't save the *Centurion* for you. His ammo blew and scattered him all over the neighborhood. Must have been an older model, you know, no CASE?"

Messner knew what Colonna meant. Cellular Ammunition Storage Equipment would have channeled the blast of a catastrophic ammunition explosion out and away from the 'Mech.

"Colonna, you okay?" Messner asked.

"Yeah, I'm okay. Well, sort of. I think I've got a couple of busted ribs. That *Centurion* got in close and clubbed my *Enforcer* a good one. Like to stove my head in, and I don't mean the 'Mech's. I got thrown against the ejection seat's armrest. Sorry, boss."

It was just like Colonna to apologize for getting wounded in battle, even if it wasn't his fault.

"It's okay, Danny. You sit tight for now." Messner switched comm channels. "Knuckle, Pockets, how's it looking?"

"Knuckle is clear, Whip," the civilian partisan leading the infantry assault group answered. "We've got fifteen Capellans down and out, maybe a dozen more wounded. Least there ain't nobody left shooting at us. Sir, we tried to kneecap that *Jenner*, but we didn't bring it down. Somebody in our group dusted the pilot as he was climbing into the cockpit."

"Whip, Pockets. We got the trucks hot-wired and ready to roll. What do you want us to do about those shot-up 'Mechs?"

"What can you do with them?" Messner asked cynically. "The *Vindicator* is missing a leg, and the *Enforcer* lost an arm, not to mention that the pilot ejected, taking the command couch with him."

"Well, boss, you give us forty-five minutes or so, and we'll have that *Enforcer* ready to move," Technical Sergeant Mike Aston, the only surviving Blackwind Lancer tech still on Milos, answered. "Piloting will be a bit rough, but I think we can jury-rig something using the command couch from the *Vindicator*. I think we might even be able to save the arm, or maybe graft on one from the *Vindi*. But you know we can't do that here, 'least not right now. If they're right about the *Jenner*, and the knees ain't too badly damaged, one of the partisans ought to be able to walk it outta here as is, as long as they don't bang it around too bad until I get a look at it."

Messner thought for a bit. Adding either the *Enforcer* or *Jenner* to his depleted unit would bring him up to one full lance. Not much use against the entire Capellan garrison force, but then again, four 'Mechs would be better than three, and if both could be repaired, five would be better still.

"All right, Pockets, you've got your forty-five minutes, but no more, and that's if the Capellans leave us alone that long. What you can't fix in that time, you're gonna have to destroy. Understood?"

"Yessir."

"All right. Get to it."

Forty-five minutes later, the partisan raiders moved out of the Capellan bivouac. Aston had proved to be as good as his word. Both the *Jenner* and the *Enforcer* were able to move under their own power, though somewhat unsteadily. The *Vindicator* had been stripped of every useful component. The

cannibalized carcass was then rigged with pentaglycerine satchel charges and blown to pieces.

As the raiders faded away into the growing dawn,
one of the civilian partisans lagged behind. For a moment he stared at the burned-out hulk of the battle-
wrecked *Centurion*. Then, searching through the canvas
kit-bag hanging at his side, he produced a large
spray-can of blood-red paint. In large, careless, hasty
strokes he scrawled a Chinese ideograph on the ruined war machine's left leg. Replacing the can, he
spat contemptuously on the 'Mech's armored foot
and faded away after his friends.

Behind him, the paint ran down the *Centurion*'s
thick steel hide from where he had scrawled the char-
acter for "Revenge."

10

Eridani Light Horse JumpShip Gettysburg
Zenith Jump Point, Milos System
Xin Sheng Commonality
Capellan Confederation
27 January 3062

General Edwin Amis glared at the hateful image of the *Elias Jung*, which hung motionless in space three hundred kilometers off the *Gettysburg*'s port quarter. The Capellan destroyer had maneuvered into that position shortly after Amis had agreed to recharge his JumpShip drives and leave the Milos system. The WarShip's presence and position was a constant reminder that he had pledged his word, and a constant threat that he had better keep it. If the *Gettysburg* or any of the Light Horse's other JumpShips made an attempt to detach their BattleMech-carrying DropShips, or launch aerospace fighters, the *Elias Jung* would be in perfect firing position to engage and destroy the unarmed and lightly armored transport starships.

Over the course of the seven days it had taken to build up a sufficient charge of energy to power the JumpShips' Kearny-Fuchida drives, Amis had become familiar to the point of contempt with the menacing arrow shape of the Capellan WarShip hanging motionless behind and to the left of the *Gettysburg*'s needle-shaped hull. Every line of the elegant combat vessel had become an abomination to his eye. Four times he had attempted to contact *Kong-sang-wei* Kar, the *Elias Jung*'s commander, but was met each time with a stony silence. His mood, normally cheerful and full of rough good humor, now resembled that of an ill-tempered cat with an untreatable toothache.

Only the few pieces of intelligence that filtered into the *Gettysburg*'s Combat Information Center made the week-long period of enforced inactivity bearable. From all he could gather, based upon the often inaudible civilian news broadcasts and static-laden military transmissions intercepted by the *Gettysburg*'s passive sensors, it seemed that the Capellans had total control of the planet. Nearly every commercial channel the Light Horse ships could receive was playing Capellan programming. Everything from the daily news to educational programs gleaned by the "listen-only" sensors told of a world firmly under the influence of a Liaoist state.

The military transmissions told a different story. Intercepted messages from a Capellan training cadre in the field told of a raid on their bivouac by 'Mech-equipped partisans. The partisans had defeated the trainee MechWarriors and made off with a few of their 'Mechs before disappearing into the rolling hills and sparse forests northeast of Touchstone. These intercepts gave Amis some hope and helped him formulate a new plan of attack, one in which the destroyer dogging his heels could not easily insinuate herself.

"General, we've got a full charge and we're ready to go." Colonel David Natale, the *Gettysburg*'s skipper, had come up alongside Amis while he contemplated the situation. "As soon as we finish rigging in the sail, we'd best be on our way."

"Why? You think that Capellan bastard knows we've got a full charge up?"

"Yessir, I'm certain he does," Natale said with a weary nod. "He's been 'pinging' us regularly for about the last twelve hours."

Amis bobbed his head in reply. He knew from long contact with "black-ocean sailors" (as starship crews were sometimes called) that "ping" referred to an active sensor scan, and was a term left over from the days when all navies sailed the wet oceans of Terra.

"All right," Amis said with a sigh. "Rig in the sail and let's get the hell out of here."

An hour later, Natale reported that the *Gettysburg*'s sail was fully stowed.

Amis nodded. "All right, Captain, take us out of here."

In the space of a few minutes, the 380,000-ton vessel vanished from the Milos system, reappearing at the nadir jump point of the Kittery system thirty light years away. The rest of the Light Horse's transport vessels soon followed.

"Sir, we are in system and safe," Natale informed

his commander. "All commands reporting no problems with the jump."

"Very well," Amis said briskly. "Captain, rig out the sail and begin recharging as soon as possible. And patch me through to the *Forrest* and the *Circe*."

"Communications link established, General," the commtech said a few seconds later.

"All ELH commands, this is General Amis. Rig out your sails and begin recharging your engines. We didn't go all the way to Milos just to get run out of there without firing a shot. I want the navigation departments of each ship to plot a course for a pirate point in the Milos system. When you've got your course, transmit it to Captain Natale to make sure none of us are going to be jumping into each other. That is all, so get to it."

Amis turned to the communications tech. "Now get me General Sortek."

Establishing contact with the headquarters of the officer in charge of the operation to push the Capellan forces out of the St. Ives Compact took a little longer. Because of the vast distances between a standard stellar jump point and the planet's surface, it was thirty minutes before the marshal's headquarters replied to the *Gettysburg*'s hail.

"Amis, what the hell are you doing back here?" Sortek demanded, the communications time lag unable to completely erase the angry surprise in his voice.

"Well, Sortek, exactly what in the name of God did you expect me to do, go up against a bloody damn destroyer with a couple of transport JumpShips, 'Mech haulers, and a few fighters?" Amis snarled back. "Oh, and by the way, be sure to convey my thanks to your intel boys for their hot tip on that 'lightly defended' system. Or do they always consider a brand-new, just-off-the-ways destroyer a light defense?"

By the time Sortek's reply came back from the planet-side command center, Amis had gotten his temper under control. He explained the situation in the Milos system in greater detail, and more calmly.

"General, I'm sending you my report on the situation in the Milos system. As soon as we recharge our engines, we're going to jump back. This time, we're going in at a pirate point," he said. "Attached to my report you'll find a file containing all the raw data we could pick up with passive scans while we were in system. I've got my intelligence analysts going over it, but I'd appreciate it if you could get your intel boys in on it too. This time, tell them to think a little more about the data before giving us their estimates, huh?"

"I'll do that, General," came Sortek's reply half an hour later. "It's probably no consolation, but we didn't know the *Feng Huang* Class had entered active service yet. I wish I had a WarShip available to send back with you, but everything in system is already assigned. We've sent for a cruiser, but she won't arrive for some time. If the situation changes by the time you're charged up and ready to go, I'll let you know, but as it stands now, you'll have to go back in without an armed escort."

"What about the Nova Cats?"

"I thought of that," Sortek said. "They did bring one of their own WarShips, the SLS *Faithful*, as protection for their Tau Galaxy on Kittery. Besides that, we can't ask them to release it for political considerations."

"That's just bloody wonderful, Marshal. You'll be sure to tell that to our next of kin, won't you?"

Eight days later, the situation had not changed. There was still no WarShip available to send to Milos with the Eridani Light Horse. The news from General Sortek's intelligence staff was even less encouraging. But Sortek at least had the courtesy to make the long trip from Kittery aboard a high-speed shuttle to explain his staff's findings. Amis called his command staff together in the small conference room on the JumpShip's forward grav deck.

There were two such grav decks aboard the *Gettysburg*, each 105 meters in diameter. These two doughnut-like rings housed the vessel's recreation, conference, and briefing rooms. Access to these spaces was tightly regulated so as to give each of the JumpShip's passengers and crew their share of time in the odd rotational gravity.

"General, I've had my people going over the data you sent me for nearly a week now," Sortek began, once all the Light Horse officers had been seated. "Our best estimates now place the Capellan garrison on Milos at approximately regimental strength. We believe them to be of about second-line quality, perhaps not even that. But that isn't the worst of it.

"I assume your intelligence people have come to the same conclusions that we have regarding the mood of the local population. Nearly all the civilian news and entertainment broadcasts you managed to intercept indicate that the bulk of the Milosians have welcomed the Capellan troops back with open arms. They seem to be treating them more as liberators than as conquerors.

"But there are a few indications that there *is* a degree of partisan activity going on. For example, a fragment of a newscast that says a group of native militiamen and their Capellan advisors were out on some sort of a sight-seeing trip in the mountains outside Touchstone when they were ambushed and slaughtered by quote-end-quote terrorists. The report plainly says the act was committed by 'Davion-backed, pro-independence malcontents and traitors.' You might be able to turn that to your advantage."

"Yeah," Amis grunted. "Assuming the report wasn't some kind of propaganda planted by the Capellans."

"*Oui*, General," Charles Antonescu said. "But we must assume that it is not propaganda. We cannot afford to think otherwise, *non*?"

"That's right, Charles," Amis agreed. "If we get there and find that there is more resistance to the Capellan invaders than these reports lead us to believe, so much the better. But for now, we have to treat this as a combat drop against a prepared and hostile force.

"So, gentlemen, this is how I want to do this. We're going in in two waves. The first wave will be the Pathfinders. They'll go in on the *Circe*, hit a pirate point, launch a couple of Mark VII high-speed landing craft, and burn hard for the planet. The *Circe* will hot-load her engines as fast as Captain Morningstar thinks is safe and hop back outsystem before that bloody damned destroyer crawls up her back. Let's try to make it at least forty-eight hours, Kim. You got that?"

Captain Kimberly Morningstar, the *Circe*'s skipper, nodded her understanding. Charging a JumpShip's engines directly from the vessel's power plant was possible. In fact, it was routine procedure when a ship jumped into deep space between star systems. "Hot-loading," as it was called, was the process of feeding power to the vessel's K-F drive more rapidly than was normally possible through the use of a jump sail. In theory, it was possible to fully charge a Kearny-Fuchida drive in sixteen hours, but the chances of a lost charge, misjump, or crippling damage to the relatively delicate jump drive made such an undertaking risky. Amis's restriction of at least forty-eight hours brought the odds down from nearly impossible to about fifty-fifty.

"As soon as the *Circe* is back in system here at Kittery, the rest of the ELH will jump into Milos, hitting at different pirate points," Amis continued. "Here again, the forty-eight-hour minimum should give the Pathfinders enough time to scrounge around and find a suitable drop zone, and prepare the way for the rest of us. We got decent enough maps from the AFFC/SLDF military archives, so two standard days isn't unreasonable.

"The main body will deploy in two stages. The first wave will consist of lighter, jump-capable 'Mechs in the hands of experienced pilots. They'll make a high-altitude or preferably orbital drop into the DZs laid out by the Pathfinders. As soon as they're on the ground and the LZ is secure, the rest of the Light Horse will come in on DropShips."

"What do you have staked out as your drop/landing zone?" Sortek asked, looking closely at an electronic map-box displaying a chart of Milos.

"Right here," Amis replied, tapping a control. A small square glowed on the display, then expanded to show the area in greater detail. "This broad, relatively flat section of tundra. It's about three days' 'Mech-march northeast of Touchstone. It's far enough out of the city that the garrison won't be able to scramble any kind of serious opposition."

Amis paused and let loose a few choice obscenities.

"I'd rather bring the whole force in hot and hard, but I can't. We're so far down in good, qualified pilots after that bloody cluster-frag on Huntress that we don't have enough MechWarriors who know enough about Light Horse combat-drop doctrine to pull off a clean assault.

"And that ain't the worst of it. What about that bloody destroyer?" As he spoke, Amis's tone and language became rougher until he lapsed into the coarse speech of the Sergeant-Major he had once been. "How smart is this *Kong-sang-wei* Kar? Is he gonna figure that he scared me off, just overawed the whole bleedin' Eridani Light Horse, and sent us packing? Or is he give me credit for the guts it takes to ramrod an outfit like the ELH? Will he guess that I'm gonna pull exactly what we're planning, a pirate-point insertion? Worse yet, will he figure that I'm gonna whistle up a coupla SLDF WarShips, and jump back into Milos with our gun ports open?

"Whatever else we do, we've gotta figure that Liaoist bastard is smart enough to warrant the command of a brand-new home-grown Capellan destroyer. So, as soon as we pop the DropShips, the JumpShips will fast-charge and get the hell out of the system, away from that bloody destroyer."

Amis sat forward in his chair, leaning his elbows on the conference table.

"That means our ground forces will be on their own. I don't like it any more than you do, gentlemen, but that's the way it's gotta be."

11

"Okay, Captain, we're charged up and ready to go," said the *Circe*'s chief engineer.

Kimberly Morningstar turned to catch his eye.

"All right, Mister Walthrop, take us to Milos."

"Aye, Captain, Milos it is," Walthrop answered, sounding more like a Periphery pirate than the highly skilled military officer he was. His fingers flew across the control panel in front of him as he droned through the jump-initiation procedure. "Powering up the drives. Course plotted and locked in."

A raucous honk resounded through the ship, advising all aboard that the *Circe* was about to enter the nothingness of hyperspace.

"I hope to god General Amis knows what he's doing. If those SLDF charts are off by even a kilometer, this is going to be an awfully short ride," Walthrop said, grinning sardonically.

Morningstar shot him a pointed glance, but the engineer shrugged it off and tapped one last control. "Field initiator active. Jumping now."

The calm, ordered, rational world melted before the *Circe* commander's eyes to be replaced by a burst of color, light, and sound. Her father was a full-blooded Lakota, and he had often spoken of her ancestors and the visions they had sought by means of chants and dances. Briefly, she wondered if the ghost dance could bring any more frightening images than a hyperspace jump.

Then the nightmare images were gone as rapidly as they had come, replaced by the unfamiliar stars of the Milos system.

"Navigator, check our position," Morningstar barked, throwing off the effects of being hurled thirty light years across hyperspace. "Sensor operator, report all contacts."

"Captain, we're in system at Milos," the navigator called out. "Right where we're supposed to be."

"Bridge, sensors, I have no major contacts."

"Say again?" Morningstar snapped, as she crossed the bridge to the main sensor panel. The magnetic boots needed to maintain one's footing in freefall made it impossible to move quickly, but she covered the distance in the long, loose-legged strides of a career spacer.

"Captain, my scopes are clear. There are no major contacts anywhere in system."

"What about that destroyer?"

"I'm sorry, Captain. I've got no trace of her," the technician answered, leaning back to allow his commanding officer to have a look for herself. "She may be out of sensor range, or she may have jumped out-system while we were back at Kittery charging our engines. Whatever, she just isn't showing up on any of my scans."

"All right," Morningstar said forcefully. "Let's not look for trouble. If the *Elias Jung* is still in system, she's far enough away that she can't cause us any trouble. Keep the passive and active scans running. If there's any sign of that WarShip, I want to know about it before *you* do, got it? Signal to Captain Kyle. Tell him the Pathfinders are clear to launch. Mister Walthrop, start charging the drives. Hot-load, but watch the rate. I don't want to blow the drive coil all over the engine room."

A chorus of "Ayes" answered her long string of orders.

Morningstar turned away from the sensor panel. She knew her orders were to drop off the Pathfinders and jump outsystem again, but she felt guilty about it. No matter that they were ground-pounders, and infantrymen at that, Captain Kyle and his special operations troops were Light Horsemen, and no Light Horseman relished the idea of leaving friends behind enemy lines on a world occupied by hostile troops.

A few decks below the bridge, Captain William Kyle leaned back hard in his thickly padded seat as the Mark VII landing craft blasted away from the *Circe*'s small-craft bay with nearly four Gs of acceleration. Beside him, his second in command, Lieutenant Chatham Siwula, mimicked Kyle's tense, braced posture, as did the other half-dozen men and women occupying the landing craft's troop bay.

With their visors shut and the light scout armor purchased from the Gray Death Legion locked down tight around their bodies, it was difficult to read anything in their postures or faces, but Kyle thought he knew what was going through the minds of each of the troopers in the bay and aboard their sister landing craft, which followed them out of the small craft bay seconds after their ship blasted free. Each Light Horse Pathfinder was experiencing a mixture of pride, apprehension, and fear.

Pride because they were going to be the first Light Horsemen to land on Milos, the spearhead of the operation. Apprehension because they were going in alone, unsupported by the brigade's heavier 'Mech elements. And fear because no one wanted to fail in the task for which they had been recruited and trained. To the Pathfinders, failure would mean letting their friends and comrades down, and somehow betraying the trust the late General Ariana Winston had placed in the Light Horse's first special operations team.

"Major Kyle?" the shuttlecraft's pilot called, maintaining the tradition of giving any ground-pounding captain a temporary promotion while he was aboard ship. "We're away and on course. I figure we'll hit the atmosphere interface in about nine and a half hours, so try to relax. I'll give you a yell when I'm ready to cross the 'face."

"Thank you, Captain," Kyle answered. Try to relax?—easy for the shuttle pilot to say. As soon as he dumped them out, he'd be burning hard for the *Circe*, and then back to Kittery, while Kyle and his people could well be dropping into a meat-grinder.

"Major Kyle, we've hit the 'face. Get ready for drop. Twenty minutes."

Captain Walthrop's voice jerked the Pathfinder commander awake. He was grateful for the thick armored visor of his powered scout armor. Its heavily shielded faceplate concealed his embarrassment. He had surprised himself by falling asleep during the fast in-run to Milos.

"Got it, Captain," he croaked, his voice thick. He switched comm channels and cleared his throat. "All right, Pathfinders, we're crossing the 'face. Twenty minutes to drop."

Each man repeated the call of "twenty minutes" to make sure that each of the armored infantry scouts got the message. Kyle unsnapped his restraining harness and lurched to his feet, bracing himself against the shuttle's jarring entry into Milos's upper atmosphere. In twenty minutes, the landing craft would arrive at the proper altitude for his team to make a safe insertion.

Well, as safe as dropping into an enemy-held planet can be, he told himself with grim humor.

"All right, stand up," Kyle called. The six armored troopers lurched to their feet and turned to face the forward end of the bay.

"Check equipment."

Each man ran his hands over the gear of the trooper in front of him, checking the fit of his suit, ensuring that all the vital seals were in place, that his drop harness was properly attached, and that all his equipment packs were anchored to the armor's outer surface. As each man finished his check, he slapped his mate on the hip, informing him that his equipment had passed muster. Then the line turned around and the process was repeated. Such procedures were vital for the safety of the Pathfinder team. More than once in the long history of air-mobile forces, an improperly secured piece of equipment had broken loose during the violent maneuvering of a high-altitude jump, costing the life of the jumper and putting his buddies at risk. The safety checks had been developed over long centuries of practice. Kyle was not about to circumvent them now.

"Sound off for equipment check!" the scout captain snapped. Each man in turn called out the positive results of the check.

"Six, OK."

"Five, OK."

The count continued until Captain Kyle said, "Leader, OK."

A glance at the chronometer built into the suit's helmet displays showed only three minutes remaining, so thorough had been the safety inspection. The instrument repeater attached to the bay's forward bulkhead indicated that the landing craft was leveling out of its steep dive at slightly less than twenty thousand meters above ground level. Jumps from that altitude were risky but not unheard of. At

least this time they would not need the sealed abla-
tive pods required for orbital drops.

The landing craft shuddered as Walthrop applied
power to the braking thrusters. The ship bled speed
rapidly, settling into a steady glide.

"Okay, Major, we're on station and we're depres-
surizing."

The lights in the bay went off, to be replaced a
few seconds later by a sullen blue glow, which was
supposed to aid in the acquisition of night vision
while limiting the enemy's ability to detect the dim
lamps. Sealed in his suit, Kyle was unaffected by the
rapid depressurization of the troop bay. Only the
quickly descending numbers on the repeater panel
showed the rapidly vanishing atmosphere.

When the counter reached zero, Walthrop called,
"Door opening!" A rectangular section of the hull
slid upward, revealing a patch of dark, cloudy sky.

"Major, we're on station, and you're cleared to
go."

Kyle didn't respond. Instead, he laid a hand on the
shoulder of the first man in the stick, a reconnaissance specialist named Jones.

"One, stand in the door. And . . . go."

Jones launched himself out the door, his spring out
and away from the landing craft powered by his
suit's strength-enhanced legs. Quickly, the number
two jumper leapt from the ship, with Lieutenant Siwula right on his heels. As the rest of his men cleared
the ship, Kyle fell into line in the last position, took
a deep breath, and jumped into the stormy Milosian sky.

As soon as Kyle fell clear of the ship, Walthrop

ignited the vessel's main engines and burned hard out of the planet's atmosphere, heading for the relative safety of the *Circe*. Not far away, the landing craft carrying the Pathfinder platoon's second section did likewise.

It seemed like the long fall into Milos was going to last for hours, but Kyle knew better. He and his men were accelerating toward the planet's surface at an almost constant rate of 9.6 meters per second. Even taking into account the minimal effects of wind resistance, they didn't have as much time as one might think. A cold sweat broke out on his face as he watched the altitude counter projected onto his helmet's head's up display tick inexorably down toward zero and the bone-shattering impact with the planet's unyielding surface.

As the counter flicked past the eight thousand-meter mark, Kyle heard and felt a sharp thump in the center of his back, as the suit's on-board computer deployed the first of his drogue parachutes. The canopy deployed above his head, violently jerking him into an upright position, cutting his rate of descent sharply by a third. But this chute was not the one he'd ride down to the planet's surface. After only fifteen seconds an explosive bolt fired, cutting the chute away and allowing the armored commando to drop free once more. Then a second canopy larger than the first bloomed over his head, bleeding off more speed. Kyle counted the seconds. He knew from practice that this second canopy would remain attached to his suit for a full minute before the computer jettisoned it and deployed the final, "ram-air" parafoil he would steer into the Pathfinders' targeted drop zone.

But that was the ideal, and the ideal was never realized in combat situations. The clock showed that the second drogue had been deployed for only forty-five seconds when a sharp bang heralded the premature departure of the thin, black nylon canopy. No answering thump proclaimed the deployment of the steerable air-foil chute.

For a few seconds Captain Kyle fell straight toward the planet's surface. Fighting panic, he clawed at the chute's manual release handle. Twice, the armored gauntlet's thick fingers refused to grasp the narrow, D-shaped ring. Then they caught. Swearing violently, he yanked the ring, hearing a muted rustle and snap as the ram-air canopy deployed above his head.

Looking upward, Kyle made sure that the black nylon airfoil had inflated properly. Then, glancing around, he saw that he was off course for the drop zone and below the rest of his team. Hauling on the chute's left-hand risers, he got the ram-air back on course. As he settled into a glide that would bring him down on the edge of the assigned drop zone, Captain Kyle made a mental note to have a private interview with the rigger who had packed his chutes and invite the man to make the next jump with him.

If he was lucky, Kyle just might let him have a parachute.

=== 12 ===

Sound and color blurred Ed Amis's senses as the *Gettysburg* came out of hyperspace. Hundreds of kilometers off, a burst of invisible tachyon energy heralded the arrival of the Light Horse command ship's sister vessel, the *Star Lord* Class starship *Forrest*.

"Position check!" Captain Natale bellowed before Amis's stomach had stopped roiling. "Run a full sensor sweep. Captain Morningstar said the *Elias Jung* was gone, but I want to be certain. Air boss, launch the CAP immediately."

No sooner had the sound of the Captain's orders faded than the responses started coming in.

"Captain, we're right on target. The ship is in system, and all departments report all secure."

"Sir, other than the *Forrest*, I have no major contacts. It looks like the *Elias Jung* really *has* left the system. All I'm showing is a few fighters in atmospheric flight above Milos."

"Captain, the Combat Aerospace Patrol is launching now. Four fighters spaceborne with four more on ready-five."

Amis knew that the air boss, a title held over from the days of naval aviation, was responsible for coordinating the launch and recovery of the craft associated with a JumpShip, including the massive DropShips mated to her hull. He also knew that fighters held on "ready-five" were sitting in the launch bays fully armed and fueled, capable of becoming spaceborne within five minutes of the command to launch. What constantly amazed him about naval officers was their ability to process and respond to a constant flood of information that would have overwhelmed most ground commanders. Added to that was their uncanny ability to think in three dimensions when maneuvering their vessels. Out of his element on the bridge of a starship, Ed Amis felt as useful as a set of training wheels on a BattleMech.

"General," Natale said, turning to face his commander. "Everything is secure for now. I'm going to clear the DropShips for immediate launch."

"Very well, Captain," Amis answered. "Start your power plants, quick-charge your engines, and get the devil out of here as soon as you can. I don't want to risk losing the *Gettysburg* or the *Forrest* if that Capellan destroyer is still hanging around."

"General, if I do that, you'll be . . ."

"We'll be stranded," Amis finished. "I know, Captain. It's drilled into us from the time we sign on. 'The Light Horse doesn't leave its people behind.' But if we drop into Milos and leave you hanging around here, and the *Elias Jung* is still in-system, it's *us* who will be leaving *you* behind. You've got your orders, Captain. Charge up and take the JumpShips back to Kittery. We'll call you back in if we need to be extracted."

"I still don't like it," Natale growled.

"Neither do I, Captain. Neither do I."

"General, we are beginning our descent into the atmosphere." The voice of Lieutenant Carol Govi, the *Red Legs*'s commander, sounded like it was in Amis's ear, although the *Overlord* Class DropShip's bridge was eight decks above the vessel's lower 'Mech bay.

Amis looked at his watch. The black-on-metallic-gray numbers read 1439. It had been twelve hours since the *Gettysburg* and the *Forrest* emerged from hyperspace at a pirate point on the rim of the Milos system. Eleven hours ago, the *Red Legs* and her sister DropShips had broken away from the massive transport vessels to begin their high-speed in-run to the planet below. Amis allowed himself a brief chuckle. To those unfamiliar with modern warfare, the term "high-speed run" suggested that the massive, BattleMech-carrying DropShips were pushing their engines hard, pulling several Gs worth of acceleration in a hell-bent-for-leather dash for the planet's atmosphere.

The truth was less glamorous. A high-speed in-run meant that a DropShip would accelerate at one-and-a-half to two Gs and then maintain that speed throughout its journey. A sustained high-G acceleration would put far too much strain on man and machine alike and would deliver the troops to the planet in no condition to fight.

For half an hour, Amis and the men and women under his command had been strapped into the command couches of their BattleMechs, waiting for the moment when the DropShips would arrive over the targeted Drop Zones. Then they would be kicked out of the security of the massive armored vessels into the hostile world of BattleMech combat.

"Acknowledged, Lieutenant," Amis said. "How long until we drop?"

"I make it twenty-eight minutes, General."

"Two-eight minutes it is," Amis confirmed. "Any sign they know we're coming?"

"No, sir. All scopes are clear."

"Good." Amis smiled behind the closed visor of his neurohelmet. "At least we're done with all that *batchall* foolishness."

"Aye, sir. What a stupid way to run a war, huh? Telling the enemy who you were and where you'd be—aw crud . . ."

"What is it, Lieutenant?"

"Looks like I spoke too soon, General," came the reply. "Sensors just detected eight aerospace fighters coming in hot and hard."

"Eight fighters?" Amis said in disbelief. "That's all?"

"Yes, sir. But we've also got a couple of real big readings moving low and fast across the planet's surface. It looks like the bad guys might have scrambled a couple of DropShips, too."

"Think we can duck them?" Amis was surprised to hear himself asking if the Light Horse might avoid a fight.

"Not a chance, sir. The fighters have already changed their vector, and they're pushing their overthrusters to the limit. We're gonna have to fight this one out."

It felt as though a giant hand had picked up Lieutenant Erica Keffer's *Visigoth-A* and flung it bodily through the narrow, slot-like launch bay door. The powerful myomer-operated catapult accelerated her heavy fighter free of the *Red Legs*'s hull and into the cold blue-black of Milos' upper atmosphere. Twisting in her seat, Keffer looked around, trying to visually locate the equal-armed T shape of her wingman's ship. Reassuringly, the small, white-painted shape had settled into its accustomed position a few kilometers off her starboard quarter. Together, they made up Avenger Flight of the Fiftieth Heavy Cavalry Battalion. Painted just above the twin tubes of her forward-firing medium lasers was the image of a whirlwind sporting muscular arms and a fanged mouth. Below the comic figure was the word "Hericane" in red letters. The nose art was a play on Keffer's call-sign: Hurricane.

Both ships had been designed by an unknown Clan engineer in a factory on remote Huntress. The *Visigoths*, like many Clan machines, had fallen into the hands of the Eridani Light Horse following Operation Serpent. It had taken long hours of practice for Keffer to acclimate herself to the strange layout of the captured Clan fighter's cockpit. Her wingman, Warrant Officer Daniel Osler, on the other hand, had taken to the new fighters with the same ease he demonstrated in every pursuit he undertook.

A low tone sounded in Keffer's ear, telling her that her fighter had been targeted by a hostile fire-control radar. Automatically, she threw the control stick hard to the right, kicking the right rudder pedal almost to the cockpit firewall. She knew without looking that Osler had performed the mirror image of her maneuver. Keffer's *Visigoth* rolled onto its right wingtip and dove away while Osler pulled up into a climbing turn to the left. The maneuver was intended to confuse the fire-control radar, breaking its targeting lock by having two exact radar images merge and diverge in the course of a few seconds. This time, it worked exactly as it was designed to. The insistent tone faded and died.

Keffer glanced at her primary radar, locating the red triangle that represented an enemy fighter. Grateful that the Clanner who had designed her fighter had stuck to the battle-proven concept of the Hands-On-Throttle-And-Stick, she pressed a stick-mounted stud and designated the nearest enemy ship for her weapons system's deadly attention. A discrete next to the icon revealed that the enemy ship was a Capellan TR-10 *Transit* medium fighter.

Working her controls with a feather touch, she brought the incredibly responsive fighter into line with the icon. A small square representing the targeted enemy fighter snapped into existence on the *Visigoth*'s HUD. Again using the "coolie-hat" control set into the top of the HOTAS stick, she selected the massive LRM 20-packs slung under each of the *Visigoth*'s long, narrow wings. The powerful Artemis IV Fire Control System pulled data from the fighter's radar system, compared it with images from its sensors, and produced a firing solution in seconds. The letters INRNG flashed across the bottom of her HUD, and she tapped the thumb-trigger.

The fighter's ferro-aluminum skeleton shuddered as forty missiles streaked away from their launch pods. At the missiles' maximum range, she could not see the arrow-shaped enemy fighter, but she could follow the white contrails left by the missile exhaust in the upper atmosphere. The missile tracks seemed to merge into a single line, then erupted a few seconds later in a series of pinhead-sized, strobing flashes.

The *Transit* weathered the storm of steel and explosives, though it had to have suffered serious damage under the pounding LRMs. As though to demonstrate that he was not completely out of the fight, the Capellan pilot kicked his fighter up to its maximum overthrust speed and closed the distance between Keffer's fighter and his own. A stuttering blast of orange-glowing tracers burned past the *Visigoth*'s starboard wing. Laser fire gouged a line of steaming pits across the Clan-built fighter's nose and fuselage, furrowing the small canard attached to the port side of the forward fuselage.

Muttering an oath, Keffer locked up the enemy ship again and let another volley of missiles fly, adding a blast from the *Visigoth*'s extended-range PPC. The Capellan pilot rolled his ship onto its right wing, allowing the hastily aimed missile volley to pass harmlessly within centimeters of his fighter's armored belly. He could do nothing about the stroke of charged particles that ripped into his lightly armored cockpit. The extended-range PPC, designed by Clan technicians to be devastating, slagged the thick pla-steel of the cockpit canopy and turned the fragile human tissue within into a pink-tinged billow of steam. The *Transit* staggered and dropped away, pi-lotless, out of control.

"Avenger One to *Red Legs*, splash one bandit," she said coolly, watching the fighter tumbling end-for-end toward the ground.

"Good shooting, Boss," Osler said over the com-municator. "I'll confirm that kill."

"Roger that, Danny-boy," Keffer replied. "Now let's go find one for you."

"Gee thanks, Hurricane," Osler said. "Mighty nice of you not to hog all the action for yourself."

Less than an hour later, the *Red Legs* and her con-sorts arrived over the appointed Drop Zone.

"General?" Lieutenant Govi called from her sta-tion. "There's the markers. Looks like Captain Kyle and his boys are gonna get paid this month."

"Yes, it does," Amis said, looking at the main bridge display screen. The computer-generated map projected a series of red dots on the three-meter-square screen, each representing a small, infrared beacon placed on the surface of a broad, flat plateau, concealed in the rolling hills several hundred kilome-ters northeast of Touchstone.

"Lieutenant, any surface contacts?" Amis asked.

"Nothing on the scanners other than Kyle and the Pathfinders."

"Hmmm." Amis rubbed his chin and considered the situation. "All right, message to all commands. There's no need to risk our 'Mechs in a combat drop if there are no hostiles in the area. All DropShips will ground at Captain Kyle's LZ. The *Red Legs* will go in first. The rest of the ships will touch down according to plan."

"Aye, sir," Govi replied, turning to relay his command through her communications officer.

Before she had finished passing the orders to the rest of the Light Horse DropShips, the *Red Legs* had swung in over the arrow-shaped pattern of landing lights and touched down. A short while later, as such things are reckoned, all six DropShips were grounded and their cargoes of BattleMechs, infantry carriers, and mobile artillery pieces were disembarked. Amis set up his command post in the shadow of the *Red Legs*'s massive hull.

"General, all units are grounded and deployed. We will be ready to move out within the hour," Charles Antonescu said formally. "The engineers and ships' crews are rigging camouflage nets over the DropShips."

"Good, Charles. Thanks," Amis said, looking up from the electronic map box before him. "Have the DropShips power down their engines and shut off all their non-vital systems. Let's minimize their signatures in hopes that the Capellans will miss them. If the Liaoists are out hunting us, and they find the DropShips, well, there goes our ride home."

"Yes, sir," Antonescu answered flatly and turned as if to go.

"Colonel? A word?" Amis stopped him.

"*Mais oui*, General."

Amis waved the rest of his staff out of the command post and waited until he and his subordinate were alone.

"Listen, Charles. If Captain Natale does as he is told, and I have no doubt he will, he'll recharge his engines and jump outsystem within forty-eight hours. Then the Light Horse is gonna be stuck here." Amis paused and stared levelly at Antonescu. "We're in a win-or-die situation here. If we get our heads in a vise, we're gonna have to fight our way through to the hyperpulse generator station at the Touchstone spaceport before we can get off a shout for help or a call for extraction. So let's try to keep the troopers' minds on their jobs. If they get to thinking about being left here alone, it's gonna hurt morale."

"*D'accord*, General," Antonescu said with a nod. "I agree."

"All right, get the regiments formed up and ready to move out. Our first objective is Touchstone."

Antonescu saluted and started to leave, when his commander stopped him again.

"And Charles? When we're alone, how 'bout calling me Ed?" Amis smiled thinly. "It's kinda lonely having everybody calling me general nowadays."

"*D'accord*." Antonescu paused, and smiled gently. "I'll do that, Ed."

13

Querien Hills, northeast of Touchstone,
Milos
Xin Sheng Commonality
Capellan Confederation
09 February 3062

"Flash! SITREP!" The sharp cry rang in Ed Amis's ears. "Strawberry Six has contact with enemy forces. Grid November-Yankee-niner-one-four, by Alpha-Mike-seven-three-seven. Enemy force is one-five Bravo Mikes, primarily mediums, supported by a large body of conventional armor and infantry. Enemy force is in an apparent defensive position across highway five-five. Unit identification is unknown. The insignia is not in the warbook. Enemy is under current observation. Strawberry Six requests instructions."

Amis consulted his *Cyclops*'s Tactical Data Display. The device automatically painted an enemy combined-arms force icon, an open square bearing the upper-case letters CA, drawn in red in a shallow valley about ten kilometers west-southwest of his current position. A much smaller blue square crossed by a single diagonal line rested in a sparsely wooded area, about a thousand meters east of the enemy. This small azure icon represented the recon team code-named "Strawberry Six."

"Strawberry Six, this is Stonewall. Hold position and observe. Do not engage unless fired upon," Amis snapped into his communicator. "Tiger is moving to engage."

A tap of a single control switched communication channels and brought Amis into contact with Colonel Paul Calvin.

"Tiger, this is Stonewall. Shag it, Paul. Strawberry Six has contact with the bad guys. If we can grease them now, we may be able to push straight through to Touchstone. I want you to ram the Nineteenth straight down their throats. I'll have Charles do a mass rabble bypass and flank those beggars."

"Right, boss," Calvin replied, the joy of battle turning his reply into a war song. "Tiger is moving in."

Amis gave a half-amused snort. "Watch yourself, Colonel. Just because they're indig militia doesn't mean they can't hurt you."

Now where did that come from? Amis wondered to himself. For a minute there he sounded just like General Winston warning Amis himself not to stick his neck out so far that it got chopped off.

Pushing aside the startled realization that, with command, had come moderation of his recklessness in battle, Amis switched channels again, this time contacting Colonel Charles Antonescu.

"Magyar? Stonewall. Tiger is moving to engage an enemy force at N-Y-niner-one-four, by A-M-seven-three-seven. I want you to move the One-fifty-first up behind him. As soon as he's engaged, send one battalion around each flank and take the Capellans in the flank. Hold one battalion in reserve as backup. I'll bring the command company in behind you to catch any leakers or provide additional support if necessary."

"Wilco, Stonewall. Two battalions to make a flank sweep, one in reserve."

The maneuver Amis had ordered was referred to in military circles as a "double envelopment." But in typical Light Horse fashion, the common tactic had come to be known as a mass rabble bypass. The flanking units would often push so far beyond the enemy's flanks that it would seem that the foe was being pinned in place while the bulk of the Light Horse units were intent on passing the engaged units by. Then, as the ends of the enemy's line turned to follow and defend against the flankers, the Light Horse troopers would sweep in and crush the enemy against the pinning force like a hammer crushing an egg against an anvil. At least that was the way it worked in theory. Amis was aware that theory rarely held up on the modern battlefield.

With another tap on the communications console, he barked out a final order. "Command Company, mount up. It's time to earn our pay."

The sudden crash of exploding shells rocked Paul Calvin's *Victor*, sending the eighty-ton war machine staggering. Expertly, with a coolness that surprised him, Calvin brought the reeling BattleMech back under his control. A quick glance at his TDD showed a line of enemy 'Mechs crouching in a gully a few hundred meters to the southwest. Looking up, he keyed a command into his combat computer to locate and designate the nearest enemy unit.

A scarlet frame snapped into existence on his 'Mech's head's up display, revealing the location of the closest hostile unit. The alphanumeric CHP-2N beneath the frame told him that the aggressor was an old model *Champion*. The enemy 'Mech did not mount as much armor as his *Victor*, nor were its weapons as powerful, but the heavy Mydron B autocannon mounted in the *Champion*'s right breast could produce nasty results if the enemy MechWarrior was skilled enough.

"Contact! Tiger One has contact with the enemy at N-Y-niner-one-three, by A-M-seven-four-six. We are engaging."

With that, Calvin leveled his 'Mech's right arm at the birdlike enemy machine. A sharp, popping hiss coincided with his brief squeeze on the trigger, as a basketball-sized chunk of nickel iron sped downrange at hypersonic velocity. The Gauss rifle's projectile smashed into the *Champion*'s left thigh, sending fragments of splintered armor plate spiraling through the air. The Capellan machine staggered, as the dense metal pellet blasted away the relatively thin leg armor and shallowly gouged the aluminum, silicon-carbide, and titanium bones beneath.

Calvin counted off three seconds while the Gauss rifle's breech mechanism cycled a fresh slug into the firing chamber. The weapon discrete, which had gone red when the first round was fired, now flashed green. The Light Horse officer tapped the trigger once again, adding a volley of four short-range missiles and a pair of laser lances to the mix. The heavy slug shattered the thin armor on the *Champion*'s left arm, while the lasers sliced away the armor protecting its chest. Two of the corkscrewing missiles dropped short, scattering clods of earth and bits of rock across the *Champion*'s clawed feet. The others burst against the Capellan 'Mech's already abused left leg. The explosions cracked the lightweight metal thigh bone and sent sparks flying from the unfortunate machine's hip and knee actuator packages.

But the Capellan was far from out of the fight. He let loose a long, rolling barrage of high-explosive armor-piercing shells from the chest-mounted autocannon, which pocked the thick armor covering the *Victor*'s chest. A pair of laser bolts, flashing a ghostly green where they crossed through the smoke of battle, cut blackened furrows into the 'Mech's camouflaged belly, and a full flight of six short-ranged missiles, guided by luck, skill, or both, slammed into the heavier war machine. One of the ten-kilo rockets exploded against the *Victor*'s helmetlike cockpit armor. The blast left Calvin's ears ringing despite the noise-attenuation gear built into his neurohelmet. Calvin peered through the thin, red-tinged fog that swam before his eyes, then dropped the wheel-like targeting reticle across the *Champion*'s wavering form.

Damn, that hit must have been pretty severe, Calvin thought, struggling to clear away the cobwebs. It really rang my bell.

The reticle flashed once, and he triggered his full weapon complement. A wave of heat flooded into the cockpit, threatening to intensify the wooziness caused by the hollow-charge warhead's detonation against the *Victor*'s head armor.

Before his heat sinks could bring the temperature in the cockpit back to a more tolerable level, Calvin saw the heavy Gauss slug rip into the shallow laser gouge on the *Champion*'s right breast. The wound widened as reinforced steel gave way. It was deepened when a short-range missile splintered the enemy's metal ribs.

An explosion tore through the Capellan 'Mech as the missile's bursting warhead touched off nearly a full magazine of heavy autocannon shells. The bird-like 'Mech staggered, sank onto its hips as though it intended to sit down, then toppled backward, trailing black, oily smoke from the jagged wound in its torso. The pilot did not attempt to escape from his crippled machine. Calvin knew, with the sickening certainty that comes only from experience, that the valiant, but poorly trained warrior was dead in his cockpit. Calvin turned to seek out another foe.

Accompanied by a sharp cracking sound, a fusillade of nearly invisible laser darts streaked past the *Victor*'s faceplate.

"Tiger, this is Boxer One-One." Calvin recognized the call sign as that of Captain Robert Jones, leader of Second Striker Battalion's Eighth Company. "We are taking fire. Boxer One is under heavy long-range enemy fire. I have two 'Mechs down and three more damaged. Request immediate assistance."

Another stuttering blast of laser fire flashed the

half-frozen ground beneath the *Victor*'s feet into muddy steam before Calvin could reply. A low-slung Manticore tank had poked its nose above the rim of a shallow gully to take potshots at the Nineteenth Cavalry's command 'Mech. This time, it added a cloud of semi-guided missiles to its attack. The anti-armor warheads flayed the thick hide off the *Victor*'s legs and feet. Calvin popped a hastily aimed shot from his Gauss rifle at the tank, missing by half a dozen meters.

"Steady on, Captain," Calvin barked. Jones was a transferee officer, a Lyran Alliance major who had taken a reduction in grade just to get a spot with the ELH. Calvin had always been a little suspicious of the transferee officer program, stating in no uncertain terms that you never knew what kind of officer you'd get until it was too late. Now, fate seemed to be proving his suspicions correct. Jones was beginning to panic. The TDD revealed that the First was a few klicks southwest of his position, well ahead of where they were supposed to be. "Pull your troops back to grid N-Y-niner-one-one, by A-M-seven-four-three. Reform on Boxer Three."

"We can't, sir. The Capellans are keeping us pinned with long-range artillery fire. If we try to move, the short-range stuff in front of us hammers us flat."

"Well, then, dammit, if you can't go back, go forward!" Calvin roared. "If you get in among their own 'Mechs, they can't very well drop in arty, now can they?"

"But, Colonel—"

"Dammit, I said go forward, Captain. I'm too busy

here to argue with you." Calvin leveled his Gauss rifle and fired again. The slug struck home, deeply creasing the tank's turret armor. "I gave you a flipping order. You'd bloody well better do what I say, or I'll frag you myself when this is all over."

There was no reply to Calvin's enraged outburst.

"Boxer One, do you copy?"

There was still no response.

"Crud." Calvin switched channels. "Is there anyone available to go check on Jones?"

"Yessir. Boxer Three is not currently engaged," Captain Thomas Graeme replied, glancing at his tactical map. Eighth Company was a few klicks west of the spot where his Sixth Heavy Assault Company had just finished a short, bloody scrap with a platoon of machine gun- and satchel charge-armed infantrymen. One of Graeme's 'Mechs was down, its right foot blown off at the ankle by a sapper's knee-capping charge. Another had deep gashes in its back where a machine-gunner had managed to rake the 'Mech from behind, but the bulk of his company was intact.

"All right, Graeme, go pull that idiot out of the fire."

"Okay, Sixth!" Graeme shouted into his boom-mounted communications mike. "You heard the man. Form up and move out, at the double quick."

Graeme shoved the control sticks of his captured *Cauldron-Born-B* fully forward, launching the elegant, birdlike, Clan-designed OmniMech into a loping run. All around him the men and women of his assault company were doing the same. For a moment, in his mind's eye, Graeme saw armored knights with leveled spears charging across the battlefield. The distance fell away rapidly. Graeme knew that the Capellans had become aware of his presence when a howling volley of heavy artillery shells burst among his charging ranks. The tactical display showed that he was almost on top of Eighth Company's position.

Shrapnel rang off his 'Mech's armored carapace, but did him no further harm. A *Bombardier* from his Strike lance was not so fortunate. A heavy shell penetrated the artillery 'Mech's armor and detonated the machine's supply of long-range missiles. Only the Cellular Ammunition Storage Equipment surrounding the magazine saved the pilot's life. The special blow-out panels had directed the blast away from the *Bombardier*'s vital systems. But the explosion shredded the internal structure supporting its right arm, where its only other offensive weapon, an SRM launcher, was mounted. With that limb useless, the sixty-five-ton machine was unarmed.

While the enemy gunners were reloading their pieces and adjusting their aim, Graeme's company charged past the few operational 'Mechs remaining to the Eighth, determined to close with the half-dozen or so Capellan BattleMechs and their supporting conventional armor and infantrymen. On his way through the Eighth's position, Graeme noticed the smoldering hulk that had once been Captain Jones's *JagerMech*. He later learned that Jones had tried to obey Colonel Calvin's order but had been struck by a volley of long-range missiles that ripped into his 'Mech's head, killing him instantly.

Graeme had no time to pity a fallen comrade. Their charge had carried the Sixth straight into the midst of the Capellan positions. A gangly-looking *Enforcer* stood in his path, as though daring him to fight. Graeme obliged the Liao warrior by unleashing a paired blast from his 'Mech's twin PPCs. The man-made lightning ripped into the lighter 'Mech, all but severing its left arm and leaving a huge blackened scar high on its chest.

Heat flooded into Graeme's cockpit, stealing his breath. He hesitated a few heartbeats until the highly efficient, Clan-designed heat sinks brought his Omni-Mech's internal temperature down to a more manageable level. Selecting a different weapon, Graeme added a series of heavy, pulsing laser bolts to the incredible energy already absorbed by the *Enforcer*. The reeling Capellan tried to reply, but the burst of autocannon shells only stitched a line of shallow divots across the *Cauldron-Born*'s rounded torso, while the blast of laser energy scoured paint and armor from the bird-like machine's right leg. Another blast from Graeme's right-hand PPC smashed the tall enemy 'Mech into the ground. It did not get up again.

"Tommy, they're running!" Lieutenant John Morosini, the commander of Graeme's Strike lance, bellowed gleefully.

Indeed, the Capellan troops seemed to be in full, headlong retreat, their will to fight broken along with their defensive line.

"Tiger, this is Boxer Three-One. The Capellans are falling back in disorder," Graeme reported to Colonel Calvin. "Looks like we've got a clear road all the way to Touchstone."

14

A glance through the fading afterimages of the coruscating colored lights projected on his retinas by the nothingness of hyperspace told *Kong-sang-wei* Tullio Kar that the *Elias Jung* had emerged from the void exactly where it was supposed to, at the nadir point of the Maladar system's primary star. Several billion kilometers away, a second sun gleamed dully against the black curtain of space. Due to the paradoxical nature of JumpShip travel, the actual travel time from Milos had been only a matter of seconds. But the actual journey had consumed more than two weeks. Traveling in a direct line, the *Elias Jung* had been forced to jump into deep space and recharge its jump engines from its own power plant, rather than collecting solar energy with its jump sail.

"*Kong-sang-wei*, we are in-system, and all systems are functioning properly," his First Office reported from his bridge station.

"Very well, *Kong-sao-wei* Yip," Kar acknowledged, turning his attention to another crewman. "Communications, establish contact with Confederation headquarters on Maladar. I wish to speak with their *zampolit*. Notify me when you have established a secure link. I'll be in my cabin."

Without waiting for acknowledgment from the young man seated at the communication console, Kar turned and walked casually off the bridge.

He'd only been in his cabin a few moments when the ship's intercom bleeped, and the communications tech informed him that a secure communications link had been established between the *Kong-sang-wei* and the *zampolit*—Confederation Political Officer—on Maladar.

"Greetings, *Kong-sang-wei* Kar," the *zampolit* said. "How good of you to join us. You were to be here over a week ago. Would you care to explain your dereliction of duty?"

"It was no 'dereliction of duty,' *Zampolit* Oroz," Kar snapped back, reading the man's name from the identification bar in the lower-right corner of the screen. Even allowing for the thirty-minute lag in communicating with the planet's surface, he was still irritated by the *zampolit*'s insinuation. Like most active-duty combat officers, Kar disliked having a political officer looking over his shoulder at everything he did, but there was something unsettling about Oroz. The man's silky manner and slicked-back black hair reminded Kar of a shiny black viper in need of being exterminated.

"We were detained at the Milos jump point by a fleet of transport JumpShips, all bearing the crest of the Star League Defense Force. From the number and type of these vessels, and the DropShips they carried, I deemed them to be an invasion force, and I prevented them from detaching the DropShips. I remained on-station at Milos until they had recharged their engines and jumped back out of that system. Then I jumped out myself."

"Why did you not simply destroy the transports and continue your mission according to your time table?" Oroz scoffed.

"Because one simply does not open fire on SLDF JumpShips, unless one wishes to make enemies of the rest of the Inner Sphere!" Kar growled back. "And one does not destroy unarmed transports, most especially when those ships belong to the Eridani Light Horse! Have you ever heard of Sendai, *Zampolit*? Need I remind you of what happened when the planetary head of Sendai had helpless Light Horse personnel and dependents massacred? Do you want a force of avenging angels descending upon Milos, or Maladar, or Sian?"

"The Eridani Light Horse was at Milos, eh?" Oroz murmured, seeming to have heard only those three words. "Why did you not notify the Confederation command authority of this invasion fleet before now?"

"Have you ever heard of scanners, *Zampolit*?" Kar

was rapidly wearying of the political officer's smarmy voice and insulting questions. "If I had sent a message to the Milos HPG station instructing them to forward my report on to the CCAF, the enemy would have been certain to intercept it. Even if it were coded, or a tight-beam transmission, no form of communication is one hundred percent secure. There is always a chance of intercept. Who can gauge the Light Horse's reaction to such a message? The size of the invasion fleet suggested nothing more than a raid in force. They may have decided to risk having me fire upon their.ships and launch their invasion. Believing that I was calling for reinforcements, they may have wanted to take the planet and then hold it against a relief force. It is far easier to defend than to attack. They may have even summoned reinforcements of their own, turning Milos into the site of a major battle rather than a backwater skirmish. I was not willing to take that risk."

Oroz did not seem impressed by Kar's analysis of the situation. "You will, of course, include all details of this invasion fleet in your report," he said in a tone that suggested boredom.

"Of course, *Zampolit* Oroz," Kar snarled, his patience at an end. "Prepare to receive a download."

Celestial Palace
Zin-jin Cheng (Forbidden City), Sian
Sian Commonality
Capellan Confederation

"Say that again, Zahn." Sun-Tzu Liao's tone was one of mild curiosity.

"Chancellor, I said we have just received a report that a Star League Defense Force invasion fleet was sighted at Milos." *San-jiang-jun* Talon Zahn, Sun-Tzu's closest military advisor, repeated slowly and carefully. "The fleet was comprised of three JumpShips, one *Invader*, one *Star Lord*, and one *Monolith*. Each was laden with heavy 'Mech-carrier DropShips. All bore the insignia of the Eridani Light Horse."

"I see," the Chancellor of the Capellan Confederation murmured, slipping his hands into the pockets of his drab green military uniform. A solid gold pin the shape of the new Confederation crest, an armored hand clutching the hilt of a *darn-dao* sword, glittered from each side of his collar. No other form of decoration or insignia was to be seen, nor was any needed. Everyone in the command center knew who this green-eyed young man was, and when one held ultimate power over one of the Successor States, one had no need to shout one's importance to the world.

"Please continue."

"*Kong-sang-wei* Tullio Kar, commanding the War-Ship *Elias Jung*, ordered the invaders back outsystem, and remained on station until the Light Horse ships recharged their engines and jumped away.

"Upon arriving at Maladar, *Kong-sang-wei* Kar reported the situation at Milos to Desmond Oroz, the local *zampolit*. Oroz forwarded the report to us. The information is two weeks old at least. If the Light Horse had decided to return to Milos, possibly via a system-rim jump point, they may have been in-system for at least a week."

"Have we received any word from Milos regarding the reappearance of this invasion fleet?"

"No, Chancellor," Zahn answered. "Following the raid by your cousin, the only activity we have seen on Milos has been the odd attack by partisans and guerrillas."

"Bring up a map of the Xin Sheng Commonality," Sun-Tzu said to no one in particular, but a technician on the far side of the command center went to work. A holographic map sprang into existence against the center's blank east wall. The Capellan Confederation was displayed in a pleasant jade green, with the worlds recaptured from the rebellious Xin Sheng Compact illuminated in white. A lighter green showed worlds not yet reclaimed, while those where fighting still raged were denoted by a scarlet dot. Beyond the edge of the region of Xin Sheng was an expanse of mustard yellow, delineating the territory held by the Federated Commonwealth, the nation-state of the hated Davion family.

"Now, show me Milos."

In response to Sun-Tzu's command, a white circle glowed a little brighter, while a window opened in the lower left-hand corner of the holographic map, displaying all the pertinent data on the Milos system. For a few moments he studied the map closely, watching as the system data scrolled by, then realization flooded across his handsome features.

"Zahn, look here. This is Milos, a little nothing of a world in the center of our lines. By itself, it is of no major significance, but look." Sun-Tzu picked up a holo-pen and scribed a half-circle through the Xin Sheng Commonality, with Milos as its center point.

"Look," he said again. "These three worlds are among those that lie within one jump of Milos: Huistang, Harloc, Gei-Fu. And see here?" He described a second, wider circle. "If the enemy stages out of Milos and uses lithium-fusion batteries to power a double jump, they could descend upon Capella, or even Sian, with little warning."

Zahn's face paled as he grasped the situation.

"Give me the name and location of the nearest unengaged line combat unit," Sun-Tzu demanded.

St. Loris, a system nearly thirty-six light years away from Milos toward the border with the Federated Commonwealth, lit up. The insignia of MacCarron's Armored Cavalry snapped into existence next to it, along with an alphanumeric code indicating that the unit occupying that world was the MAC's Second Regiment, under *Sang-shao* Samuel Christobal.

Zahn studied the map briefly, working out the navigation in his head.

"Chancellor, if we dispatch Christobal's Regiment immediately, they can be on Milos in under three weeks."

Sun-Tzu nodded, refusing to give in to the frustration caused by the circumstances that were forcing him to pull a main-line combat unit away from the front in order to re-secure a supposedly pacified world.

"Do it," he ordered.

As technicians scrambled to forward the Chancellor's command across nearly eighty light years of space, Talon Zahn stepped back from the map and rested his chin in his right palm, cupping that elbow in his left hand. He stared thoughtfully ahead.

"What are you thinking, *Sang-jiang*?" Liao asked.

"I am thinking, Chancellor, that perhaps this is nothing more than what *Kong-sang-wei* Kar said it was, a massive raid in force."

"Perhaps it is, but I cannot take that chance. Cheng Shao, the garrison commander on Milos, will have only a company or two of BattleMechs at his disposal. With those few 'Mechs and such militia units as he can muster, he would stand little chance of driving any main line-of-battle 'Mech force off planet, to say nothing of the Eridani Light Horse.

"No, if it were any other world than Milos, or any other unit than the Light Horse, or even if it were a single Light Horse regiment, then I might be tempted to believe that this was only a diversionary strike. But given the target, the timing, and the invading unit, this must be a strike against the Confederation. It could be nothing else."

"But if they've withdrawn, why divert Christobal's Regiment to Milos at all?"

"Again, Zahn, this is the Eridani Light Horse. From the classes and number of JumpShips and DropShips *Kong-sang-wei* Kar reports, we may assume that the enemy is sending at least two regiments to Milos. If they failed to gain entry through the front door, they will attempt to break in through a window. They will be back. In fact, they probably are back already."

"In that case, Chancellor," Zahn said respectfully. "Will one regiment of MacCarron's Armored Cavalry be enough?"

Liao considered the question for a moment, then shook his head sadly.

"It is all I have to send." He brightened a bit and continued. "But I happen to know that the Light Horse suffered heavy casualties on Huntress. There *are* advantages to having been First Lord, you see. I also know that they have yet to make them up out

of new recruits and personnel transferred in from
Successor State units. So we may assume that any
invasion force will be short-handed. Of the forces
they *do* have, about half will be either untested recruits or transferees who are not yet fully integrated
into the Light Horse's style of maneuver warfare.

"And, *Sang-jiang*, do not forget Cheng Shao. I
know this man." The Chancellor paused and allowed
himself the ghost of a smile. "If he survives the initial
invasion, he will find some way of making life *very*
uncomfortable for the Eridani Light Horse until
Christobal's Regiment can arrive."

Sun-Tzu stopped speaking abruptly, all expression
draining from his face. He reviewed the hard copy of
Kong-sang-wei Kar's report that he had been handed
upon his arrival in the command center, which had
remained unread until now. The report was concise
and clear, a commendable effort on the part of the
destroyer *Kong-sang-wei*, but a chilling lapse in the
officer's judgment and devotion to duty was obvious.
If the *Elias Jung* had remained on station at Milos,
she might have turned back any second invasion attempt, or notified CCAF command, or both.

In an instant, The Chancellor's mask of neutrality
hardened.

"Zahn, send a message to Sasha Wan Li. Have the
Maskirovka arrest *Kong-sang-wei* Tullio Kar. He is to
be court-martialed for gross negligence in his duty
to the Confederation."

Talon Zahn read in the Chancellor's jade-green eyes
the unspoken remainder of the order. Kar was to be
found guilty and executed.

15

Touchstone Spaceport, Milos
Xin Sheng Commonality
Capellan Confederation
10 February 3062

Cheng Shao took his hands from his *Anvil*'s control sticks, stripped off his fire-resistant nomex gloves, and rubbed his sweaty palms across the rough ballistic nylon cooling vest. A few hundred meters away, a low, hunched-over *Sentinel* kept silent electronic watch on his northern perimeter. Aside from his own, and the medium 'Mech being piloted by *Saowei* Claus Basara, Shao had only four BattleMechs left under his command. An older-model *Centurion* and its complementary *Trebuchet* would serve as his primary base of fire. The third, a small, quick *Raven*, designed before the Fourth Succession War, could only act as a harrier. The last was a brand-new *Exter-*

minator seized intact from the Blackwind Lancers. This modern machine was under the command of another of Shao's Death Commandos.

Beyond this lance-and-a-half of mixed weight class machines, Shao had only a handful of conventional armored fighting vehicles and a small mob of half-trained militia infantrymen to oppose the well-equipped, superbly trained, powerful combat force that was bearing down on him.

What scouts remained to him had spotted a force of light BattleMechs, supported by a few dozen infantry carriers and light hovertanks, skirting along Touchstone's southern edge. Knowing the Light Horse from intelligence reports, Shao determined that the units closing in on the spaceport from the south were only a pinning force. The Light Horse was well known for its efforts to avoid civilian casualties and would probably not send a heavy combat unit into the city of Touchstone. Thus, the primary strike must come from the north.

Shao wiped the sweat from his hands again, pulled on the close-fitting gloves, and settled back to wait. He knew it would not be long.

From his vantage point, secure in the cockpit of his *Hercules*, Colonel Charles Antonescu could see little more than the low, rolling hills and thin, scrubby woods that had come to represent Milos for the Eridani Light Horse. Gray winter skies that were beginning to release wet snow completed a bleak picture. Fortunately, he was not limited to what he could observe through the armored viewscreen of his heavy BattleMech's cockpit. A small computer-controlled tactical display showed the location of each company command 'Mech in his attack force. If he set the instrument to display every war machine under his command, the small monitor screen would be flooded with tiny blue icons representing each 'Mech and armored vehicle in the One Fifty-first Light Horse Regiment.

Antonescu had initially questioned General Amis's notion of fighting a limited battle against the Capellan forces defending Touchstone.

"It is foolish to hold back any of our strength, General," he had protested formally. "You know as well as I that when you attack you must hold nothing back, *non*? So why attack using only the Dark Horse Regiment's lightest elements? Why not commit to one crushing blow?"

"Charles, do you remember Lootera, the capital of Huntress?" Amis asked. "Remember what it looked like after we got through with it? I made myself a promise that I'd never be a party to destroying civilian areas again unless it could not be avoided. If we go in with a full 'Mech-to-'Mech assault, we're gonna wreck a lot of civvie property, and we'd rather not have the people here siding with the Capellans any more than they already are.

"No, we'll do it my way. If things get bogged down, *then* we'll call in the heavy stuff, not before."

Antonescu gave the oddly Gallic shrug he often used when speaking to his commander, making the restraining straps of his ejection seat bite into his shoulders as he lifted them in resignation.

"Magyar, this is Hawkeye One," a radio message

interrupted his musings. "We're in contact with the enemy. Looks like things are gonna get hot now."

A pair of laser lances scored deeply into the thick armor covering the chest of Chen Shao's *Anvil*, making the big machine stagger as a ton of hardened steel was turned to slag. High-explosive rounds burst at his machine's feet as a barrage of autocannon shells fell short. Shards of ferrocrete snapped and clattered against his armored ankles.

At first Shao had thought the Light Horse commander was going to attempt to take the spaceport solely with armored infantrymen, because it was they who opened the battle against him. Hardly had the SLDF power armor moved into the port and begun firing upon the Capellan tanks and unarmored infantry than the Light Horse BattleMechs arrived and the battle was joined in earnest.

In one corner of his viewscreen he saw a militiaman who, until a few weeks ago, had been a simple farmer, kneel in the shadow of a spaceport hangar door and unleash a pair of short-range missiles at a gray- and green-painted *Falcon*. The projectiles didn't burst on contact with the Light Horse 'Mech's armor. Instead, they were triggered by a proximity fuse a few meters before impact, spraying the skinny war machine with a mixture of naphthalene palmitate, white phosphorus, and other incendiary chemicals. The sticky, burning liquid showered the *Falcon*, wreathing it in dark, greasy flames.

For a few moments, the MechWarrior desperately tried to scrape the burning fuel off his 'Mech's armor, but he only succeeded in spreading the stuff around.

In an act more worthy of a petulant child than a professional soldier, he fired his 'Mech's pulse laser, burning down the man with the missile launcher, before ejecting from his crippled 'Mech.

Shao had little time to contemplate the needless death of the militia trooper, for at that moment a second volley of autocannon shells, this one better aimed, slashed across his *Anvil*'s legs. Twisting the machine at its waist, he located his tormentor, a bird-like *Cicada*, and treated it to a stuttering blast of heavy laser fire that ripped armor from the Light Horse machine's right leg and arm. The *Cicada* must have taken damage earlier in the fight, because it sagged toward its damaged leg and toppled onto its side, the right leg snapping in half at the knee. The pilot was dead, or unconscious, or playing things smart, because the forty-ton 'Mech lay still.

Before he could savor his victory, another Light Horse 'Mech, this one an *Enforcer*, took the place of its fallen comrade. The enemy 'Mech opened up with its full complement of weapons, risking a heat-induced shutdown for the sake of launching a devastating "alpha strike" against the enemy commander.

A warning indicator flared to life on the *Anvil*'s 'Mech Status Display, revealing a serious gap in the armor of his right leg below the knee. Armor-Piercing Discarding-Sabot rounds from the *Enforcer*'s dual-purpose autocannon had ripped away two thirds of the leg's protection in a single burst. A nearly invisible bolt of coherent light cored into his *Anvil*'s right breast, widening and deepening the wound inflicted by the earlier laser strikes from an unknown assailant.

Shao replied with a paired blast from his heavy pulse lasers, which sent a wave of heat spiking into his cockpit. Ignoring the dangerously increased core temperature, he clamped down on the triggers again, this time adding his slightly less powerful medium lasers to the incredible energies savaging the Light Horse 'Mech. The *Anvil* became sluggish, and an oddly sexy female voice advised him that automatic shutdown procedures had been initiated. Contemptuously, he slapped the manual override, panting for breath as his overtaxed heat sinks struggled to bring the 'Mech's internal heat level down to a manageable level.

As he shook the sweat from his eyes, Shao realized that the *Enforcer* had stopped firing on his 'Mech. The mangled Light Horse machine stood quiet. Both arms lay on the ground, the lightly falling snow steaming when it hit the hot metal. The *Enforcer*'s leg joints had been locked in place by its onboard computer when the pilot ejected from his severely damaged machine.

Across the compound, a coruscating flower of flame blossomed next to the terminal building as the *Trebuchet*'s ammunition exploded. Nearby sat his two Po heavy tanks, both wrecked and burning. Clearly, the battle had been against them from the start.

In a move that the uninitiated would hardly have expected from a Death Commando, Chen Shao opened a broad communication channel, which would reach all of his surviving troops.

"All Milosian troops, this is Chen Shao," he sent in clear, plain language. "Pull out. I say again, pull out and head for the rally point."

Not waiting for acknowledgments from his men, Shao fired his *Anvil*'s jump jets and bounded away backward. All across the compound, militia troopers and regular CCAF training officers alike began to disengage and withdraw from the fight.

As his vaulting 'Mech crashed back to the ground, urged into a loping trot by its human pilot, Shao cursed bitterly at having to leave the fight and the battlefield to the enemy. But he also knew he could better serve the Chancellor by staying alive and continuing the fight as a guerrilla than by dying a hero.

16

As General Edwin Amis slid down the chain ladder dangling along his 'Mech's torso, he felt a flush of pride rise into his heart. Under his command, the Eridani Light Horse had fought two engagements, albeit small ones, and had taken only a handful of casualties. Most of the battle losses were the result of damage to steel and myomer, rather than to flesh and bone. All but one of the damaged 'Mechs were repairable. That one, an *Enforcer* belonging to the Fifth Recon Company, would have to be scrapped out for spare parts.

A more difficult task than combat now lay ahead of the Light Horse. The Capellans had possessed

Milos for nearly a year. The intelligence briefings he'd received on Kittery said that there had been Capellan military personnel, political officers, and training cadres on planet almost from the day it was captured. Amis also knew the former Blackwind Lancers had waged a desperate guerrilla campaign for months before the Light Horse arrived. Too bad it wasn't in time to save them.

How many of the citizens had been turned to the cause of Capellan expansionism? How many had become so indoctrinated by the Xin Sheng propaganda that they were willing to fight a guerrilla war? How many partisan snipers, bombers, and general troublemakers would his troops face until the planet could be secured? He knew of their existence from the news reports of political murders he had intercepted on his initial, abortive foray into this system.

Then, too, there would have to be a response from the Capellan Confederation Armed Forces. No one knew exactly how many troops Sun-Tzu Liao had at his disposal. Most of the military planners on Kittery believed that the Capellan forces were stretched dangerously thin across the active military front between the Confederation and the rapidly dwindling St. Ives Compact. Did Sun-Tzu have enough troops to launch a counterattack against the now-occupied Milos?

"General? We've got a bit of a problem here." Amis recognized the voice in his headset communicator as belonging to Major Gary Ribic, Antonescu's second in command.

"Go ahead, Major. What's up?"

"Well, sir, some of our armored infantry troopers chased a bunch of Capellan militiamen into the secure ComStar facility over here on the north edge of the spaceport," Ribic answered. "Seems they asked for refuge, or sanctuary, or some damnfool thing, and the local Precentor gave it to them. They're holed up in the HPG station, and the Precentor says ComStar has claimed neutrality, which the Star League forces must honor. One more thing, sir—though this is still a ComStar installation, it seems that the head honcho is kinda sympathetic to the Wobblies."

Dammit, Amis cursed silently. The somewhat derisive term "Wobblies" meant the Word of Blake faction that had split from ComStar some years earlier over the parent organization's abandonment of its quasi-religious trappings.

"All right, Major," he said, after considering the situation for a moment or two. "Tell the Precentor that we'll leave him and his alone. The militiamen can have their sanctuary, so long as neither they nor any ComStar personnel inside that facility attempt to give aid and comfort to the Capellan forces still active on Milos. Tell him . . . What's his name anyhow?"

"Precentor Jamie Micone."

"Tell Precentor Micone I'll stop by and see him some time in the next few days. Maybe we can work this thing out without shooting."

Amis changed a setting on his transmitter and opened a wide-band command channel.

"Attention to orders! All ELH commands, this is Stonewall. Get your people organized. Rearm and repair are at the top of the list. Have your ground-pounders go over every centimeter of this facility. The Capellans have probably left behind booby-traps, or sabotaged some of the port facilities, or some such thing. I don't want anyone getting killed if we can avoid it.

"Colonel Antonescu? Give your troopers a 'well done' for me, will you?" Amis could sense his subordinate's narrow smile of pleasure at receiving an unwonted compliment from his former peer.

"And someone call in the DropShips," Amis continued, a smile creasing his lips. "Sunny-boy may not be able to throw all that much at us. But, what he does throw is gonna be good. I want the ELH to be as ready for 'em as we can be."

One who was not a member of the Eridani Light Horse watched coldly as an enemy officer with the single pip of a Star League Lieutenant General adjusted the headband of his radio transceiver and turned toward the spaceport's main terminal building.

From her vantage point on top of a warehouse fronting on the port's eastern fence, Nessa Ament peered intently through the powerful optical telescopic sight mated to the upper receiver of her accurized and suppressed Zeus heavy rifle. Instinctively, she calculated the man's pace and the distance to the target. Taking into account the slight cross-wind and the fact that she was shooting downhill, she carefully lined up the scope's mil-dot reticle, took half a breath, and squeezed the trigger.

*   *   *

"General?"

The voice came from a few meters behind him. Amis stopped in his tracks and turned sharply.

"Yeah, Dane?" Captain Dane Nichols, who had been Ariana Winston's aide-de-camp, had seemingly appointed himself to that same post for her successor.

Whatever piece of information Nichols had to impart to his commander went unvoiced, for, at that moment, a sharp crack split the air. Almost buried in the ear-hurting sound was a muted *paff*, as a frangible rifle bullet struck the ferrocrete a half-dozen meters from where Amis was standing.

Neither man had to be told what the sounds meant, nor did either stop to consider their consequences. Both set up the age-old cry of "Sniper!" and dove for the cover of a spaceport cargo-hauler, parked only a few meters away.

Armored infantrymen rushed to the scene and hustled the pinned-down officers into the relative safety of the terminal building. Other AI troopers swarmed around the terminal building, searching for any sign of the sniper, but found none.

Six hundred meters away, Nessa Ament silently lowered her rifle. Beside her, equally as silent, her spotter, Jin Racan lowered his electronic binoculars and shook his head. Her shot had been a clean miss.

Ament hissed through clenched teeth as she snapped the magazine from the rifle's lower receiver.

She should never have missed such an easy shot, she thought in angry self-reproach.

Racan shook his head again, as Ament slipped the

rifle into its thickly padded "drag-bag." She took the simple gesture as he had meant it. "Everyone misses now and then."

"Next time I won't." Her hoarse voice was raw with anger and disappointment. "Next time, I'll blow his head off."

=== 17 ===

"**R**epairs are almost complete. We should be up to nearly pre-operation strength by nightfall." Regimental Sergeant Major Steven Young read from the electronic clipboard lying on the table before him. "We've lost four 'Mechs, non-recoverable, and two more than could be fixed if we had enough spare parts. Problem is, we ain't got the spares."

Amis listened carefully to what was called, with gallows humor, "the butcher's bill," the list of casualties from any battle or campaign. Under ordinary circumstances, he'd have said the Light Horse got off easy, losing only six 'Mechs and a dozen supporting infantry or armored units to enemy action, and capturing an enemy-held spaceport in return. But, given that the enemy had been a poorly trained and equipped local militia supported by Capellan military advisors, the casualties were high.

When Young finished his report and sat down, Lieutenant Sebastiano DiGiovanni, head of the Command Company's Security Lance, and also the officer who usually served as a liaison officer between the Brigade and the local population, took his place.

"General, we still have no idea who took a pop at you the other day," DiGiovanni said without consulting his notes. "We ran a sweep of the surrounding buildings and found a whole lot of traces on a whole bunch of rooftops. Seems that a fair number of folks had turned out to watch the battle, and then took to their heels once the shooting started. We were able to figure out roughly where the shot came from, but that's about it. I've ordered our perimeter guards to keep an eye on the rooftops adjoining the spaceport. But since those buildings are civilian property, I can't order them closed down.

"I tried going through the local civil authorities, and that's where we ran into a problem."

"How so?" Amis asked, leaning back in his chair. True to form, he showed up for the staff meeting with a thin black cigar clenched tightly in his teeth.

"Well, sir, when I talked to the local Chief of Police, he was kinda blunt with me. He said they'd 'check on the incident'—his words, sir—but he didn't have much hope of finding out who the shooter was. As you know, it's our policy to buy at least some of our supplies from local sources. About half the merchants we approached treated us with what can

best be described as sullen resignation. A few were
openly hostile. I'm told one produce wholesaler
bodily threw one of our commissary sergeants out of
his shop. Said he'd burn the place down before he'd
sell to us. I gather a lot of the locals have taken similar attitudes."

"My men report similar incidents throughout the
city," Major Kent Fairfax put in. His Fiftieth Heavy
Cavalry Battalion was well-known for its concern for
the safety of all civilians and non-combatants, not
just those belonging to the Eridani Light Horse. "We
went into town to check on the locals. You know, to
see if there was anything we could do for them, to
make sure that none of our people got out of hand,
or anything of the sort. Well, General, I actually got
the impression that the locals were angry that we're
here. Some even said they were happy to have the
Capellans back, and why did we have to come in
and mess everything up?"

Amis puffed silently on his cigar for a moment.
He was surprised that any planetary population that
had been living free under a democratic government
would eagerly welcome the return of a repressive,
totalitarian state like the Capellan Confederation.

"All right, Lieutenant, why?"

"I don't exactly know, sir."

"Perhaps I might offer an explanation, General?"
Antonescu said formally. "Again, the hard records
are rather thin, many having been deleted, redacted,
or otherwise altered, but it seems that prior to the
Capellans launching their campaign to retake the St.
Ives Compact, Maskirovka *agents provocateur* were
sent to various worlds, Milos included, to stir up the

local populations against the government they had initially embraced, but which they now resented. News accounts show that the number of anti-Davion, anti-St. Ives, pro-Capellan demonstrations grew dramatically just before Sun-Tzu sent his 'peace-keepers' into the Compact. Apparently, things were getting so hot just prior to the Capellan invasion that the Blackwind Lancers were prisoners in their own base. Demonstrations were a daily occurrence and were growing more violent day by day."

Antonescu paused for a short, bitter laugh.

"If the Capellans hadn't seized Milos, it's likely that the locals would have stormed the Lancers' base, resulting in a blood bath.

"As it happened, when the Capellan 'peace-keepers' arrived and kicked out the 'turncoat' Blackwind Lancers, the Milosians welcomed them with open arms. The Capellans have been here for just about a year now. I gather once things settled down, with the exception of the odd guerrilla strike, they brought back their cultural monitors, and refrectors, their quotas, and economic-utilization programs. As a result the planetary economy has turned around. People are becoming prosperous again. I gather it is all a part of this Xin Sheng program. Seems like they don't mind giving up some of their freedoms in exchange."

Amis put down his cigar and shook his head.

"Sad, isn't it, when people value a few C-bills in their pocket more than they do their freedom?" He shook his head again and sighed. "So, Charles, what you're telling me is that the people of Milos were really happy when the Capellans came back. Now, they feel that the Eridani Light Horse, arriving under the banner of the Star League with the intent of kicking out Sunny's 'peace-keepers,' is actually a sign that the League *wants* to keep them in their poor economic state."

"That would seem to be about the size of it, General."

Amis snorted in disgusted half-amusement at the vagaries of the human mind.

"All right," he said at last. "Starting now, we do everything we can to counteract this stupidity. Charles, get a message off to Kittery. Tell General Sortek what we've got here and ask for advice from Civil Affairs or Psy-Ops. In the meantime, we keep up standard policies. No one gets into a hassle with the indigs . . ."

"Excuse me, General," Fairfax interrupted. "But that might be the best place to start."

"What?"

" 'Indigs,' sir. I know it's a common term, but a lot of locals think it's degrading."

"All right, post it with tomorrow's orders. Use of the term 'indig' is to be discouraged. From now on, they're locals. Will that serve?"

Fairfax nodded.

"To continue, I don't want any hassles with the locals. We'll reduce the visibility of our patrols as much as possible. Keep the security checks on Milosians to a minimum. Only those persons who must be in sensitive areas of the spaceport are to be checked out. Let's try to keep a lid on this thing. Sunny's bound to send more troops to try to kick us off Milos, and I'd rather not be facing a world full of guerrillas as well as 'Mech-equipped line troops."

"General, what about the Capellan and Milosian troops holed up in the ComStar station?" Colonel Calvin asked.

"Precentor Micone says he'll turf them out in a few days, so I don't think we've got any problems there," Amis answered. "Just make sure we separate the Capellans from the locals. Let the Milosians go on parole, but keep the Capellan troops locked up as POWs.

"Now, anything else?" When no one spoke, Amis dismissed his command staff.

As Ed Amis and Charles Antonescu stepped from the warmth of the spaceport's main terminal building, they paused in the shelter of the doorway to turn up their collars against the cold, damp wind that had blown up in the past few hours. Captain Bill Kole, Colonel Calvin's executive officer, touched his cap in a half-salute as he squeezed past his superiors. Kole smiled indulgently at the senior officers' efforts to shield themselves from the wind. Growing up in Tharkad's cold southern climes, he regarded the cool breeze as comfortable.

With no prior sign of distress, in the midst of striding across the spaceport tarmac, Kole pitched over onto his face, making no effort to catch himself. A sharp, high crack echoed off the brick and ferrocrete faces of the port buildings.

Amis grabbed Antonescu and shoved him inside the terminal building just as another crack rent the air. Fragments of bullet casing and gray shards of ferrocrete rattled against his field jacket.

"Dammit! This is getting out of hand!" Amis

snarled, as half a dozen voices outside set up the warning cry of "Sniper!"

A hundred meters from the main terminal building, in the direction of the port's primary hangar facility, a Light Horse infantryman brought up his assault rifle and began to blaze away at the uppermost level of a nearby building. Amis guessed that the trooper had seen, or thought he had seen, the sniper's muzzle blast, and was attempting to suppress or kill the enemy marksman.

A puff of pink-tinged spray flew from the man's wet uniform as a heavy bullet slammed into his chest. The sonic crack of the bullet was lost in the roaring chatter of the Light Horseman's full automatic burst. The infantryman collapsed onto his back. In his death agony, the trooper convulsively clutched the rifle's trigger. Tracers continued to lance into the dreary snow-laden air until the weapon's magazine ran dry.

On the rooftop of a nearby warehouse, Nessa Ament looked over the tube of her daylight sniper's scope, while Jin Racan swung his electronic binoculars in search of a new target. Her last victim, an infantryman, had been far too easy. He had not only failed to seek appropriate cover but had called attention to himself by spraying automatic fire into the wrong building. He was a fool, and he died for it.

"One o'clock ten meters. Jeep," Jin said quietly.

"Got it," Ament replied, locating the vehicle a dozen meters from the spot where her last target fell.

"There's a man behind the engine cowling. Wait a second and he'll stick his head up again."

Ament dropped her eye to peer through the scope. Sure enough, a red-haired man lifted his head a few centimeters above the drab green jeep. She watched as he crept cautiously around the front of the vehicle, gathering himself for a dash toward her first victim, the enemy officer. He had a large green nylon satchel in his left hand. Both the bag and the man's sleeves were decorated with a white circle emblazoned with a red cross.

With no hesitation, Nessa Ament settled her sights behind the man's left ear and squeezed the trigger. The medic fell dead in a heap, a bloody pulp where his head had been.

A low, whining hum reached her ears, but the sniper ignored it while she searched the compound for another target.

"Nessa, they've got a BattleMech powering up." Racan's urgent whisper explained the sound. It was the throbbing of a 'Mech power plant coming on line. "His sensors may be able to detect our position. We must go. Now."

Ament nodded silently. No matter that she was firing from a concealed position, using a suppressor that killed the weapon's muzzle flash and smoke as well as reducing the sound of her shots; three rounds was the usual tactical limit for a sniper, set forth by the Death Commandos' rigid doctrine. The BattleMech's sophisticated sensors would almost assuredly allow its pilot to locate their position. Even the big thirteen-millimeter slugs from her heavy sniper rifle stood little chance of penetrating the armor of a 'Mech.

Without a word, she backed carefully out of the

specially selected hide she and Racan had occupied for the past two days. The kills were worth the effort. One officer, a medic, and a foot soldier lay dead. Now the enemy knew that they were not going to enjoy an easy campaign. The battle for Milos would not be a clean, stand-up fight. If Nessa Ament had anything to do with it, the Eridani Light Horse would experience the horror of a guerrilla war.

18

Like many towns and cities on Milos, Orpheus was dedicated almost exclusively to the sea. Built around a small, well-sheltered harbor, it boasted a fleet of fishing boats and floating factories, which processed Milosian hurricane kelp into pharmaceuticals, or packaged the rare, delicate flesh of her marine animals for connoisseurs across the Inner Sphere. In spite of its interesting economy, to Cheng Shao, Orpheus was as uninteresting a town as he had seen in all of his thirty-nine years.

Following the stinging defeat he had suffered at the hands of the numerically and technologically superior Eridani Light Horse, Shao and his shattered command had fallen back to the small fishing village to regroup. Only thirty kilometers to the southwest of Touchstone, Orpheus was well situated for the next phase of the campaign that was now forming in the Death Commando's mind. Less than half of Shao's original command had survived the battle initially opposing the Light Horse's landing and the defense of Touchstone. His tank and infantry battalions had suffered the greatest losses.

More importantly, one of his Death Commandos had lived up to the unit's reputation by fighting to the death, taking one Light Horse 'Mech and an unknown number of infantrymen with him. The battles had left him with only eighteen operational BattleMechs, too few to stage an operation to recapture Touchstone from the invaders. Shao was grateful to the gods he didn't believe in that he wouldn't have to make the attempt.

He sat at a table in the only decent restaurant in Orpheus, the only one, in fact, where the menu did not consist solely of seafood. Aside from himself and the two men seated with him, the place was empty. An obviously nervous waiter and an equally apprehensive busboy hovered uncertainly near the kitchen doors. Across the table from Shao sat *Sao-wei* Claus Basara, the Maskirovka Agent-in-Charge of the Capellan intelligence branch on Milos. To Shao's right was Captain Petar Kredic, the leader of the now-decimated Milos Militia.

Shao waited until they had been served before he began to explain his plans. Once the steaming plates of food had been placed in front of them and the wait-staff had retreated to the relative safety of the kitchen, Shao started laying out his scheme.

"You both know I received a message from the *Elias Jung*'s captain just before she jumped outsystem, informing me of the Light Horse's first invasion attempt. I immediately had word of the thwarted attack relayed to the Confederation Command Council on Sian. When the Light Horse launched their second strike attempt, I sent an urgent, priority message back to Sian to inform them that we would probably not be able to hold out against the enemy assault.

"I am certain that the Command Council will send in a heavy combat unit to drive the invaders off-planet as soon as such a unit is available. The problem is that the Light Horse will be well entrenched by the time that unit arrives. We must allow the enemy no leisure time to dig in. We must force them to waste their time and strength in fighting us, rather than preparing improved positions for defense.

"The Death Commandos have not been idle these months we have spent here on Milos. At my instructions, my men have spent much time in training the loyal citizens in the arts of guerrilla warfare. Beginning immediately, we will make life difficult for the Eridani Light Horse. I intend to initiate a program of harassment against the enemy. We will launch hit-and-run strikes, rocket and mortar attacks; we will snipe at their officers and their sentries, and do everything in our power to weaken their morale and sap their will to fight."

"It is a good plan, Major," Basara said. "I wonder how much your harassment will affect the morale of a unit like the Eridani Light Horse. They have faced some of the toughest opponents of any main-line combat unit and have not quailed. Do you really believe that a few mortar rounds tossed into their compounds or a couple of snipers shooting at their officers will weaken their will to fight?"

"You are correct, as always, *Sao-wei*, in your assessment of the Light Horse's fighting spirit," Shao conceded with a nod. "But you have not taken into account two things. First, the Light Horse we are facing is not the Light Horse of old. They lost many of their most experienced soldiers in the fighting on Huntress. Many of their replacements have yet to become 'infected,' shall we say, with the Light Horse's belief in their invulnerability. We shall strike hardest at these weaker links.

"Second, as you observe, the Eridani Light Horse is a main-line combat unit. Their entire tactical doctrine is built around maneuver warfare on a large scale. They are not equipped, physically or mentally, to fight a guerrilla war. They will attempt to—what is the phrase?—'swat mosquitoes with a sledgehammer' by trying to use 'Mech forces against us, but this is one situation where superior firepower will not prevail."

Basara nodded his understanding.

"In the meantime, Claus, you will return to Touchstone and initiate your own special brand of warfare against the Light Horse. Begin stirring up the citizenry against the invaders. Turn them against the Light Horse by means of rumor, innuendo, and propaganda."

Basara bared his teeth in a fierce grin. As a Maskirovka agent trained in disinformation and psychological warfare, this was the sort of operation he was trained for.

"In addition, Claus, you are to use your special talents to attempt to subvert one or more of the invaders to our cause. It would most useful to have a tool of our own in the enemy's kit when the time comes."

19

Touchstone Spaceport, Milos
Xin Sheng Commonality
Capellan Confederation
22 February 3062

In most other military units, rank carried many privileges, but in the Eridani Light Horse those special considerations were few. The one duty from which many other outfits excused its senior officers was that of Officer of the Day. Not so the Eridani Light Horse. Only the Commanding General was exempt. All other officers had to stand OOD watch, even regimental commanders.

Colonel Paul Calvin, who had the dubious honor of being Officer of the Day on one of the coldest mornings since the Light Horse had landed on Milos, leaned wearily against the frigid bricks of the spaceport terminal building's main entryway. He looked with dismay at the knot of protesters gathered outside the space-port's main gate. Though few in number, the civilians were setting up a fearful clamor. Signs ranging from the unimaginative, such as "Light Horse, Go Home," to the obscene, bobbed and waved above the heads of the demonstrators. A few shouted slogans at the stone-faced MPs stationed behind a three-meter-high chain-link fence topped with barbed wire.

After the sniper attack following the capture of the spaceport, the demonstrations had been relatively peaceful. Every day a handful of pickets would show up, armed with their placards and catch phrases. They would march back and forth, wave signs, and screech imprecations against the Eridani Light Horse, but do little else. Occasionally a few rocks or empty glass bottles would be lobbed over the fence at the sentries, but those missiles didn't make much of an impression. Neither did the weather, which was growing progressively colder, seem to deter the mob. In fact, as the depth of the snowbanks drifting up against the windward side of the spaceport buildings increased, so did the anger and resentment of the crowd.

That was not to say the demonstrations had no effect whatever. Off-duty Light Horsemen were ordi-narily permitted to go into town. But the general populace of Touchstone seemed to hold the Star League troops in such disdain that few took advan-tage of the opportunity to leave the spaceport.

Nor were the protests limited to the planetary capi-tal. Most of the outlying towns and cities had their own form of protest, which they leveled against any-one wearing a Light Horse uniform. Because of the threat of sniper attacks and the anticipation of the arrival of a Capellan relief force, General Amis restricted his people to the spaceport town and some small outposts situated within a few days' forced march from Touchstone.

Watching the protesters, Calvin shook his head in disgust. He'd been on less comfortable planets, but he could not remember being on one where so many of the people seemed to have their heads bolted on crooked.

A dull, thuttering sound reached his ears. The noise seemed to come from the direction of the gate, an odd sound that reminded him of an old-time motorcycle engine. Drawn by the anomaly, he abandoned the shelter of the main terminal building's recessed doorway and trotted across the wind-blown spaceport tarmac toward the gate. As OOD, it was his job to check out unusual occurrences.

Just as he arrived, the Corporal in change of the gate guard detail was accepting a large, brown paper-wrapped parcel from a young man wearing the uniform of a local package delivery service.

"Colonel," the non-com said, noticing Calvin's arrival. "We got this package addressed to General Amis and the ELH command staff. Whaddaya want me to do with it?"

"Let me see it," Calvin replied. A standard, letter-sized envelope was glued to the top of the heavy parcel. Calvin pulled it free and extracted the single sheet of paper it contained.

"Says it's a goodwill gesture from certain members of the city council who wish to remain anonymous for fear of their neighbors," Calvin said thoughtfully.

"Hmmm. I still don't necessarily like this, though. Trooper, run over to the ordnance depot and fetch Sergeant Kilgore. Tell her we've got a suspicious package down here, and I want . . ."

Blanng!

A violent force picked up the Light Horse officer and slammed him face down on the snow-dusted pavement. He heard and felt the dull crack as several of his ribs snapped, driving the breath from his lungs. He lay there, unable to move, gasping for air. Strangely, he felt no pain, just a dull ache in his chest and an odd sunburn-like sensation across his back and legs. He knew the initial shock of his injuries was insulating him from what he should be feeling.

Dimly, through fogged senses, Calvin heard a scream of pain. It seemed to be coming from far away, perhaps even from the other side of the space-port compound.

Summoning all his willpower, he dragged his hands beneath him and pushed himself into a kneeling position. A saw-edged wave of pain ripped across his upper back as he levered himself onto his knees. Reeling, remaining upright only by the force of his will, Calvin waited until the red fog across his eyes cleared. Then, cautiously, trying not to move much, he reached over his shoulder. His probing fingers encountered a wide, jagged gash that gouged deep into the latissimus muscles. His senses reeled again as his wounded body recoiled from his own touch.

Staggering to his feet, Calvin looked around the guard post. The Corporal of the Guard was nowhere to be seen. His issue boots stood exactly where Calvin had seen the man last, but the non-com had vanished. Two other infantry troopers lay on the redstained tarmac in the grotesque huddled postures that only the dead can achieve. One, mercifully, lay face down, his wounds hidden from view. The other lay on his back, his torn and bloody face staring emptily at the sky. The front of his green and gray camouflage jacket was now a sickly red brown color.

Turning away from the horrible sight, Calvin spotted the fourth member of the guard detail, the young trooper he had sent off in search of Ordnance Sergeant Kilgore. He lay thrashing in agony on the tarmac, screaming himself hoarse, and trying to staunch the blood that spurted from his left arm, which was torn away just below the elbow.

"Corpsman!" Calvin called. His shattered ribs sent a knife of pain into his chest.

Heedless of his own hurts, Calvin ripped his torn and bloody field jacket from his back and dropped to his knees beside the wounded man. As best he could, he wrapped the sleeve of his jacket around the wounded man's severed arm, just above the head of the biceps. Using the last of his rapidly fading strength, he twisted the heavy cloth garment in his hands, desperately trying to pinch off the torn brachial artery with his makeshift tourniquet.

"I've got him, sir," a dark-skinned man said, dropping to his knees beside the swaying Colonel.

Calvin could not force his hand to release the tourniquet to the corpsman.

"I said I've got him, Colonel," the medic said again, a bit more sharply. "Let go of him, for God's sake."

Other hands were on him now, some forcing him

to relinquish his grip on the twisted jacket sleeve, others applying pressure bandages to his wounds. Then blackness closed over his mind as Colonel Paul Calvin lapsed into unconsciousness.

A *Watchman* bearing the flaming bronco emblem of the Nineteenth Cavalry Regiment advanced on the perimeter fence, its lasers and machine guns appearing to menace the fear-stricken, morbid curiosity-gripped mob just outside the wire. Around the forty-ton monster's feet swarmed a platoon of armored infantrymen, their anti-personnel weapons held at the ready. They same equine crest adorned the shoulders of their heavy armor. In the background, a white-painted ambulance sped off in the direction of the spaceport medical facility, while a squad of Light Horse Military Policemen struggled to keep ELH troopers from rushing to the scene to help their fallen comrades.

Unfortunately, that was not how the reporter who provided the voice-over for the evening holovid news spun it. According to him, the MPs were trying to prevent the enraged Light Horsemen from pouring through the gate to take revenge on the crowd for the bomb blast that killed three of their comrades and wounded four more, including Colonel Paul Calvin, the commander of the Nineteenth Striker, the very unit to which the menacing *Watchman* and the armored infantrymen belonged. The newsman mentioned this fact at least three times in his report.

With a snarl of anger and disgust, Ed Amis stabbed the control pad with his finger. The holovid clicked off.

"There," he said furiously. "You see how they're playing it? They deliver a package to our front gate, claiming that they want to be our friends. The bomb inside blows the Corporal of the guard to pieces, kills two other troopers. Not to mention they damn near killed Colonel Calvin and three more. *Then* they have the nerve to go on planet-wide holo and twist the facts to make it look like *we* were the bad guys."

Amis flung his unlit cigar across the room and turned his angry gaze on his command staff.

"All right, people, I wanna hear our options."

"General, I have already set our MPs to working on the scene." Predictably, Charles Antonescu was the first to respond. He was the most familiar with Amis's volatile but usually well-hidden temper, and was thus the least affected by it. "Unfortunately, we have never needed the kind of investigators such a case requires. I do not believe the MPs will have much luck in determining the origins of the bomb. They have been trained to handle field security, traffic control, and management of POWs. They have no experience in investigating terrorist bombings.

"Nor have we any troops who are trained to counter guerrilla or terrorists attacks. The closest thing we have would be Captain Kyle and the Pathfinders, but even they aren't trained for this kind of situation."

"Sir, what about the local police?" Dane Nichols asked. "Their crime labs would be better suited for analyzing bomb fragments. Do you think it would do any good for us to ask for their help on this one?"

"I dunno, Dane," Amis answered. "I've already sent a carefully worded request to their chief asking for assistance on this case, but I'm not sure they'll even answer me. If they do give us a hand here, they probably 'won't be able to find much evidence.' "

Amis shook his head, then continued, "All right, nobody's gonna like this one, but it can't be helped. As of now, all off-base passes are canceled. Double security patrols inside the fence. I want four-man teams of armored infantrymen patrolling *outside* the wire. They are to stick to the streets adjoining the spaceport and to avoid confrontations with the locals, if possible.

"Also, all civilians normally employed at the spaceport will have their passes revoked. That includes the civilian areas of the port. We can't risk having a terrorist slip into our compound from the civvie part of the port. Maybe when things calm down again, we can let them come back, but until then, I'm not willing to take that risk."

"General," Antonescu said quietly. "Some of the troopers are not going to like this. Major Fairfax and the Fiftieth Heavy Cavalry, for example."

"I know, Charles. I know," Amis said bitterly. "I know that the Fiftieth and the Eighth Recon are dedicated to the protection of *all* civilians, but we have to do it this way. We both know these steps are necessary to protect the Brigade. Fairfax and his boys will simply have to understand."

20

The poorly insulated nyleath gloves protecting her fingers creaked faintly as Nessa Ament flexed her hands in an attempt to relieve the stiffness that presaged a full-blown cramp. It had been snowing when she first crawled into the shallow gully in which she lay, but that had been five hours ago. In the last forty-five minutes, the snow had turned to sleet. The narrow ditch was now half-filled with icy, frozen mud.

A dozen meters away stood a low earth berm topped with a concertina fence of razorwire strengthened with a web of tanglefoot, the latter being a snarl of barbed wire strung a few centimeters off the ground. Throughout the previous day, Ament had lain hidden beneath the low, twisted thorn trees that bordered the firebase's killing zone. She watched as Light Horse infantrymen set up simple barricades with the assistance of construction equipment commandeered from a local contractor.

How like them, she thought as she watched the big yellow-painted bulldozers scrape up the thick, yellow-brown clay into a chest-high embankment. They dropped onto Milos, where they had no business and were not wanted. Then they stole Capellan state property to build themselves a little fort from which to spread their oppression of the Milosians. Well, tonight she was going to raise the price of doing so.

It had taken her almost three hours to crawl to within a stone's throw of the Light Horse firebase. In all that time, she only glanced at her intended target a half-dozen times. Even then, her gaze never rested on the man for more than a second. She knew from experience that, if one stared for too long at a man, some sixth sense would warn him that he was under surveillance, even if he could not see the one watching him. Her target was young and obviously unprepared for the combat environment.

He would never gain any experience now.

Moving so slowly that the water pooled beneath her body barely rippled, Ament freed a bulky pistol from its waterproof holster. The weapon was an adaptation of the standard dart pistol used by zoos to sedate animals. It had been retrofitted with a set of self-luminous tritium night-sights, which she settled over the green infantryman's lower abdomen. When she squeezed the trigger, the cough of the pneumatic weapon was buried in the grunt of pain from her target.

Dropping the dart gun, she slithered forward as hastily as her need for silence would permit. She arrived at the edge of the rampart just as the youth was beginning to stagger from the effects of the fast-acting tranquilizer the dart had injected into his system. She surged to her feet, caught the young trooper, and lowered him smoothly to the ground. Shoving aside his bulky assault rifle, she hauled her victim into the drainage ditch. Moving quickly, she dragged him away from the Light Horse firebase, using the ditch as cover. She knew the invaders would send out a search party for the missing trooper. The frozen mud left few traces for the enemy to follow. Even if they had experienced trackers, which she counted unlikely, they'd have a hard time following her trail. She had what she came for. If they really wanted him back, they could have him *after* she had finished with him.

The sun was barely peeking over the western horizon when Sergeant Tae Je Kwan, Gamma Company's senior non-com, stepped out of the command bunker in the center of the small firebase.

"In all the years I've been a soldier, and all the worlds I've been on," he said quietly to himself, "I'll never get used to seeing the sun come up in the west."

Kwan arched his back, taking pleasure in the feeling of vertebrae settling into place, before picking up his assault rifle and beginning his rounds of the perimeter sentries. To the sergeant, it seemed a waste of time to build a firebase out in the middle of nowhere to guard a mining site that the locals probably wouldn't want to damage anyway, but, as always, the General's word was law.

The first three troopers he checked on were cold and sleepy, but they were awake and right where they were supposed to be. The fourth was missing. Kwan scanned the open ground outside the base for signs of the sentry. A few meters away from the perimeter berm, a Light Horse-issue assault rifle lay on the ground. A thin coat of ice covered the grass around the weapon, but the rifle was only wet. It had not lain there long.

Sergeant Kwan raced back to the command bunker.

"El-Tee," he shouted, roughly shaking the sleeping officer's shoulder. "Lieutenant, wake up, we got a man missing. Private Davis, second squad. He was on perimeter watch last night. Now he's gone."

Lieutenant Anthony Fesh, who had been dozing in his chair, jerked upright. He jumped to his feet, knocking over the folding camp chair with a clatter. To his credit, he did not ask Kwan to repeat himself.

"Get a patrol together, Sergeant," Fesh snapped. "Make a three-klick sweep. See if you can find out what happened to him. I've got a bad feeling that tells me I already know. If I'm right, you won't find a trace, but he's Light Horse, and we've gotta try."

Six hours later, Kwan and his men straggled back into the firebase. They looked weary. Fesh and Major

I.K. Njemanze, the Battalion commander and the CO of Firebase Kiowa, met them at the gate.

"No luck, sir," Kwan said before either officer could ask. "We found a few scrapes in the ground where whoever grabbed him hauled him into the ditch, and then again about five meters this side of the trees, where they dragged him out again. Damn frozen ground." He kicked at the earth. "Doesn't hold any tracks."

"That's all right, Sergeant," Njemanze said, his handsome black face furrowed with concern for his lost trooper. "I know you did your best."

Kwan nodded wearily and turned to follow his squad. As he made his way across the snow-dusted compound, he heard Major Njemanze say in a tired voice, "It's time we called in the experts."

Ten hours after Major Njemanze placed his radio call to the Light Horse headquarters at the Touchstone spaceport, and twenty hours after Private Davis took a tranq dart in the stomach, Sergeant Lisa Rolls brought her Pathfinders section back into Firebase Kiowa. Their light powered armor was heavily caked with mud and frosted in some places with ice and snow. Despite the fact that they were totally encased in their armor, Major Njemanze was able to read the dejection in the Pathfinders' postures. Even the highly trained special-purpose troops had been unable to locate the missing infantryman.

An armored figure indistinguishable from the others stopped in front of the battalion commander. The Pathfinder reached up and opened the armor's thick helmet visor to reveal the broad, freckled visage of

Sergeant Rolls. A stray wisp of flame-red hair was plastered to her forehead by sweat. It had never occurred to Njemanze that it must get hot in those suits, regardless of the temperature outside.

"I'm sorry, Major," Rolls said. "Your boy's been gone for almost twenty-four hours, and we can't find a trace of him. Aside from the marks your people made, there's no sign of anyone entering or leaving this compound within the last day or so. I really hate to say it, but I don't think you're going to get him back. Not in one piece anyway."

Before Njemanze could respond, the cold night air was filled with the harsh sound of a man's scream.

Rolls snapped her visor back into place and brought up her heavy gyrojet rifle. The weapon's ugly muzzle swung slowly from side to side as though the rifle were searching for a target independently of its operator's will. Others in the firebase ran to the north barricade, desperately peering into the darkness, straining to locate the source of the sound.

"That's Davis!" Njemanze said with chilling certainty.

"I do believe you're right," Rolls said. "I can't see a thing, even on thermal scan. They can't be that far away, so whoever's got him must be pretty well hidden."

Another howl of agony rent the night air, sliding up the scale like a file being dragged across a saw blade. The cry broke off suddenly, falling into a muted series of gasping sobs.

A few meters down the perimeter, a Light Horse infantryman vented his anger and frustration by sending a long, full auto-burst of rifle fire out into the night.

A sharp yelp of pain, followed by a weird, high-pitched moan, begging for mercy.

"I'm sending a patrol out to find him." Njemanze turned to his aide as though to give the order.

Rolls caught him by the elbow.

"Major, that's exactly what those buggers want you to do. They're probably sitting out there, just a few dozen meters away, waiting to ambush your troops the moment they're out of sight of the base. They're using the kid as bait. Even if it isn't an ambush, the guerrillas will kill the kid and slip away quietly before your patrol ever gets close enough to spot them."

"What do you want me to do, Sergeant, just sit here and listen while they torture one of my troopers to death?" Njemanze shook his head. "That may be the way in the Pathfinders, or whatever House special forces unit they dragged you out of. But that is not the way it is in my battalion. The Light Horse does not forsake its own. Captain Redmond . . ."

Njemanze walked away, rattling off orders to his executive officer. Moments later, a lance of light BattleMechs strode off into the darkness, their battle lamps dark, their pilots relying solely on the light-amplification gear built into their viewscreens. As the last of the four combat machines left the compound, Davis gave one shriek of agony and terror. Then all was silent.

The 'Mech patrol was unable to find any trace of Private Davis or his captors. Shortly after dawn the next day, an infantry squad stumbled across the horribly mutilated corpse of their missing comrade. His headless body was covered with deep ragged cuts and ugly blackened patches where a neural lash had been applied. His head had been set on a stake nearby, as though to keep watch over its mangled body. Only the name tape stitched to the front of the tattered uniform jacket and the stainless steel dogtag forced between the teeth identified the corpse. Davis had been so badly abused before he died that his own mother wouldn't have recognized him.

Pinned to the man's torn and blood-stained field jacket was a hand-lettered placard. The words had been written in a red-brown stain. They read:

"Light Horse Go Home."

21

DropShip Farwell, *Approach vector to Milos*
Xin Sheng Commonality
Capellan Confederation
05 March 3062

The DropShip *Farwell* shuddered as heavy High-Explosive Armor-Piercing rounds detonated against its thick armor. Even the massive 35,000 thousand-ton vessel was jarred a little by the slamming impact of two volleys from the Class 20 autocannons mounted in the nose of the attacking *Hammerhead* aerofighters. The light gray ships streaked past the 'Mech hauler's bridge so close that it seemed to *Sang-shao* Samuel Christobal, McCarron's Armored Cavalry, that he could see the color of the Light Horse pilots' eyes.

"Well, they rattled our teeth with that one," the *Farwell*'s *Kong-sang-wei* said with a grin, as a pair of large lasers reached out to swat at the withdrawing fighters. One of the azure lances sliced the tip from the trailing *Hammerhead*'s portside vertical stabilizer, causing the fighter to juke suddenly to the right. "And we're giving better than we get."

Christobal was unused to being a helpless passenger while a battle raged around him. He was more accustomed to the stifling heat and stench of his *Thug*'s cockpit than he was to a DropShip's deck. Several times he forced himself to stifle the urge to shout orders to the ship's crew. He was a ground-pounder, and his presence on the *Farwell*'s bridge was only tolerated by the experienced spacers. If he began trying to run the battle rather than allowing the professionals to handle it, he'd find his welcome swiftly revoked. He bit his lip and tried to stay out of the way while the battle unfolded around him.

In the bridge's main viewscreen, he saw Milos's gray and blue orb looming below him, while tiny DropShips and tinier fighters darted and wheeled through the blackness of space around the *Farwell*. It was obvious from the spirited counter-attack he and his regiment were facing that the Eridani Light Horse had been expecting the arrival of Capellan reinforcements, but the slowness of their response showed that they had not expected fresh troops to arrive so soon.

That was exactly what Christobal had intended. By pushing his JumpShips, hard, perhaps harder than he should have, he was able to arrive at Milos a week ahead of the best estimates calculated by the CCAF Command Council. By entering the system at a so-called pirate point, he'd managed to achieve a measure of surprise against the tough and wily Light Horse and reduce his intrasystem travel time significantly. Christobal found it ironic that his regiment was jumping into a non-standard jump point that the Light Horse had used to seize Milos in the first place.

A fiery rose bloomed at the edge of the viewscreen, dragging Christobal's attention back to the battle. The rapidly expanding ball of flame and debris marked the spot where a warrior had died as his fighter disintegrated around him. Christobal wondered if the lost ship had been Capellan or Light Horse.

Two more Light Horse *Stuka* strike fighters headed for the *Farwell*. Lances of laser light and man-made lightning reached out to savage the attack ships. One crumpled and died under the unbelievable energies that melted armor and reduced human tissue to red-tinged steam. The other delivered its payload of missiles at point-blank range, following it up with a long burst of laser fire. Again, the *Union* Class DropShip trembled as more armor was shattered or turned into vapor.

The *Stuka* rolled onto one wingtip and pulled around into a tight arc, deftly avoiding the *Farwell*'s counterattack. Christobal could only imagine the G-induced physical torture the fighter jock must have been enduring to pull so tight a turn at so high a speed. As the heavy fighter flashed past the DropShip's nose, Christobal caught a glimpse of a surprisingly lifelike drawing of a Terran skunk, and above it, the word "Polecat," decorating the nose of the attack ship.

Missiles leapt from the *Union*'s starboard batteries, but most failed to lock onto the twisting fighter. A few laced the *Stuka*'s wings with armor-breaking explosions.

"*Sang-shao*, we're coming up on the drop zone," the *Fallwell*'s *Kong-sang-wei* shouted over the din of battle. "If you want to go in with your troops, you've got five minutes to get down to the 'Mech bay and get strapped in."

"Right, *Kong-sang-wei*," Christobal answered as he headed for the bridge's elevator. "And thanks for the lift."

Many kilometers below, on the ground at the military compound attached to the northern edge of the Touchstone spaceport, General Edwin Amis watched a sensor repeater display as his aerospace assets tried to stave off the incoming relief force. He knew that the fighters attached to his two regiments would neither be sufficient to halt the Capellan troops nor to reduce their numbers enough to make a difference in the coming fight.

Guerrilla activity had forced the Light Horse to pull in its Area of Operation to within a few score kilometers of Touchstone, and yet the attacks continued. The sniping and bombings and mortar attacks were having their intended effect on his task force. Morale was low and sinking lower. Now, with the inbound 'Mech-haulers, the Light Horse would be forced to fight a two-front battle—against the mainline combat unit now identified as Christobal's Regiment of McCarron's Armored Cavalry as well as against the partisans.

Well, at least his people knew how to fight 'Mechs, he told himself. And if Christobal really wanted to fight for Milos, the Light Horse would certainly oblige him.

22

Sleet and freezing rain clattered against the boxy armored sides of the Eridani Light Horse mobile headquarters truck, sounding like static, but failing to completely blanket the incoming radio message.

"Goshawk Six to Stonewall. Goshawk reports six Delta Sierras, one *Leopard*, two *Overlords*, and three *Unions* on the ground, one-one-zero kilometers southwest your position. Goshawk Six confirms previous ident. The inbounds bear the markings of Mac-Carron's Armored Cavalry. Estimate the enemy should be able to begin off-loading his 'Mechs within the hour."

Ed Amis turned to face the mobile command post's

communications console. His face settled into an impassive mask as he interpreted the words that crackled from the small, high-quality speakers mounted on the heavy vehicle's roof. Five Delta Sierras, the Light Horse brevity code for DropShips, had grounded one hundred ten kilometers southwest of Touchstone, three hours 'Mech-march away.

Major Ted Goslen, "Goshawk," commander of the Light Horse aerospace fighter assets, said that three of the enemy vessels were *Union* Class ships, each capable of hauling a company of BattleMechs. The fourth was identified as a *Leopard*, the smallest 'Mech-hauler in common service, with space for only a single lance of four 'Mechs. The remaining two were massive *Overlord* Class DropShips, armored monsters capable of transporting a full battalion of thirty-six BattleMechs.

That meant the Light Horse could be facing as much as a full regiment of fresh combat veterans, whose reputation as tough, resourceful warriors was almost as great as their own. Still, Amis had little doubt he could defeat a single regiment of MacCarron's Armored Cavalry. In theory, the Light Horsemen had a near two-to-one advantage over MacCarron's troops. That advantage was somewhat diminished by the guerrillas, whose attacks were forcing the Light Horse to hold back a portion of their strength for use as counter-insurgency patrols, security details, and the like. In the final analysis, Amis would have no more than a three-to-two edge over his enemy. But he still had some of the most highly trained, best-equipped troops in the Inner

Sphere, and that would go a long way toward tipping the scales back into his favor.

There was only one factor that nagged at the back of his mind. Having survived the blood bath on Huntress, he had no desire to be in the position of being forced to hold a hotly contested planet against a determined enemy until relieved. Milos could turn into just such a situation. If the Capellans were serious enough to send a full regiment of their best combat troops to Milos in an attempt to force the Light Horse off the planet, how much more of their overall force would they be willing to commit to the retaking of what was essentially a backwater world? Milos's importance lay in its proximity to several important worlds in the Confederation, making it a convenient staging area for a massive strike at the heart of the Capellan state.

That, of course, was why the Eridani Light Horse had been sent to this frozen ball of mud, to draw the enemy's attention away from the front and to force him to siphon off troops from the assault forces stabbing into the St. Ives Compact. But here on Milos, the Light Horse was being treated to the same tactics, only in microcosm and in reverse. The partisans were forcing main-line combat units to be pressed into service as security troops, just when those troops were needed to combat a counterattacking 'Mech force.

If there could be one positive thing said about the arrival of the Capellan MechWarriors, it was that the morale of the Eridani Light Horse troops, which had suffered under the constant harassment by the pro-Capellan guerrillas, was beginning to come back.

Here at last was an enemy the Light Horsemen had been trained to fight.

"Captain Nichols," Amis said, hastily scrawling a message across the face of an old-fashioned paper notepad, "I want you to run this over the HPG station. Tell the ComStar boys I want that sent out priority. Pay whatever fee they set. Ask for a return receipt. As soon as you get it, haul yourself back over here. I'm gonna need every staffer I can get my hands on today."

"Right, sir." Nichols quickly snatched up the handwritten note, saluted, and ducked out of the command post. Amis heard him scrabble for purchase at the side of the vehicle in the treacherous ice that was slowly building up on the spaceport's tarmac.

Amis turned back to the comm console. "That message was to General Sortek on Kittery, advising him of our situation," he told his commanders. "I'm pretty certain we can paste the MAC boys, but these guerrillas have got me stumped. I'm asking Sortek for instructions.

"So, gentlemen, this is the kind of fighting we were trained for. Saddle up both regiments, except for those troops on security duty. I want to be on the field in an hour. With luck, we can hit the Capellans before they're completely unloaded."

"Target, one full company of 'Mechs moving in the open. Grid: Eight-eight-five-six-seven-zero. Request one fire mission, circular target, with a two-five-zero meter radius," Colonel Paul Calvin said slowly in a clear voice. He spoke in low tones as though he feared the enemy might overhear his words. There was little chance of that. Calvin was strapped into his VTR-9B *Victor*'s command couch, the transmission was heavily encrypted, and the map references he used appeared on only a handful of charts that were held exclusively by the Light Horse's command echelon. His manner of speech was a factor of Calvin's normal soft-spokenness and of standard communications practices of speaking clearly and without undue haste.

Calvin wished that his stomach was as calm as his words. This was his first major engagement as the head of the newly re-formed Nineteenth Cavalry Regiment. In that moment, his fervent prayer was that of every new commander since before Hannibal crossed the Alps:

"Dear God, please don't let me screw up."

The BattleMechs he referred to were picking their way cautiously across a broad expanse of muddy farmland five kilometers northeast of where he and the bulk of the Nineteenth Cavalry Regiment lay hidden behind a series of low, rocky hills. The 'Mechs of First Company, Second Striker Battalion, his lead elements, were even closer to the enemy, a few hundred meters away from the enemy's left flank, hidden behind a line of trees.

Before Calvin could draw his next breath after transmitting the fire-support request, a rough New Syrtis drawl rasped in his headset.

"Stand by, Tiger. The stuff's on its way."

At that moment, the *Victor*'s external microphones picked up the freight-train howl of outgoing artillery shells. Three ugly black flowers blossomed to life above the enemy 'Mechs, followed seconds later by a random series of smaller explosions. This latter string of grenade-like bursts peppered the enemy war machines and churned up the muddy earth beneath their feet.

Captain Solomon Hendrich, commander of Calvin's artillery assets, had delivered a trio of Improved Dual-Purpose Conventional Munitions. Each Thumper artillery shell held dozens of small anti-armor bomblets that rained down over the enemy 'Mechs, scattering their deadly effects over a wide area. In addition to the shaped-charge warhead, which punched holes in the enemy's armor, the bomblets would scatter small bits of shrapnel across the battlefield, shredding any infantrymen unfortunate enough to be caught in their area of effect. Fortunately for MacCarron's ground-pounders, the 'Mechs were operating without direct infantry support.

"On target," Calvin reported to the battery commander. "Hit 'em again, but increase your range by five hundred."

"Up five hundred and fire again," Hendrich confirmed. A few seconds later, another triplet of submunitions delivering shells burst over the enemy lines, a half-kilometer northeast of the first set.

Unfortunately, the effect of the shelling was more psychological than physical. The Light Horse had lost many of its artillery assets on Huntress. Still, the sudden, unexpected blast of any artillery can have a surprising effect on enemy troop cohesion and morale, and Calvin had no intention of allowing the enemy to recover from the unanticipated attack.

"Broncos, this is Tiger," he growled into his neurohelmet's boom-mounted mike. "At the double-quick, advance."

The BattleMechs of the Nineteenth Cavalry Regiment, whose flaming bronco crest gave it the nickname "Calvin's Broncos," swept out of their concealed positions to smash into the enemy's reeling left flank.

"Stonewall, Magyar, this is Tiger," Calvin said, after switching to the brigade command frequency. "Tiger is attacking."

"Roger, Tiger, Stonewall copies," General Amis answered. "Go get 'em, Paul."

Calvin could almost see General Amis, leaning forward in his chair in the Light Horse's mobile HQ truck, chewing one of his thin black cigars unmercifully, champing at the bit to get into this battle. He knew that it galled Amis to be stuck "skulking behind the lines," as he put it, while the rest of his troops rode out to engage the enemy.

More artillery shells howled overhead, their smears of black smoke bursting forth a kilometer away from the center of their last volley. The attack was going as planned. Calvin's regiment would smash the enemy's left, while the artillery tried to pin the center. Colonel Antonescu's lighter, faster regiment would sweep into the enemy's rear, hoping to damage or destroy the MAC's DropShips.

Something smashed into Calvin's 'Mech, forcing him to take a few mincing steps in the slick, snowy mud to maintain his balance. A glance at his damage display told him that he had lost a ton of armor from the relatively thin angled plates covering his *Victor*'s right shoulder. Another hit like that in that location and he would lose the Gauss rifle that replaced the 'Mech's forearm and hand on that side.

Tall, massive, its cockpit painted to resemble a repulsively grinning skull-face, a huge *Atlas* stepped out of the falling snow. A bright, actinic flash lit the monster's side. Another basketball-sized sphere of nickel iron streaked across the battlefield to shove in the muscle-like bulge in the armor covering his left lower-leg myomer bundles.

The *Atlas* outweighed Calvin's *Victor* by a good twenty tons and mounted half-again as much armor, and more weapons, than his lighter assault 'Mech. The *Victor* had a slight edge in speed, but not enough to make a real difference in the ugly situation that was beginning to shape up. Calvin's 'Mech did have one advantage that he fully intended to exploit.

Stomping hard on the pedals beneath the control panel, the Light Horse officer lit off the massive Lexington jump jets built into the *Victor*'s torso and legs. The eighty-tone assault 'Mech bounded into the air like some ponderous, two-legged insect, just as the Capellan pilot laced the smaller machine's torso with nearly invisible beams of coherent light from its two heavy lasers. Calvin tried to hit back with his Gauss rifle, but the slug only ripped a furrow in the soil at the big 'Mech's feet.

Manipulating his controls, Calvin brought the *Victor* jarringly back to earth, landing one hundred meters away, in the *Atlas*'s "eleven o'clock" position. Calvin snapped off another quickly aimed shot from his Dragon's Fire Gauss rifle. This time, the massive chunk of dense metal found its mark in the *Atlas*'s left elbow. Shards of armor flew from the impact point, but Calvin knew that an assault 'Mech could withstand more than twice the amount of damage he had just dealt to that limb. A volley of green, flickering laser darts, followed by a barrage of short-range missiles, added to the damage his Gauss rifle had inflicted on the *Atlas*, but none of those exploited the deep crack in the enemy's left vambrace.

The Capellan responded by triggering his lasers and Gauss rifle once again, and adding a flight of long-range missiles to the mix. The laser blasts scored deep black furrows in the *Victor*'s left arm and side. The Gauss rifle's nickel-iron slug ripped past Calvin's cockpit. His tech would later discover that three centimeters of the lower edge of the *Victor*'s helmet-like head armor had been shorn away, probably by the Gauss slug. Just half a meter to the left, and Paul Calvin would have been washed from his ruined cockpit with a hose.

The missiles were either better aimed or guided by luck. Most of the flight of deadly, armor-piercing warheads smashed into the already-battered *Victor*, ripping away armor and widening the gash in the assault 'Mech's wounded left leg.

Calvin stomped on the jump jet controls again, ignoring the computer's warnings about the dangers of jumping with a damaged lower leg. The *Victor* rose on three narrow columns of superheated steam and reaction mass, coming to rest squarely behind the sluggish *Atlas*.

The Capellan pilot's profligate use of his entire weapons complement must have pushed his 'Mech's internal heat index up to dangerous levels, making the *Atlas* even more balky than it normally was. The enemy MechWarrior had forgotten one of the most basic rules of BattleMach combat—watch your heat.

Calvin smiled grimly. This time, the enemy's inattention to this rule was going to cost him.

He leveled his Gauss rifle at the *Atlas*'s relatively thin back armor and let fly. The Gauss slug smashed into the enemy machine's armored spine. Armor shattered under the impact of the nickel-iron pellet, leaving the big assault 'Mech's innards partially exposed to enemy fire.

Calvin brought up his *Victor*'s left arm and fired both pulse lasers. He gasped as heat spiked into his cockpit. Slapping the manual override, he decided to risk the very danger the Capellan had gambled against and lost. He triggered his chest-mounted SRM pack, sending four anti-'Mech warheads spiraling across the battlefield. The Capellan 'Mech was fitted with an anti-missile chain-gun, which clawed two of the four projectiles out of the air before they reached their target. The others, and the laser pulses, ripped up the *Atlas*'s already savaged back armor. One missile smashed into the big 'Mech's already damaged left arm, widening the jagged crack left by the Gauss slug.

Apparently aware that he could not turn his recalcitrant 'Mech about in time to deliver a more telling blow to his tormentor, the Capellan fired both of his rearward-facing medium pulse lasers. Both scored hits on the *Victor*'s armor, but did little damage.

Calvin responded by pumping still another slug into the *Atlas*'s spine. This time, the ugly whine of a damaged gyroscope could be heard. Without that massive instrument, the big machine would be unable to maintain its balance long enough to stand, let alone to move and fight. The *Atlas* staggered, dropped to one knee, and struggled to rise against actuator packages made sluggish by heat and a gyro partially wrecked by enemy weapon fire. As coldly as his namesake might eye a weakened buffalo calf, Paul "Tiger" Calvin leveled his Gauss rifle, taking careful aim at the gaping holes in the enemy's back, and fired again. Carbon fiber-reinforced aluminum was reduced to shrapnel by the heavy Gauss slug. Calvin's lasers slagged the thick shielding around the Capellan 'Mech's engine, sending even more heat flooding through the already incredibly hot machine.

Apparently having had enough of the fight, the MAC pilot tipped the *Atlas*'s head back and punched out. The ruined assault 'Mech sagged forward and fell on its face in the snow and mud of the battlefield.

Calvin turned to his tactical monitor. The MacCarron's Armored Cavalry 'Mechs were withdrawing in disorder. Reports filtering in from his subordinates suggested that the battle had gone exactly as planned. Surprise and superior numbers had driven the MAC troops from the field, while Colonel Antonescu had succeeded in destroying a *Leopard* Class DropShip on the ground and damaging several of the enemy's heaviest security 'Mechs.

But three 'Mechs failed to respond to Colonel Calvin's hails. Three Light Horsemen were either dead or their 'Mechs were disabled.

"Broncos, this is Tiger," he said, panting against the heat in his cockpit and fighting the sadness of losing comrades in battle. "The enemy is retiring.

We're gonna let him go. First Company, Second Battalion will shadow them back to their drop zone. The rest of us will hold up here. We've raised enough hell for one day."

23

Tsingtlit Hills, east of Touchstone, Milos
Xin Sheng Commonality
Capellan Confederation
05 March 3062

"**M**agyar, Magyar, this is Typhoon," Major Benedetto Porliss intoned into his neurohelmet microphone. "Magyar" was his immediate superior, Colonel Charles Antonescu. "FLASH, sitrep. Grid: Six-eight-eight-zero-five-niner. Typhoon has contacted unknown 'Mech force, approximate company strength, probable hostiles. The bogies appear to be headed in the direction of Touchstone. Have deployed Typhoon Two-three to follow, request instructions. Over."

"Typhoon, this is Magyar. Maintain surveillance of the bogies," Antonescue replied. "All Typhoons will prepare possible intercept of bogies. Stand by for further instructions."

"Roger, Magyar. Typhoon Two-three will maintain surveillance. Typhoon Group will prepare intercept. Be advised, Magyar, I do not have the Pathfinders."

"I know that, Major," Antonescu replied acidly, even though both officers knew that it was Porliss's responsibility to advise his commanding officer that the Pathfinder Company was still on detached duty, tracking down guerrillas.

As the command channel went dead, Porliss reviewed the situation in his mind, formulating his next set of commands.

One of his scout elements, a reconnaissance lance belonging to the Second Recon Company, spotted a dozen or so enemy BattleMechs moving into Goshen, a large village forty kilometers southwest of Touchstone. The 'Mechs all bore the green triangle and sword crest of House Liao and the Capellan Confederation. From the traces the recon lance could find, the Capellans had been moving on a roughly northeasterly track, heading straight for the planetary capital. Colonel Antonescu had ordered him to move his entire Sixth Recon Battalion into a position where he could halt the enemy force's advance. A scan of his *Exterminator*'s electronic map system revealed a suitable ambush site to Porliss's experienced eye.

"Attention, all Typhoons, this is Typhoon Actual. Typhoon Two-three will maintain contact with the hostiles. Do not allow yourselves to be drawn into a fight. You are there to observe and report, do you understand me, Sergeant Chilzer?"

Chilzer signaled his understanding, and Porliss continued, "Typhoon Group will execute a flank march, heading for Grid Six-seven-eight-zero-five-eight. If we knock on it, we'll intercept the bad guys just north of Goshen. Any questions? No? Then move out."

Two blasts of heavy pulse laser fire ripped across his 'Mech's belly as Major Porliss fought to keep his *Exterminator* under control. The *Anvil*'s pilot was good, almost as good as some veteran Light Horsemen Porliss had seen. Regaining command of his mechanical mount, he directed a flight of long-range missiles at his opponent. As soon as the last of that flight left the launch tubes, the Sixth Recon Battalion's commander fired his jump jets, intending to close the range with the *Anvil*, where he could bring his own medium lasers into play against the heaviest enemy machine he'd seen in this engagement. In response to his leaping charge, the Capellan lit off his own jets and bounded away, but the *Anvil*'s jets weren't as powerful as Porliss's, so the distance between them was closed.

Porliss brought up his 'Mech's arms, intending to unleash a blast from each of his four medium lasers, but a shattering hit to his *Exterminator*'s right side caused him to miss the opportunity. The *Anvil* jumped backward again, landing more gracefully than a sixty-ton pile of armor and weapons had any right to. The Light Horse officer was forced to break off his attack against what might have been the enemy command 'Mech and face the new threat blasting away at his right side. He turned in time to see flame gout from the chest of an old-model *Hermes II*. Shells from the forty-ton 'Mech's Class 5 autocannon burst against his heavier machine's left leg, making it stumble, while the enemy's laser sliced nearly half a ton of armor from the *Exterminator*'s right arm.

Porliss shuddered, imitating his 'Mech's response to the relatively light damage the enemy had inflicted. It was neither the autocannon nor the laser that gave Porliss a qualm; it was the bell-shaped muzzle of a flamer where the *Hermes II*'s arm should have been. One of the few weapons that every sane warrior, whether 'Mech pilot or infantryman, dreaded was fire, and the *Hermes II* had initially been built with that fear in mind.

The Capellan was bringing the gaping, carbon-lined bore of the flamer on line with Porliss's *Exterminator*. Reacting on instinct mixed with fear and revulsion, the Light Horseman unleashed his medium lasers, adding a volley of missiles to the green-flickering assault. The *Hermes* staggered, but hosed down the bigger war machine with a wave of burning fuel. Heat flooded into Porliss's cockpit, making the atmosphere oppressive almost to the point of being deadly. The pumps beneath his feet kicked in, flooding his cooling vest with a life-saving ethylene glycol solution. His 'Mech's heat sinks struggled to counteract the suddenly elevated heat levels. If the *Hermes* pilot pressed the attack now, while his heat-crippled 'Mech was fighting against the enveloping flames, he'd be in trouble. If the *Anvil* chose to get back into the action, Porliss would be lucky to survive the assault.

Close by, a deep-throated chattering roar sounded across the muddy ground north of the village of Goshen. Dimly, through the flames and heat-crippled instruments, Porliss caught the outline of a gray-green *Enfield*, its Class 10 dual-purpose autocannon spitting smoke and death at the *Hermes*. The Capellan incendiary 'Mech staggered, caught its balance, and sprayed a burning gout of jellied petrochemical fuel across the *Enfield*'s torso. Almost as suddenly as he began, Porliss's would-be rescuer stopped firing and tried to scrape the sticky fuel off his 'Mech's torso and to beat the flames out with his *Enfield*'s single hand. All he succeeded in doing was to spread the burning stuff around, ensuring that the fiery heat would affect all of the 'Mech's vital systems.

Under the cover of that flaming attack, the *Hermes* withdrew into the village of Goshen, pursued by two Light Horse 'Mechs. Of the *Anvil*, thankfully, there was no sign.

Ten minutes later, the battle of Goshen was over. The Capellans had tried to turn the fight into a street-to-street brawl, but the Light Horse's numbers and superior firepower drove the enemy troops away with little difficulty, to the Eridani Light Horse at least. The village of Goshen was another story.

During the short, desperate struggle within the village proper, several houses and businesses were damaged or flattened outright. Two homes and one apartment building were burned to the ground, probably, Major Benedetto Porliss thought, by the same *Hermes II* that had tried to roast him alive.

"Damn," Porliss said, surveying the ruined village through his slightly blackened viewscreen. "Attention all Typhoons, this is Typhoon Actual. Typhoon Four and Typhoon Eight, take your 'Mech elements and set up a defensive perimeter around the village. All Typhoon infantrymen are to report to the town hall. We'll use that as a command post. We've got to render aid and comfort to these people. Captain Hayford, see if you can raise Stonewall and Magyar. Tell them what we've got here, and let them know that some of these people might need med-evacced to Touchstone."

"Roger that, boss," Frances Hayford, Porliss's executive officer, replied.

Unplugging his helmet and cooling vest and switching the heavy combat gear for a lighter jumpsuit, synthleather jacket, and fatigue cap he pulled from a small locker in the corner of the cockpit, Porliss then undogged his cockpit hatch and climbed out onto his 'Mech's shoulder.

Already, in the finest traditions of the Eridani Light Horse, infantrymen were swarming across the ruined village, opening their personal first-aid kits to render what medical attention they could to the dazed and wounded inhabitants. Several light 'Mechs were attempting to fight the still burning fires. In most cases, that meant simply pushing the involved structures into themselves so that the flames wouldn't spread to nearby buildings.

But for all the good the Light Horsemen were doing, the inhabitants of Goshen seemed to resent the help. One infantryman, wearing the age-old symbol of a white brassard emblazoned with a red cross, was roughly shoved away from a badly burned child. A pair of the medic's buddies ran to his aid, but were met by twice their number of angry men and women, each armed with a stick or a rock. The troopers unslung their rifles to cover the mob. While the medic got to his feet, the trio backed away slowly, their faces showing anger, sorrow, and confusion.

Porliss snatched his personal communicator from the pocket of his jacket.

"All Typhoons, this is Typhoon Actual. Do not, I repeat *do not*, get involved in a scuffle with the locals. If they want our help, fine, give it to them, but do not force the issue."

Before he finished speaking, a cry of agony and terror rang out. Porliss looked up the street just in time to see a Light Horse MechWarrior, a veteran of Operation Serpent who had come through that bloodbath without a scratch, being dragged off the chain ladder of his BattleMech and struck to the ground by a huge man wielding an axe-handle. Porliss later learned that the trooper had dismounted from his *Commando* to help a young man staunch the blood flowing from his pregnant wife's severed left arm. The mob had apparently taken a single look at his Star League uniform and turned on him violently. The crowd beat him to death before anyone could intervene.

That wanton murder seemed to signal a general riot. A wine bottle filled with petro-fuel, its mouth plugged with a burning rag, shattered on the pavement only a meter from the feet of Porliss's *Exterminator*. A pair of rifle bullets spanged off the big 'Mech's cockpit glazing near where he balanced on the machine's curved shoulders.

Diving through the open hatch, Porliss shouted for all Light Horse troopers in the village to withdraw as quickly as possible.

"Pull out!" he screamed into the communicator. "All Light Horsemen, pull out. Do not engage the civilians. I repeat, do not fire upon the civilians. All Light Horsemen, pull out. Just get out of the village. We'll worry about re-forming companies later."

As he was struggling into his command couch, Porliss saw two young men dart out of a doorway half a block down the street. Each carried a large canvas bag slung over his shoulder.

"Sappers!" he bellowed into his communicator.

Before he could call in the location of anti'Mech infantrymen or warn their intended victims, the men jumped onto the feet of a *Javelin* and a *Hammer*, clambered partway up the legs, and stuffed the bags into the machines' vulnerable knee joints. As they dropped free, one man was cut down by machine gun fire from a Light Horse hover APC, but it was too late.

The satchel charges exploded with the characteristic dull thump and sullen orange flash of a low-grade homemade explosive device Still, jammed as they were into one of a BattleMech's most vulnerable areas, the charges were just as effective as military-grade pentaglycerine. One of the blasts left the *Javelin* with a twisted knee joint, which, though crippling, was not enough to immobilize the medium 'Mech. The second "knee-capping" charge had been placed better. The *Hammer* lay on its back, its right leg blown off at the knee. The pilot, a transferee from the Twelfth Vegan Rangers, was dragged, stunned and bleeding, from his cockpit by the furious villagers. Because of the rioting mob between the fallen warrior and his comrades, neither man nor machine could be recovered.

"Pull out," Major Porliss repeated dully. "There's nothing more we can do here."

24

An infantryman clad in Star League-issue combat fatigues charged across the narrow street, his mouth open in a shout that could not be heard over the clamor of the riot. The gold disk bearing the prancing black stallion of the Eridani Light Horse flashed briefly as the trooper lifted his assault rifle high over his head. The sharpened cutting edge of the blackened steel bayonet fixed to the weapon's muzzle glittered faintly in the weak sunlight filtering through the overcast. Then the trooper swept the rifle back down, dealing a vicious butt-stroke to the side of a youth's head. The boy probably wasn't out of his teens. The civilian dropped like a string-cut marionette. There was little doubt that the blow had been fatal.

"God *damn* them, those bloody, lying sons of diseased rats!" Colonel Paul Calvin swore, hurling the holovid remote against the far wall of the spaceport lounge with enough force to shatter the device's plastic case. "General, that wasn't how it happened at all."

"I know it wasn't, Colonel," Amis said. He removed the self-contained headset communicator and laid it on the table. Gingerly, he touched the place behind his left ear where the device had rested against his skull with a thick callused fingertip. The lightweight communications unit never seemed to fit properly and tended to rub a sore on both the back of his ear and on his scalp. He started to replace the device, then dropped it on the table top. The abraded spot was not particularly large, or tender, but protracted wearing of the communicator would quickly change that.

"We're facing more than Capellan troops here," he said. "We've got a whole planet of hostiles. Why should the press be any different?"

Amis gazed at the broken remote control before crossing the lounge to thumb the holoset's power stud, cutting off the pretty, empty-eyed female news reader mid-sentence in the weather forecast. He already knew the forecast; stormy, and he was not thinking of the heavy banks of dark clouds forming over Milos's planetary capital. Amis knew that the coming storm was going to be more violent, more hazardous, and longer-lasting than any blizzard the god-cursed planet could throw at them.

True to form, the local news service ran a holovid clip, ostensibly shot by a civilian, of the riot in Goshen. The "news cameras" showed men and women in Star League green with the gold-backed black horse crest of the Eridani Light Horse brawling with the inhabitants of that village. The clubbing of the teen-aged boy seemed to be a favorite. What the cameras didn't show was that same trooper helping a bleeding, barely conscious female Light Horse medic to her feet. The youth had been kicking the medic in the chest, belly, and face, until her comrade intervened, probably saving her life.

Other clips included a particularly graphic shot of a Light Horse Maxim heavy hover transport machine-gunning down a small group of men and women dressed in work clothes. Again the carefully edited footage failed to reveal that those "workers" had just knee-capped two Light Horse BattleMechs. One of those, a *Hammer*, had its leg blown off at the knee. Its unfortunate pilot was dragged from his cockpit, hanged from a lamp post, and set on fire while he was still alive.

Since the holovid footage had become public, first as a "news flash," later as a staple of the evening and late night holocasts, the number of civilians gathered around the spaceport's main gate had grown from about a dozen malcontents to upwards of fifty. And these did more than carry placards and howl curses at the guards. The new batch of protesters threw rocks and bottles. Occasionally, one would produce a civilian hunting rifle or handgun and pop off a few rounds at the Light Horsemen. The soft-pointed hunting bullets stood little chance of damaging the flak-jacketed infantry troopers. Still, a few Light Horsemen had been wounded badly enough to prompt General Amis to station armored infantrymen at the gates.

Oddly, most of the crowd tended to melt away around sundown, leaving only a few die-hards clustered around the metal barrels in which they'd built fires of scrap wood, trying to ward off the cold. Colonel Antonescu speculated that they were either fair-weather partisans or were afraid of getting caught in a crossfire between the Eridani Light Horse and the guerrillas, should the latter attempt to attack the spaceport under the cover of night.

Whatever the reason, the balance of the mob was back in the morning, their hatred of the Light Horse, House Davion, and the Star League seemingly refueled by a good night's sleep.

"Gentlemen," Amis said. "The situation on Milos has become intolerable. And, in my opinion, it is rapidly becoming untenable. If the sentiment among the civilian inhabitants of this world continues to go against us, as these news broadcasts seem to be leading it, we will soon find ourselves placed in the unacceptable position of being forced to fire upon civilians to protect ourselves. I do not want to be the first general in Light Horse history to order his troops to commit such an act. We need to find some alternative.

"Captain Nichols." Amis turned to his aide. "Any word from Star League command on Kittery?"

"Nothing new, sir." Nichols shook his head. "General Sortek said he has no troops to spare for us. He refuses to even release the rest of the Light Horse to come in. Says he needs them elsewhere. He wouldn't say where, because it was an open transmission, and he doesn't trust anyone, including the local ComStar personnel, not to leak anything he says to the Capellans.

"What he *did* say, sir, doesn't make me any happier. He says continue to hold for as long as practicable. Then call for extraction. He also says, if the situation demands it, we are authorized to surrender to the Capellans."

"That's awful decent of him," Amis snorted. "Well, gentlemen, there it is. We aren't getting any backup, not even from our own people . . . What was that, Major Porliss?"

Porliss, whose troops had been the first attacked by the civilians at Goshen, looked up with a defiant light in his dark eyes.

"I said, sir, I wonder if Colonel Eicher knows we're in trouble here."

Amis cocked his head to one side and chewed briefly on the butt of his cigar. The Major had a point. Amis had left Colonel Eveline Eicher and her Twenty-first Striker Regiment on Kittery. If she had gotten word that the Light Horse expeditionary force on Milos was in trouble, she would be agitating General Sortek to allow her to either effect a rescue or to reinforce her comrades on planet. If Eicher did know of the rapidly deteriorating situation on Milos, and Sortek had forbidden her to launch a rescue or reinforcing mission, how long would she continue to obey while her comrades were being picked off one by one by guerrillas, angry civilians, and Capellan House troops?

A deep, protracted *wuff* interrupted Amis's thoughts. A few ragged pops, sounding like fire-crackers, spattered the air before the odd, breathy sound died out. A short burst of automatic fire fóllowed and overpowered the sound of small arms gamely banging away outside the fence. Snatching up his headset communicator, Amis called for a situation report.

"General," the communications officer-of-the-watch answered immediately. "Looks like the indigs are trying it again. Somebody just tossed a firebomb over the fence from the roof of one of those damned warehouses."

"Patch me into the net."

A second later, the watch officer replied. "You're in, General."

"All Light Horsemen. This is Stonewall Actual." The use of his codename and the word "actual" con-firmed that the message was coming from Amis him-self, rather than through one of his staff. "Do not retaliate against the crowd. I say again, there will be no retaliation against the crowd."

"Stonewall, this is gate two." The alto voice on the communicator packed more than a bit of fear and anger into those simple words. "No one here is firing on the crowd. That's all incoming."

"Say again, gate two."

"General, I say again. We aren't shooting. The indig bastards have gotten hold of automatic weap-ons, and they're spraying our position. They also heaved a firebomb off the roof of a warehouse. I have two men down. We're pinned behind the guard shack. Every time we make a move toward my casualties, they start shooting again. Sir, if we don't get to those men soon, they're gonna die, if they aren't dead already."

Amis spat out a curse, then bolted from the conference room.

"Somebody get an APC over there!" he bellowed into the communicator.

As though his speaking the words had made it so, a black, white, and gray camouflaged Blizzard hover APC streaked across the tarmac, only twenty meters from where Amis stood. Heedless of his own safety, Amis vaulted into the driver's seat of a hoverjeep parked near the entrance of the terminal building and gunned the engine to life. Antonescu and Calvin also vaulted into the vehicle even as their commander was engaging the drive fans. Remotely, Amis realized that his staff was yelling at him and, in the same remote portion of his mind, he had to admit that they were probably right. Commanding Generals and senior regimental commanders did not risk their lives for two line infantrymen. But those were his men, Light Horsemen, and the Light Horse did not abandon its people.

Above and behind his head, Amis heard the slippery metallic clatter of a machine gun's bolt being drawn back. He turned slightly in his seat and glanced over his shoulder to see Antonescu release the charging handle of the jeep's heavy machine gun and then hang on to the weapon's firing grips for balance against the speeding jeep's twisting path.

"Let's try not to hose down the whole town, Charles," Amis bellowed against the roar of the wind, fighting for control of the wildly skidding vehicle. Navigating between 'Mechs was proving to be a challenge at this speed.

"*D'accord*, General," Antonescu replied grimly. "But those were *my* men on gate two."

Antonescue didn't have to say anything more. If there was one thing greater than the Light Horseman's love for the unit, it was the commander's love for his men. As far as Colonel Charles Antonescu was concerned, the wounded men lying on the snow-covered tarmac at gate two might as well be his own sons.

As the hover jeep rounded the corner of a spaceport hanger building, Amis saw the APC skid to a halt between the wounded men and the perimeter fence. Four men, each of them wearing the red-crossed white brassard of a combat medic, dashed from the squad bay before the ramp was fully lowered. The black latticework of light exoskeletons lined their arms and legs. The strength-enhancing mechanisms were essential if the medics were to rescue their power-suited comrades. Two men grabbed each of the casualties by the shoulders and dragged them into the relative safety offered by the Blizzard's armored hull. The APC's lift fans howled and blew the snow covering the tarmac into miniature whirlwinds as the vehicle rose onto its cushion of air and sped off in the direction of the spaceport infirmary.

Only then did the inconsistencies strike Amis. The injured men were armored infantrymen. Their battle armor should have been painted in winter camouflage colors weeks ago. The men dragged into the APC were all dressed in shades of black and off brown. Despite the snow that had drifted deeply around the base of every building on the spaceport, the wounded men had been lying in a five-meter-wide circle of clear, if wet pavement, from which steam was still rising.

A coldness settled into Amis's guts. The realization finally sank in that the anti-Davion, anti-Star League crowd, who were by now increasing the volume and variety of their shouted slogans and invective until it sounded like the rumble of an inbound DropShip, had hurled a firebomb directly at his troopers. If not for their armored suits, they would have been burned to death before anyone could get to them. As it stood, the injured troopers stood about a fifty-fifty chance of surviving the injuries they had suffered at the hands of the hate-filled mob.

For a fleeting moment, Amis fought the urge to leap into the firing position, wrest the heavy machine gun from Antonescu, and avenge his dead and wounded troopers on the crowd outside the fence. But the impulse was brief. His long adherence to the Light Horse tradition of protecting the helpless, even if they were the enemy, helped bring his anger and revulsion under control.

He sagged against the jeep's steering wheel.

"All right," he sighed. "Pull all the infantrymen off the perimeter. I can't afford to risk losing any more lives to partisan action. Replace them with light 'Mechs, but make sure the pilots know that they are still forbidden to fire on civilians except in self-defense.

"We know that MacCarron's Armored Cavalry is still out there. Since the partisans have got us bottled up here in Touchstone, the MAC will have to come to us. That means a push on the spaceport and capital city, and we're going to need every man and machine we've got."

"Boss," Calvin said, from his position in the front passenger seat. "Charles and I understand the reason for your order. You wanna keep as many of our people safe as you can. But I gotta tell you, morale is running pretty low. First, we get pushed back into this god-forsaken spaceport with no way out except to surrender, unless Sortek sends our JumpShips back in, and it don't sound like he's gonna do that.

"There's been a lot of grumbling in the ranks, 'specially among some of the younger troops and those who transferred in after Op Serpent. Most of it's 'Why won't they let us win,' but some of it is against you and the SLDF command structure in general."

"I know, Colonel." Amis shut down the jeep's internal combustion engine and turned to face Calvin. "The decaying morale is what's got me the most worried. That's gonna hurt us more than the MAC and the guerrillas combined, and we're gonna need every man we've got at his physical and mental best when the Capellans launch their assault on Touchstone.

"If the troops are wallowing in depression, or if they get well and truly honked off at their officers, we lose one leg of our tactical doctrine; the ability to act as a single unit. It we lose that, all the firepower and mobility in the world ain't gonna matter a damn.

"If that doesn't happen, they begin to look at all Milosians as potential enemies and start taking their troubles out on the locals under the cover of fighting the Capellan troops, and that's just as bad.

"Either way, if the troops lose their will to fight or

their ability to fight as a controlled, organized team, then we will be forced to surrender to the enemy, something the Light Horse has never had to do throughout its long history. And that, gentlemen, is not going to happen on *my* watch.''

25

Ed Amis leaned heavily against the hardened 'Mech hangar's thick steel bay door. The cold winter wind whipped around his legs. Even in wintertime, the massive reinforced panel stood wide open, allowing the armored behemoths inside easy egress from their dark, cavernous shelter. Only during an actual attack would the heavy doors be closed and locked to protect the valuable BattleMechs inside.

As things stood now, the doors were partially closed. Fitting, Amis thought, because the Eridani Light Horse found itself being caught in a sort of half-siege situation. Since the initial broadcast three days ago of what the local media called "the Goshen massacre'' tapes, the crowds gathered outside the Touchstone spaceport's main gates had steadily increased in size and fury. But, following his replacement of the infantrymen guarding the perimeter fence with light BattleMechs, the incidents of violence directed against the Light Horse had dropped off dramatically.

But, as with any siege, time was on the side of the besiegers. Amis knew that the supplies he had brought in with him would last the Light Horse another two or three months, even assuming that they would be called upon to fight at least one more pitched battle against the McCarron's Armored Cavalry troops who were being welcomed as conquering heroes by the citizens of Milos. It was this odd attitude of the civilians that puzzled Amis and put a strain on the morale of his troops.

He could not remember being in a situation where a people liberated from an oppressive form of government, and re-conquered by that regime, so welcomed the return of a totalitarian state that they would turn on the troops who sacrificed their lives to once again secure their liberty.

With a snarl of disgust, he turned his back on the ugly gray skies and icy wind and slipped into the gloom of the 'Mech hangar.

"Curse it," Nessa Ament muttered, lifting her head from the cupped rubber eyepiece of her powerful telescopic sight. "I waited too long."

Even as she was taking up the minimal slack on the Zeus heavy rifle's trigger, the big man wearing the uniform of a Star League Defense Force general turned away from the open 'Mech hangar door and vanished into the hardened shelter's interior.

"I told you, Nessa, you should have taken him." Jin Racan's voice carried a mixed tone of reproof and disappointment.

"Yes," Ament hissed. "But when the trophy gets away, one must be content with smaller fry."

She dropped her cheek to the slightly raised comb of the big rifle's stock. Her ice blue eyes searched the compound nearly eight hundred meters away for a victim. Beside her, Jin scanned the spaceport, his abnormally sharp vision augmented by a pair of electronic binoculars.

"Okay, got one." His voice was a low whisper, though no one was around to overhear the hushed words. He and Ament were a highly trained, successful sniper team, and the discipline of strict silence came as second nature to them both. Carelessness could become a fatal habit. Neither Jin Racan nor Nessa Ament planned to fall victim to negligence.

"Where?"

"Hangar bay doors, two o'clock, fifty meters," Jin replied, guiding the sniper's eye to the target. "Maintenance tech and what might be a MechWarrior, standing on a repair lift."

"Got it."

Ament adjusted the rifle a bit to line up her telescopic sight with the target. Dialing back the variable power setting, she widened her field of view, allowing an assessment of the situation. A young woman wearing the stained uniform and hard hat of a technician was leaning back against the rail of an elevated repair lift to allow a thin man to peer into

an open maintenance hatch in the torso of a gray-
and-white-camouflaged *Centurion*. The skinny man
wore a cloth cap with the divided square of a Star
League corporal sewn to its front. A laser pistol hol-
stered cross-draw fashion on his left hip declared that
he was no tech, but probably the 'Mech's pilot.

"I'll take the 'Mech jock first."

This was a long step down from a general, Ament
thought as she settled her breathing into an easy,
regular rhythm. But it was a start.

She settled the scope's cross hairs on the tip of the
MechWarrior's right ear, where the heavy, 700-grain
bullet would instantly destroy the man's motor neural strip. She inhaled, then exhaled two normal
breaths. On the third, she took half a lungful of air,
checked her aim carefully, and gently squeezed the
big rifle's trigger.

The sear broke cleanly at just 1.5 kilos pressure.
The suppressor coughed harshly, and the Zeus
bucked against her shoulder, jarring the sights off
target, but the bullet was already on its way.

"He's down," Jin whispered, but Ament gave no
sign of hearing him. She was already lining her sights
up on the tech, who was staring open-mouthed at
the bloody corpse at her feet.

The rifle bucked and coughed again. The technician dropped headfirst from the repair lift, a thumb-
sized hole through the center of her chest. If she
wasn't already dead when she fell from the lift, the
sickening impact of her head and neck on the ferrocrete below left no doubt as to her condition.

Ament wasted neither time nor pity on the young
female tech, who, she remotely noticed, couldn't have

been a day over nineteen. She was busy leveling her rifle's sights over the open maintenance hatch. Three quick shots smashed into the massive target, the steel-jacketed slugs shredding myomers and ripping through power feeds in the *Centurion*'s chest. A loud bang, audible even at the distance from which she was firing, accompanied the last of the rounds she sent through the open hatch.

"That's it. Time to go," she growled, lowering her weapon. Even suppressed, the big thirteen-millimeter, hypersonic slugs made enough of a crack and muzzle blast that an astute observer might spot the sniper's hide. Three rounds was her normal tactical limit, but the inviting target of an open maintenance hatch had been too good to pass up. Nessa Ament had fired five rounds in all. It was past time for her and Jin Recan to escape and evade.

Only her disappointment at missing the enemy's commanding general a second time marred the sense of satisfaction she got from reducing the enemy's fighting strength by two and doing untold harm to his morale.

Besides, Ament promised the officer she could no longer see, she'd be back, and his damnable luck wouldn't hold out forever.

26

"**C**olonel, you've got to let us try. This is getting way out of hand." Captain Bill Kyle's normally soft drawl had grown harsh with the intensity of his emotions.

After several days of harassing sniper attacks, the Pathfinder commander's patience had finally snapped. The latest victim of the unseen marksman had been a promising youngster from his own platoon. According to Doctor Fuehl, the brigade's chief surgeon, the boy would live but would likely lose his right leg at about mid-thigh. Even if the wounded trooper could be fitted with an advanced prosthetic, the severity of the wound meant he would be cashiered from the Pathfinders, perhaps even from the Light Horse combat arm. That was the final blow for the normally reserved commando leader.

Colonel Calvin stared at the drab tan walls of the spaceport manager's office, which had been pre-empted for the Nineteenth Cavalry's command center. Finding no answer there, he shook his head and gazed directly into Kyle's eyes.

"I'm sorry, Captain. I truly am. Nobody wants these attacks stopped more than I do. And nobody is more torqued off about this sorry state of affairs than the general, but we have our orders. We can't send infantrymen out to hunt down the snipers, and BattleMechs are worse than useless for the job. That would be like hunting mice with an Odessan raxx.

"We've all seen how the media twists every move we make into grounds for a war crimes trial against the general and the whole Light Horse. The Capellan state news service is calling for an emergency meeting of the SLDF council to indict the whole outfit for violations of the Ares Conventions, specifically for our actions in the 'Goshen massacre.' "

"I know all that, sir, but . . ."

"No buts, Captain." Calvin waved aside his subordinate's protest. "I can't give you a hunting license. Suppose you were caught? Suppose you thought you spotted the sniper and ended up popping some civilian, or, worse yet, some newsman? Just imagine what the media hacks would do with *that*!"

Kyle bit off his angry retort as to what the news media could do with their altered and fabricated stories. "Yes, sir," he said. Then he touched his brow in a ghost of a salute, turned on his heel, and stalked from the command center.

"Well, Boss?" Lieutenant Chatham Siwula, Kyle's second-in-command, had been waiting in the hallway outside.

"No go, Chat," Kyle said in a low, angry voice. "Colonel Calvin won't let us go out, 'cause the general is afraid of what the media might say or do if we get caught."

"What the hell happened to Amis, anyway?" Siwula asked. "He used to be a hell-bent-for-leather fighter. What? He decide he's a politician all of a sudden?"

"*Stow it, Lieutenant!*" Kyle growled. "General Amis is still the best there is. He knows if he orders us to go out there, and we screw up and get caught doing it, the politicians are gonna hang the whole outfit, not just us. Maybe then the 'suits' decide that the Star League isn't such a good idea, and the whole business falls apart. Then what? Huh? Then maybe we fall back into another round of Succession Wars, then maybe we really do become the barbarians the Clanners think we are. Then, the whole business of Operation Serpent becomes a sham, and all those people who died on Huntress died for nothing. You can question the politicians. You can question the SLDF command authority. You can even question me. But, by God, don't you *ever* question General Amis again. Got it?"

Siwula came to a halt, his mouth hanging open like an unhinged cockpit hatch. Kyle read the shock and surprise on his second's face, and felt a little bit of it himself. Siwula had been a transferee officer, coming over from the Twenty-second Dieron Regulars. Despite that unit's solid reputation and inculcation into the ways of bushido, there was no way Siwula could have been prepared for the fierce love and loyalty the Light Horse line troopers felt for their unit and for their commanders.

" 'Sokay, Chat." Kyle let out a small self-deprecating laugh. "Sorry I blew up at you."

"*Shigataganai*, Boss," Siwula answered in formal Japanese, telling Kyle it didn't matter. "But what are we gonna do about that sniper?"

"Well, now that you ask . . ."

An unearthly vista painted in shades of black, green, and white was revealed through the eyepiece of the variable power spotter's scope. A light-amplification device attached to the scope pierced the darkness of the cloudy night.

"Anything yet?" The voice in the dark was a barely audible whisper.

"Nothing. Maybe everybody's still asleep."

"Hmm, maybe."

Bill Kyle lifted a pair of electronic binoculars to his eyes and scanned the area before him. The only movement was near the spaceport's main gate, where a dozen or so pickets huddled around a fire in a heat-rusted steel petrol drum. Just inside the three-meter-high fence a solitary BattleMech, a thirty-ton *Battle Hawk*, walked a ponderous sentry-go along the port's perimeter. Nothing else moved in the pre-dawn gloom.

Kyle lowered the binoculars, rubbed his eyes, and glanced at his companion. It had taken a mere thirty seconds to convince Lieutenant Siwula to accompany him on his order-breaking mission. Following his abortive attempt to convince Colonel Calvin to allow the Pathfinders to hunt down and neutralize the enemy snipers, Kyle decided to take matters into his own hands.

As soon as dusk began to fall, he and Siwula slipped quietly out of the compound, scaling the perimeter fence at a point well removed from any gate. In spite of the awkward, heavy packs strapped to their backs, the commandos easily climbed the three-meter-high, razor-wire topped, chain-link barrier. Neither man wore armor or any unit insignia that might identify him as the Eridani Light Horse, in case he was caught or killed. Instead, each wore a plain, dark gray coverall looted from the port facility's civilian maintenance depot The only military gear they carried were the heavy rucksacks and the weapons cradled in their hands.

It had taken less than an hour to locate the tallest building in the immediate vicinity of the spaceport, a task made easier by the afternoon the pair had spent walking around the compound, studying the warehouses surrounding the port. Kyle and Siwula spent another ninety minutes carefully searching the storage building whose sign declared its owners to be O'Keefre Importers-Exporters. Twice in that period, the commandos swung their sound-suppressed submachine guns to cover an unexpected noise or sudden movement, only to find that they had nearly engaged a couple of rats with lethal force, or perhaps it was the same rat twice.

Three hours after climbing the spaceport's south

fence, the commandos found themselves a comfortable spot on the warehouse roof. While Kyle checked the Minolta 9000 sniper's rifle and its magazine of soft-pointed hunting ammunition, Siwula carefully scanned the surrounding rooftops for the enemy snipers. Both men knew that the use of soft-nosed, expanding ammunition against enemy troops was forbidden by the Ares Conventions. At that moment, neither cared. The two were only interested in neutralizing the enemy sniper by whatever means possible. The heavy slugs, with their exposed, soft lead tips would almost guarantee a killing shot, provided a good hit could be achieved.

Through the rest of that night, Kyle and Siwula scanned the rooftops, hoping to catch a glimpse of the terrorists who had been conducting their murderous campaign against the Eridani Light Horse. Now, with the sun about to creep over the western horizon, they were beginning to wonder if the enemy marksmen had decided to call it quits.

"Boss, I've got movement here," Siwula whispered.

"Where?"

"Ten o'clock, white building, six hundred meters."

Kyle picked up the sniper's rifle, set the weapon's integral bipod on the raised parapet of the roof, and pointed the weapon in the direction Ziwula had indicated.

"Got it," he whispered, locating the structure his spotter had given as his first reference point.

"All right. From there, four o'clock, one hundred meters, rooftop," Ziwula continued, designating the target building by a system called the clock-ray method. "You've got a couple people moving around up there."

Kyle easily located the building, settled the Minolta against his shoulder, and dropped his cheek to the stock. His eye lined up perfectly with the powerful telescopic sight affixed to the weapon's upper receiver. The night scope would only be useful for another half-hour. By then, the rising sun would blind the sensitive light-amplification system. It would be a half hour after that until there was enough light to employ a standard optical sight.

Turning the night scope's gain all the way to maximum, Kyle managed to pick out two man-shaped black shapes making their way across the rooftop from a stairway door. The figures were moving roughly west toward the edge of the roof, where they would be overlooking the Light Horse compound at the spaceport.

"It's gotta be," Kyle drawled, thumbing off the high-precision rifle's safety.

Holding the rifle by its firing grip and allowing the heavy weapon to rest securely on its bipod, he brought his left hand back to grasp the toe of the buttstock. The awkward-seeming grip was actually more stable, permitting more long-range shooting. He settled his breathing into an easy rhythm and dropped the sight over the trailing silhouette, the one that most tactical doctrine said should be the sniper.

"Range check?" he whispered.

"Range is five hundred twenty-six meters." Siwula read the numbers off his spotting scope's laser range finder.

"Right. Here we go," Kyle said, dialing his scope

to the appropriate range setting and turning the magnification up to its highest power. At this greater magnification, he coldly noted that one of the figures was a young girl with long, dark hair. The other was a fair-haired boy of about the same age. To his mind, this was no anomaly. Some terrorists began their training as young as twelve, and were full-fledged, blooded killers before they were sixteen.

As his finger tightened on the weapon's trigger, the targets sat down on the edge of the building's roof and twined their arms around one another, the girl resting her head on the boy's shoulder.

Kyle eased his finger off the trigger, feeling embarrassed. The black and green figures he had taken for an enemy sniper team were a couple of young lovers stealing a few private moments. In some ways, he envied them. They could innocently stroll across a rooftop in the pre-dawn gloom, completely unaware that over half a kilometer away, some stranger was about to snuff out their lives.

He dialed back the scope, lowered the rifle, and grinned sheepishly at Siwula.

The spotter did not answer his smile. Instead, he frowned. Reacting on instinct, Kyle twisted, bringing the Minolta up in the direction of Siwula's gaze. Dropping his eye to the scope, he caught a glimpse of a light-haired figure with a long rifle set against its shoulder. The weapon was aimed into the spaceport. Before he realized what he was doing, the heavy Minolta rifle thumped him hard in the shoulder, and an ear-splitting crack pierced the pre-dawn darkness.

The figure in his sights jerked. Kyle stroked the trigger again, and the fair-haired target pitched onto its back. A second figure lifted himself a few hand-breadths above the warehouse's roof parapet, trying to locate the source of the unsuppressed shots that had just killed his partner. Through his scope, Kyle could see the distinctive outline of a Kogyo-Ryerson-Toshiro assault rifle, with the fat tube of a grenade launcher slung beneath the rifle's barrel.

Must be the spotter, Kyle thought dispassionately, settling the glowing arrowhead-shaped targeting reticle over the man's breastbone and squeezing the trigger. The man pitched onto his face. His weapon tumbled over the edge of the roof into the street below.

"They're both down," Siwula said. "They're not moving."

"All right," Kyle said quietly. "We're gonna change location and resume our overwatch, just in case we get other visitors."

As Siwula began breaking down his spotter's scope, Kyle looked through his scope once again at the huddled corpses, realizing for the first time that he had instinctively made three solid hits at nearly five hundred meters. Moving to a new hide was a standard precaution after firing on the enemy, as was the resumed surveillance. However, he knew in his heart that the enemy sniper lay dead on the warehouse roof.

"What in the ever-frigging hell did you two think you were doing out there?" General Amis bellowed at the top of his lungs as Captain Kyle and Lieutenant Siwula stood at ramrod-stiff attention before their commander's desk. He paused in his angry pacing long enough to glare at each of his subordinates. When, as he expected, he got no response, he resumed his marching back and forth.

"You disobeyed a direct order from Colonel Calvin, who was *obeying* a direct order from me! You two are *not* the Immortal Warrior. You do not have the right to make up your own bloody orders. You were told to stay put, and what did you do? You stole the gear you wanted, went over the wire, and spent the night outside this compound on some kind of personal vendetta mission.

"Well, what do you have to say for yourselves? Make it good, 'cause I'm just one millimeter from busting you both right out of the outfit."

Captain Kyle cleared his throat and spoke. "Yes, sir, we did violate your orders, and we did break faith with the rest of the Light Horse, but something had to be done, sir. If we'd stayed put, we'd have lost two or three more men today. And, sir? When we finally moved over to the target rooftop and confirmed our kills, we found the enemy sniper's log book. It says she had *you* in her sights *twice*. Once, the day we took the spaceport, and again a couple of days ago when this whole business started."

Amis stopped pacing with a jerk and made a half-strangled noise.

"Do you honestly think that changes anything, Captain? And, for now, you still *are* a Captain. Colonel Calvin tells me that he explained the reasons for my orders to you, and you still went out hunting. Your report says that you came within a red cat's hair of capping some teenage kid and his girlfriend. What would have happened then, huh?

"So far, everything the Liaoist media has been saying about us has been either a badly twisted account of what really happened or an outright fabrication. If you'd been one second quicker on the trigger, they wouldn't have needed to make up the story. The Capellans would have a couple of real war criminals on their hands, and I would be forced to turn you over to them."

Amis paused a moment to allow the full weight of his words to sink in. He saw the dreadful truth of what they had almost done to the Light Horse, and to the Star League Defense Force, settle onto their faces.

"That's right. You guys screwed up. Big-time," Amis growled. "Now, as of this moment, you two heroes are restricted to the base. You'll take a one grade pay cut, but no reduction in rank. The difference in your pay will go to the Light Horse Legal Affairs Division. And if either of you *ever* pull a suck-egg play like this again, I'll drop-kick you out of this outfit so fast your feet won't touch the ground. Got it?"

"Yes, sir," the commandos responded in unison.

"That's it. Dismissed."

As Kyle and Simula turned to leave his office, Amis reached into an inside breast pocket of his uniform jacket.

"Hold it," he snapped.

The pair stopped and turned cautiously to face their commander again, as though each was convinced that Amis had changed his mind and decided to have them shot.

"Off the record," Amis said gruffly, extending his right hand toward them. "You guys did good."

"Thank you, sir." Kyle and Siwula gratefully accepted the thin black cigars General Amis held out to them.

27

Cheng Shao's face twisted as he stared at *Sang-shao* Samuel Christobal. The loss of his Death Commando sniper team seemed to affect him more than it should have. When Christobal first landed on Milos, he'd gotten the impression that a relationship existed between Shao and the silent, unsmiling Nessa Ament, but there had been no evidence to support that suspicion. Now, that speculation seemed to be borne out by what might, in another, be described as stoically concealed grief. In the Death Commando, even that emotion seemed to be repressed, as though Shao drew a flinty strength from any sense of loss he might feel.

"Sang-shao," Shao said. "Now is the time to launch a final attack on the Eridani Light Horse. We must strike soon, before they launch a counterattack, and before the Star League decides to reinforce them."

"I tend to agree with you, *Zhong-shao,*" Christobal said stiffly. He was aware that, even though he technically outranked Cheng Shao, the Death Commando was a man used to being obeyed by all but the most senior officers. "May I assume that you have already worked out a plan of battle?"

Cheng eyed him carefully, as though seeking derision in the *Sang-shao's* politely worded reply.

"Yes, I have, *Sang-shao.*" There was a trace of a threat in his voice, like the first whirr of a rattlesnake's tail. "Look at this map, and I shall lay it out for you."

Twelve hours later, Cheng Shao glanced at the time display set into the back of his combat suit's heavy gauntlet. The faintly back-lit numbers read 0359. In one minute his phase of the operation would begin.

The black-on-gray numbers flicked over to 0400. Shao nodded, then, with a slight motion, signaled his commandos to move out. Silently, like flickering shadows, the four men and two women ghosted rapidly out of the gloom toward the three-meter-high chain-link fence surrounding the compound. Each was armed with a heavy blazer carbine. Most carried bulky satchels or rucksacks. One young man cradled a power compound crossbow in his arms. The archaic weapon had paradoxically been fitted with a complex night sight and infrared targeting laser.

Shao also knew that the youth coated his arrows' razor-sharp points with a concentrated form of sea wasp venom.

As the commandos reached the fence, one of the nearly invisible forms knelt and began cutting the wire with a small laser torch. Soon she had opened a gap in the barrier large enough for her companions to wriggle through. Shao watched as his warriors slipped silently into the compound, each fanning out toward his or her respective targets. Two of them had been assigned to cripple or destroy each of the massive *Overlord* Class DropShips that sat arrogantly in the middle of the spaceport's landing stage. Shao wanted to make sure that both of the enormous vessels were out of commission when Christobal's men attacked the spaceport. If the DropShips were operational, their massive firepower might be employed against the attacking MacCarrons' Armored Cavalry BattleMechs. Or, if the fight went against the enemy, the *Overlord*s might be employed to transport the enemy force away to some distant location from which they might initiate a guerrilla campaign of their own. Shao wanted a clean victory, and to have it, those ships had to be disabled or destroyed.

Shao slipped from his shelter in a doorway opposite the gap in the fence and slithered through the opening. Through the night-vision goggles strapped to his eyes, he saw the crossbow-armed commando drop to one knee and point his weapon across the compound. A few score meters away, a young man in an SLDF uniform collapsed silently to the ferrocrete pavement, an arrow jutting from his chest. Far too many soldiers nowadays trusted in their heavy ballistic armor to protect them from injury and death, but a solid, non-deforming penetrator, like a thick, razor-sharp arrowhead, could slice through even the thickest ballistic cloth into the flesh. The deadly neurotoxin coating the weapon's point guaranteed that the youth would not survive to learn of his error.

Shao turned away, caring as little for the dead Light Horseman as he might for an ant he had inadvertently squashed underfoot, and continued his personal mission. When Nessa Ament's body had been found, half her chest shot away by soft-nosed slugs, he had vowed to avenge her, not upon the men who had ended her life, but upon the man who had ordered her death.

He flitted from shadow to shadow, avoiding pools of light. He had studied the compound for so many hours that he could have drawn a sketch of the place by hand, and not been more than a meter off on a building's location. He knew exactly which one was being used as officers' quarters. He intended to go in there and kill General Edwin Amis.

San-ben-bing Akai Yeng stepped over the rapidly stiffening corpse of the Light Horseman who had stood guard duty at the foot of the massive, egg-shaped DropShip's personnel loading ramp. Above Yeng's head, dark blue letters arrogantly proclaimed, "You are now entering Red Leg country." She was aware enough of the Light Horse's history and subculture to know that the vessel's name, *Red Legs*, was a direct reference to horse-mounted dragoons of Terra's ancient past.

Yeng and her partner, *Shia-ben-bing* Tolland Ou,

darted up the ramp and made their way quickly toward the vessel's engineering section. Less than a kilometer away, a second team of Death Commandos began a similar assault on the second *Overlord*. As the pair entered the vessel's engine room, a technician who had been dozing in his seat came fully and unexpectedly awake. Before either Death Commando could react, the man lashed out, smashing his palm down on a large red button in the center of the console. A rapid, deep-toned raucous honk sounded throughout the ship.

Yeng spat a curse. Bringing up her double-barreled laser carbine, she settled the sights over the technician's abdomen. Even as she fired, the man, who seemed to be blessed with unnaturally quick reactions, drew a heavy automatic pistol from his side holster. Before he could aim the weapon, her twin laser blasts took him in the chest, less than a centimeter apart. He dropped to the steel deck, twitching as his life swiftly faded away. But out in the passageway, the alarm horn continued to shriek.

Leaving Ou to watch the door, Yeng set about placing the heavy demolition charges they had brought with them. She set the first of the big, twenty-kilo blocks of pentaglycerine against the primary fuel intake unit and set the detonator. A tiny LED in the unit's face glowed red. In five minutes, the charge would go off, destroying the intake system and igniting the DropShip's fuel bunkers. Even if the ship's fuel did not go up in a sympathetic detonation, the engine room would be wrecked.

The second demolition charge was placed against the vessel's primary power converter. Although it was unlikely for the *Red Legs*'s engine to survive the blast, Yeng believed in hedging her bets. The second charge would wreck the equipment that powered the DropShip's massive weapons system. Either way, the vessel would be finished as a combat asset.

A loud, flat snap from the hatchway behind her announced the arrival of the enemy ship's crewmen. Coolly, Tolland Ou aimed his blazer down the passageway and touched the firing stud. Again, the snapping discharge of the blazer, accompanied by the stink of ozone, filled the engineering space. In the passageway beyond, a soft thud was heard. Ou grinned slightly in satisfaction.

Yeng's smile was less satisfied and more grim. She knew that, if this way out of the engine room had just been cut off, the *Red Legs*'s crew would even now be moving to secure other exists. With a sigh, she brought her personal communicator on line and clicked her tongue against the roof of her mouth.

Tich-tich. Tich. Tich-tich-tich.

Cheng Shao nodded to himself as he heard the clicking sound in his communicator's earpiece. The static-break signal in a two-one-three pattern was the pre-arranged sign indicating that *San-ben-bing* Yeng had completed her mission. Such low-key messages had been in use for centuries, starting with the special operations forces of the late twentieth century on Terra. The clicks and pops minimized the risk of an enemy overhearing the transmission of the signal, and prevented him from understanding the message even if he did.

A similar series of clicks had come in a few sec-

onds earlier from *Si-ben-bing* Mohr's team aboard the
Light Horse DropShip *Hussar*. In less than five minutes, both 'Mech-haulers would suffer catastrophic
explosions in their engineering plants. If the situation
dictated, Shao could also detonate the carefully
planted demolition charges with the radio control
unit in a pouch at his hip.

Shao peered carefully around the corner of the storage shed in whose shadow he had been concealing
himself. Not far away stood a pair of Light Horse
infantrymen clad in heavy armored vests, holding
Magna laser rifles at the ready. The door behind the
infantrymen was the entrance to Shao's objective,
the structure that careful, day-by-day surveillance
of the starport had revealed to be the Light Horse
officers' quarters.

A few moments before he had received Akai
Yeng's "mission completed" signal, a rumble of activity had rolled across the spaceport. Lights had
come on in all of the buildings designated as bar-
racks, and a jeep filled with armed men had careened
across the tarmac only a few meters from Shao's hiding place. The vehicle sped by, its occupants paying
him no notice, and headed out across the landing
stage. Though he had no word from his men to prove
him correct, Cheng Shao surmised that at least one
of the teams attacking the DropShips had been detected. In a few more minutes, the Light Horse would
be on full alert. If he was going to move, it would
have to be now.

Drawing his sidearm, he sighted over the weapon's
bulky integral sound suppressor, aligning the tritium-
coated sights with the far sentry's throat. At less than

thirty meters, there was no possibility of a missed shot. The heavy automatic pistol coughed harshly as he squeezed the trigger. The sentry's eyes grew momentarily wide in surprise before closing forever. Shao switched targets and fired again even before his first victim's laser rifle had clattered to the ground.

Swiftly, smoothly, Shao moved from the concealing shadow of the storage shed, stepping over the guards' corpses as he would a pair of fallen logs in his path. Time was of the essence. He knew he had only a few more minutes before he would be discovered. A door swung open in the corridor ahead of him. Reacting on instinct, Shao aimed and fired. The bullet took the half-dressed man high in the chest and punched him back into the room. An alarmed shout rang out. A pair of warriors appeared, each brandishing drawn handguns. Shao considered retreating, but that option was closed for him by the squeal of tires as a jeep lurched to a halt just outside the door.

With a yell of hatred, Shao charged the pistol-armed men. Both fell with heavy hollow-point slugs from his silenced pistol in their chests. A weapon boomed in the corridor behind him, and a blow like a sledgehammer crashed into Shao's back. He fell heavily to the floor, recovered, and flipped onto his back to meet the new threat. A gray-haired warrior, uncharacteristically armed with an old-fashioned, pump-action shotgun, its barrel sawed off to less than forty-five centimeters, was pointing the weapon down the corridor. Shao brought up his pistol, knowing he was about to die, but determined to take just one more enemy of House Liao with him.

The enemy trooper fired first. A heavy load of buckshot missed Shao's armored vest, tearing into his lower abdomen. Shock slammed down like a wall of iron between Shao's mind and the agonizing pain of the horrid, gaping wound. His pistol fell from his hand.

Fighting for breath, Shao reached painfully for the pouch on his left hip. The Light Horse warrior dashed up the corridor, his shotgun at the ready, but he was too late. Shao's hand closed over the black plastic box of the radio detonator. His fingers found and closed the tiny, shielded switch on the device's face.

A booming roar echoed across the compound, and a bright orange-white glare silhouetted the enemy trooper against the open door. A second explosion followed so closely as to be almost indistinguishable from the first.

Shao rested his head against the cool tile floor, gazing calmly up at the Light Horseman. The man, whose shoulder patch declared him to be a senior sergeant, lowered his weapon and knelt beside the fallen Death Commando. In a display of compassion that might be thought hypocritical by one who had not been raised in a warrior culture, as both Shao and his assailant had been, the man pulled a thick pressure bandage from a small pouch high on his combat harness.

A faint hiss escaped Shao's lips. The heavy lead shotgun pellets had so saturated his body that he could barely force enough air into his lungs to breathe, let alone speak. He mustered all his strength.

"No, Sergeant Young," he gasped out, reading the

nametape above the man's right breast pocket. "Save your bandage for one who may benefit from it."

Young ignored him and slapped the thick pad across the hole in Shao's belly.

Another man came into view. A bit younger than the Sergeant who labored over the wound he had inflicted, the newcomer had gray-shot brown hair and bright blue eyes. The single pip of a Star League general shone softly on his jacket collar.

Shao nodded once, let out a ragged, gasping laugh, and died.

28

Touchstone Spaceport, Milos
Xin Sheng Commonality
Capellan Confederation
22 March 3062

Lifting his *Thug*'s right arm, *Sang-shao* Christobal tapped the firing grip's trigger and speared a Light Horse *Mongoose* with a jagged bolt of artificial lightning. The light recon 'Mech staggered under the heavy impact of charged particles. As the pilot recovered his balance, Christobal could see the endo-steel framework of the 'Mech glowing faintly where the PPC blast had burned through the relatively thin armor.

Valiantly, the Light Horse warrior tried to reply, triggering all three medium lasers. The verdant threads of energy spattered against the *Thug*'s thick hide, leaving only shallow pings in the assault

'Mech's heavy armor. An insistent tone in his ears told Christobal that his short-range missile packs had locked on to the enemy 'Mech. The Capellan warrior thumbed the launch button. Twelve anti-armor warheads leapt corkscrewing from his machine's torso-mounted launchers. When the strobing explosions faded, the *Mongoose* lay on the tarmac in smoking ruins.

Glancing at his tactical monitor, Christobal saw the 'Mechs of his First and Second Battalions swarming across the spaceport fence. His Third Battalion was out of the instrument's limited range. Christobal had taken a page from his opponent's tactical handbook and had divided his force in the face of the enemy. His Third Battalion was making its way around the southern boundary of the facility, in a rapid, flanking movement.

He briefly considered trying to contact Cheng Shao one more time, but cast the notion aside. The Death Commando had not answered his previous hails, which meant he was probably dead. It looked as though Shao had completed his final mission. One *Overlord* lay in a still-burning heap of twisted metal, gutted by the explosion that had signaled Christobal to open the second phase of the operation. Sensors indicated that the other heavy 'Mech transport was so badly crippled that she would probably never fly again.

An ape-like *Kintaro* stepped from the shadows of a shell-scarred hangar, showering Christobal's *Thug* with a mixture of long- and short-range missiles. One of the high-explosive armor-piercing warheads detonated against the assault 'Mech's outward sloping

cockpit, jarring Christobal and leaving him with ringing ears. He was still trying to shake the cobwebs
out of his head when the Light Horseman laced his
'Mech's legs and right arm with coruscating beams
of laser fire.

Christobal recovered and repaid the enemy warrior
stroke for stroke, though the *Thug*'s attacks were far
more telling. The *Kintaro* reeled as twin PPC blasts
ate into its left thigh and shoulder. Armor plates
shattered into high-velocity shrapnel as hollow-
charge missile warheads impacted against every section of the Light Horse machine's armor. Heat
flooded into the *Thug*'s cockpit, but began to bleed
away rapidly as the 'Mech's high-efficiency heat
sinks, aided by the cold winter air, kicked in.

Though not enough to put the *Kintaro* out of the
fight, the generalized damage was sufficient to rattle
the fifty-five-ton 'Mech's pilot. His answering blasts of
laser fire cut deep scores in the ferrocrete fifteen meters
behind Christobal's 'Mech. Only four of the seventeen
missiles volleyed from the Light Horseman's multiple
launch racks found their intended target. The rest
scattered across the spaceport compound.

Urging his ponderous mount into a lurching run,
Christobal circled the *Kintaro* to his right. The Light
Horseman was forced to turn with him, in order to
protect his much-abused left side. Conserving his
fire, Christobal picked his shots, sending a blast of
PPC fire into the wide-hipped enemy 'Mech's knee.
A second stroke of man-made lightning ripped into
the already weakened chest armor, peeling it back
like the skin of an orange.

The *Kintaro* tried to reply, but Christobal hammered the lighter machine again and again until its pilot gave up and ejected from his 'Mech.

The Capellan House warrior searched his displays for another target, and found a *Cauldron-Born* bearing the flaming bronco crest of the Nineteenth Cavalry Regiment. He blasted the OmniMech, seized from the now-annihilated Smoke Jaguars on Huntress, with PPC fire, but the big Clan machine seemed to shrug the damage off.

The odd, birdlike 'Mech turned and extended its right arm, which ended in the gaping maw of a gun barrel, toward Christobal's *Thug*. A flat actinic flash ringed the muzzle. A massive slug of nickel-iron sped across the spaceport to smash into the Capellan 'Mech's left elbow.

While every foeman must be considered a threat, the *Cauldron-Born* was far more threatening than either of Christobal's prior opponents. Its heavier armor and deadly, Clan-designed weapons placed it on a level with his *Thug*, if not a step or two higher. Taking careful aim at the *Cauldron-Born*'s backward-acting knee joint, Christobal squeezed off a blast from his right PPC, waited a few temperature-quickened heartbeats until the heat sinks began to bring the oven-like atmosphere in his cockpit under control, then touched off a shower of missiles against the Light Horse machine.

The brilliant blue streak of energy missed the *Cauldron-Born*'s knee joint, instead scorching through the big 'Mech's torso armor just below the boxy long-range missile launcher. The Light Horse machine barely seemed to notice the attack, but replied with yet another basketball-sized slug from its Gauss rifle, following the devastating attack with a long, chattering burst of autocannon fire and a volley of laser darts.

Indicators began to light up Christobal's 'Mech Status Display, showing that all sections of his *Thug*'s frontal armor had taken damage.

Before he could call for help or withdraw, a hulking shadow moved into his peripheral vision. Glancing to the right, he saw a *Cataphract*, the triangular McCarron's Armored Cavalry crest painted just below its out-thrust cockpit, unleash a blast of autocannon fire at the enemy 'Mech.

The *Cauldron-Born* staggered under the hammering impact, recovered its balance, and showered the *Cataphract* with missiles and autocannon shells. Before the smoke of its volley cleared, the Light Horse Omni-Mech began walking backward, deeper into the spaceport, alternating its fire between the two Capellan 'Mechs besetting it. Christobal knew that, despite the Clan-designed 'Mech's inherent toughness, the *Cauldron-Born* must eventually fall or flee.

Christobal leveled his PPCs once again, blasting more armor from the Light Horseman's leg and torso. Gaps were beginning to show in the *Cauldron-Born*'s tough hide, and its steps were becoming less sure. But, like its namesake, it could absorb incredible amounts of damage before dying, as it proved by slamming a Gauss round into the *Thug*'s chest. A rolling burst of cannot fire and a pair of heavy short-range missiles followed the heavy metal pellet. By ill luck, or excellent aim, all three attacks smashed into the *Thug*'s torso.

Christobal's 'Mech began to tilt backward. Beneath

his feet the massive gyroscope started to whine like an aerospace fighter engine spooling up for launch, as it struggled against an axis moving rapidly off the vertical. Christobal yanked his control sticks back so hard that he nearly tore them from their mountings. He felt the heavy, jarring steps as his *Thug* began running backward in an attempt to maintain its balance. It failed. The off-balance machine stumbled and fell with a shattering impact. Christobal heard his teeth click together. The coppery taste of blood filled his mouth. A sharp pain ran along his jaw, somewhat dulled by the shock of the *Thug*'s fall. Christobal realized that he had bitten his tongue.

A white-hot, blazing anger set in. Furiously, he worked the controls, bringing his fallen 'Mech to its knees. The *Cauldron-Born* was nowhere in sight, but the Capellan *Cataphract* that had come to his aid stood, wreathed in flames, exactly where he had last seen it. The bodies of infantrymen wearing Light Horse uniforms lay scattered around its feet. One clutched an empty short-range missile launcher.

"Dammit," Christobal said aloud, looking at the faint blush of pink coming into the snow-laden western sky. "The sun's going to be up in a couple of hours." Daylight would allow the Eridani Light Horse to bring their superior firepower to bear with less chance of hitting a friendly unit by mistake.

"Forge ahead!"

The joyous shout cut across the MAC's comm channel like a sword through paper. Christobal levered his *Thug* to its feet with an inarticulate yell. The battle cry was the prearranged signal indicating that Third Battalion had joined the fray.

On his tactical monitor, Christobal could see the red triangles marking the Light Horse positions begin to fold back in an attempt to meet the new threat, while still opposing the thrust by his First and Second Battalions. One of the large scarlet rectangles representing a *Leopard* Class DropShip winked out as three of his warriors poured the combined firepower of their BattleMechs into the spacecraft's slab sides. Through his viewscreen, Christobal could see a thick column of oily black smoke rising above the destroyed *Leopard*.

Though his 'Mech had suffered badly in the skirmish with the Light Horse *Cauldron-Born*, he was not out of the battle. He pushed the control sticks forward and urged his mechanical mount into a low, lumbering trot.

As he passed a shot-scarred storage building, a pair of short-range missiles lanced out of a snow-shrouded doorway. The projectiles hissed past his *Thug*'s face like angry, rocket-propelled wasps and burst against the side of another building, covering it with burning napalm. A sudden hatred flared in him. Christobal savaged the front of the warehouse with paired blasts from his PPCs. When the explosions faded, nothing moved in the doorway.

A Light Horse 'Mech, a Kurita-built *Wolf Trap*, stepped around the corner of an intact hangar. Before the enemy MechWarrior could bring his deadly dual-purpose autocannon into play, Christobal ripped deep smoking gashes into the enemy's left side, slagging armor and destroying one of the paired lasers nestled beneath the *Wolf Trap*'s ribs.

The enemy machine rocked back on its heels. As a

testimony to the training given the Light Horsemen, the 'Mech did not fall, but dropped to one knee, like a prize fighter who had taken a particularly heavy blow. The enemy warrior, who must have been flung around inside his cockpit like a die in a gambler's cup, launched a flight of missiles at Christobal's 'Mech. The volley went wild. The range had been too short for the missiles to achieve a target lock. But the range was nearly perfect for the heavy Class 10 autocannon mounted at the *Wolf Trap*'s right arm. The weapon coughed, spitting out a stream of projectiles that ate deep into the *Thug*'s already damaged left arm.

More warning lights came on in the cockpit as the armor-piercing discarding-sabot cannon rounds shattered armor plating. Another hit, and he would lose the arm.

Ignoring the wave of heat flooding into his cockpit, Christobal blasted the *Wolf Trap* with every weapon in his 'Mech's arsenal. The enemy machine's chest burst outward as unexpended cannon shells and long-range missiles exploded. The *Wolf Trap* fell onto its face, half of its chest eaten away by the detonation of its magazines. Its pilot did not escape.

Before Christobal had the opportunity to savor his victory, two blows that hit like a gigantic double triphammer smashed his *Thug* to its knees. The 'Mech Status Display showed that the assault 'Mech's right torso had been stripped of its armor, exposing its delicate internal components to enemy fire.

Looking up, he saw a shot-riddled *Cauldron-Born*, the same 'Mech that had escaped him earlier, standing alongside a taller *Cyclops*. The second machine bore a silver horse prancing against a black background on its boxy torso. The words "Boots and Saddles!" painted on the missile launchers seemed to glow in the dim morning light.

The *Cauldron-Born* fired another Gauss slug that smashed the *Thug*'s right knee. Cannon shells and missiles peppered its chest and hips, while a volley of laser pulses ate deep into the 'Mech's exposed endo-steel ribs. A scarlet indicator, and a sudden temperature spike, told of the destruction of a heat sink.

Though some of them were piloting Clan Omni-Mechs, the Light Horsemen didn't fight according to Clan rules of engagement. The *Cyclops* got involved in the fight, blasting armor away from the *Thug*'s left leg and breast with its heavy, powerful Gauss rifle.

A sharp, squealing tone screamed in Christobal's ears, telling of a missile lock. The HUD's threat indicator told the tale. The *Cyclops* had locked both of its missile launchers onto Christobal's battered *Thug*.

In a last desperate bid for survival, Christobal reached above his head and yanked hard on a pair of yellow- and black-striped handles. The ejection seat and the *Cyclops* fired in the same instant.

Sang-shao Samuel Christobal awoke a few hours later, unable to move, his right arm and leg aching as though they were on fire.

"Ah, you're awake," a pleasant tenor voice said. A second later, a homely young man in the white smock of a medical corpsman leaned over and adjusted the pillow beneath Christobal's head.

"Wh . . . Where . . . ?" His voice sounded like the rasp of an asthmatic crow.

"Where are you?" the medic finished for him. A faint, sad smile crossed his face. "You're in an aid station. You're pretty shot up, but you're alive." The medic held a plastic cup with a straw attached to Christobal's mouth, allowing him to drink some of the tepid water.

"Prisoner?"

"Yes, I'm afraid you are." The boy actually seemed sympathetic to his plight.

"My men?" Christobal asked. His voice gradually became clearer.

"I'm sorry, *Sang-shao*, I don't know too much about that." The lie in the boy's voice was evident.

"Well, you're awake at last, hmm?" another voice intoned. Turning his head, Christobal saw a gray-bearded gentleman take a seat on a low stool next to his bed. "I'm Doctor Fuehl. How do you feel, *Sang-shao*?"

"Can't move," he replied. "And my arm and leg hurt like hell."

"I know they do, *Sang-shao*," the surgeon said somberly. "But what you're feeling is called phantom pain."

Coldness settled into Christobal's heart. He knew the term.

"You were badly wounded when they brought you in here," Fuehl continued. "Your right arm and leg were mangled beyond repair. We had to amputate them to save your life. I've seen it before. Sometimes the cockpit canopy doesn't blow away completely, and it just rips the pilot to shreds. You were lucky to survive."

"Lucky, Doctor?" Christobal felt a deep black abyss open in his soul. His attack had failed. That much was evident from the fact that he was a prisoner and was being cared for in what was obviously a permanent building, as opposed to a mobile aid station or field hospital. All his life, he had been a MechWarrior. Now he was a helpless cripple in the hands of his enemies. "No, I don't see it that way."

29

Touchstone Spaceport, Milos
Xin Sheng Commonality
Capellan Confederation
22 March 3062

Smoke rose from the burned-out hulks of destroyed BattleMechs and armored fighting vehicles, casting a pall over the Touchstone spaceport. Here and there, tongues of flame still flickered within the hull of a wrecked war machine. From his position in the doorway of the ComStar hyperpulse generator station, Ed Amis watched as men clad in green Eridani Light Horse combat fatigues moved among the fallen 'Mechs and shattered tanks carrying medical kits, cutting torches, and poncho-shrouded stretchers.

Mercifully, perhaps, it had begun snowing heavily just as the fight for the spaceport was winding down. The heavy white flakes were rapidly coating the blackened, twisted metal shapes littering the spaceport tarmac, concealing the awful price that had been paid for the facility.

His beloved Light Horse had once again proved its mettle in combat, but the cost had been high. Many of the BattleMechs he had brought with him to Milos were either destroyed or in need of major repairs. Most of his conventional armor and most of his infantrymen were out of action. Infantry losses had been particularly high.

The Light Horse had been taken by surprise, something not often accomplished by an enemy. The Capellan commander had sent one battalion around the city to strike into the Light Horse's flank and rear while they were heavily engaged with the other two MAC battalions. The surprise attack had nearly worked. The third battalion hit the Light Horse's right flank a little after dawn, throwing the line into confusion. The fight, which had been, up until then, a normal, orderly 'Mech battle at close quarters, degenerated into a series of quick, dirty slugging matches, where no quarter was asked or given. Eventually, the Light Horse's numbers prevailed, but the fight was too near a thing for Amis's comfort.

Christobal's regiment had withdrawn, leaving a good portion of their strength on the field, including *Sang-shao* Samuel Christobal. Amis shivered at the thought of Christobal lying in the port hospital. Doctor Fuehl had struggled against time, trying to save first Christobal's arm and leg, then his life. Though he knew Christobal would not blame either the doctor or himself, Amis felt at least partly responsible for the crippling injuries the Capellan had suffered. He had helped inflict those wounds. It had been his *Cyclops*, along with Captain Thomas Graeme's *Cauldron-Born*, that had shot the Capellan's *Thug* to pieces, forcing him to eject through a shattered canopy. The thought of a valiant man lying in a hospital bed, condemned to a life of useless frustration after having commanded some of the most elite warriors in the field, left Amis feeling sick. Was that what the fates of battle had in store for him?

"General, we're almost ready to begin transmission."

Amis was jerked out of his gloomy reverie. He turned to face the young ComStar technician. Gone were the robes and the trappings of techno-religion that had marked the order for so long. The youth was clad in a simple tunic and pants cut from light blue fabric.

"All right, son." Amis nodded at the clear-faced youngster and followed him inside the station.

Inside, there were still a few articles that reminded him of the Order's techno-religious origins. A framed picture of Jerome Blake, founder of the order and once revered almost as a god, hung on the far wall of the station's public waiting room, and the odd star-disk emblem of the order still graced the partition behind the counter at which one composed and received messages.

A man stood behind this counter, his gray, wispy hair lying in an unruly mat atop his bullet-shaped skull. He smiled at Amis, and indicated a small, sound-proof room where the general might record his message.

"General Sortek," he began, speaking into a table-top device that would record, compress, and encode his message for transmission. "This morning, Task Force Dagger engaged a full regiment of Capellan troops in a close-quarters battle for the Touchstone spaceport. We were able to hold on to the facility and to drive the enemy back with heavy losses. But Task Force Dagger took substantial losses, particularly of infantry and conventional armor assets.

"I fear the enemy is regrouping and may launch another attack on the spaceport at any time. Further, I fear that the enemy command structure may be planning a major assault against Task Force Dagger, with the intent of destroying this task force or driving us off-planet.

"I believe we can hold out against the Capellan forces on-planet, but we stand little chance of maintaining our position if the enemy sends a larger counter-invasion force against us.

"I respectfully submit that you dispatch the Twenty-first Striker Regiment to Milos to reinforce our positions here.

"I await your response. Edwin Amis, Commander, Eridani Light Horse."

A touch of a button popped a tiny disk from the top of the recording device. Amis took the small, rainbow-glistening circle to the tech behind the counter, who accepted it without a word and disappeared behind the partition.

Due to the time lag in interstellar communications, it was several hours before Amis had his answer.

"General Amis, I have no further support to send you. The Twenty-first Striker Regiment is no longer on Kittery. It has been redeployed to fall-back positions within the St. Ives Compact. The fighting in the

Compact has bogged down, and, to prevent it from spreading any wider, the SLDF is dialing back its response a couple of notches.

"Thus, you are hereby ordered to make a show of preparing a defensive perimeter around the spaceport. Instead, you will make your regiments ready to board their DropShips and evacuate Milos. I will be dispatching your JumpShips within the hour."

Amis's mouth hung open in shock. General Sortek was ordering him to retreat from a planet for which the Eridani Light Horse had paid in blood. With a snarl of fury, he slapped the Stop button on the record/playback device, ejected the disk, and, resisting the impulse to fling the delicate plastic recording across the room, rammed a blank disk into the recorder.

"General Sortek, I don't give a rat's behind about the fighting in St. Ives. I care about my brigade. My troopers gave their lives to take Milos, and now what? Now you're ordering me to pull out and give it back to the Capellans?

"No, sir. I demand . . ." Amis paused, backed the disk up a bit, and started again. "I strongly urge you to release the Twenty-first Striker to me and allow them to come to Milos as reinforcements."

By the time his message had been formatted and sent, General Amis had exercised his will and forced his anger to dissipate. He knew that it did little good to yell at superiors, even when—especially when—those superiors believed they were doing the right thing. Despite the four-hour time lag, there was a burning resentment in his heart as he flopped disgustedly into the padded chair in the playback room.

For a few seconds, he glared at the tiny disk, as though daring it to contain confirmation of the recall order.

When he finally played General Sortek's reply, he could almost touch the barely restrained anger and frustration in his voice.

"General Amis, your recall order has been confirmed.

"The SLCA appreciates the sacrifice your men have made, but I must insist that you withdraw from Milos. Frankly, it has become too expensive in terms of lives, machines, and assets to maintain a force on a planet that is so unexpectedly pro-Capellan. I do not want to waste any more of your men, General, on a world we would have to hold by force anyway.

"We have established a truce with the Capellan Confederation to allow your troops to be evacuated from the planet. You will be permitted to take all your arms, equipment, and personnel with you. You must leave your prisoners, if any. I am told that any of your people being held by the Capellans will likewise be returned to you before you dust off.

"The *Gettysburg* and the rest of your JumpShips are enroute to you even as I send this message."

Sortek paused for a few heartbeats, making Amis believe that the recording had run out.

"General Amis, if you are not alone now, please ask all others to leave the room."

Again, the recording paused.

"General, Precentor Martial Davion is receiving far too much pressure from certain members of the Star League Council to be able to justify intensifying or prolonging your mission by releasing your reserves.

"I'm sorry, General, but you must withdraw from Milos."

There followed a long pause, then Sortek began to speak again. Something in his tone gave Amis the impression that he was concerned about security. "The Precentor Martial doesn't trust the Capellans, I don't know if anybody does at this point. In addition to your own JumpShips, we are dispatching the Com Guard WarShips *Hollings York* and *Avenging Sword* just in case Sun-Tzu tries anything stupid.

"Trust me, General, the Eridani Light Horse will have its chance to make the Capellans pay. Right now you're needed elsewhere."

For a few minutes, Ed Amis sat staring at the silent device. Then, with a shrug, he recorded his confirmation of the Precentor Martial's orders.

As he stepped out into his last morning on Milos, he looked at the lowering gray clouds and said softly, "Revenge isn't really part of the Light Horse way, General. But, you were right about one thing, one way or another, we always take care of our own."

About the Author

THOMAS S. GRESSMAN lives with his wife, Brenda, in the foothills of western Pennsylvania. When not writing, he divides his time between worship and youth ministries, leathercrafting, and living history reenactments.

Dagger Point is his fourth BattleTech® novel. His three previous novels were *The Hunters*, *Sword and Fire*, and *Shadows of War*, which were published as part of the Twilight of the Clans series by Roc Books.

Turn the page for a preview of the
next exciting BattleTech novel

Illusions of Victory

by Loren L. Coleman

Solaris Spaceport, International Zone
Solaris City, Solaris VII
Freedom Theater, Lyran Alliance
21 September 3059

The line of steerage passengers shuffled out of the DropShip and slowly along the covered gantry, winding its way into the West Terminal of Solaris City Spaceport. Behind the passengers the large *Monarch* Class vessel sat steaming on the tarmac as residual heat from reentry into atmosphere fought a short-lived battle against the gray drizzle falling from the overcast sky. The heat made the air humid and rank with the scents of scorched ferrocrete and human sweat. People cursed as a sharp wind blew rain in under the lip of the gantry overhang. The gust was biting and cruel, bringing no true relief. Muttering under their breaths, the steerage passengers pressed forward, anxious to gain the protection of the terminal, ignoring the dark glances from those in front of them while casting similar glances at those behind.

This was how Michael Searcy arrived on Solaris

VII, the Game World. Young and eager. And *dispossessed*.

He threaded his way through the tight knot of people who blocked the gantry exit, meeting relatives or asking the harried Monopole Line official posted there for directions available on any of several nearby signs. Once he stepped aside to let an elderly couple through, blocking the way for an impatient mother towing three wrangling children from bustling into the pair. Then he, in turn, was pushed aside by security, who formed an instant corridor through the tangled mass of passengers to make way for a pair of agents escorting a man restrained by fetters and manacles. Michael spearheaded the rush to fill the void left by the departing security, breaking through the congestion at the arrival gate and into the terminal proper. To be immediately confronted by a *Gunslinger*.

The replica of the assault 'Mech stood three meters tall, only a fourth the size of the real eighty-five-ton war machine but still towering over the crowd. Several passengers had stopped to stare in awe, while Michael examined it for how well it replicated the real thing. As a MechWarrior—make that *former* MechWarrior—he'd had to study designs from all across the Inner Sphere as well as what was known of Clan 'Mechs.

The *Gunslinger* was a classic example of the war machines that ruled thirty-first-century battlefields. Built along humanoid lines, its broad-chested torso sat on thick, tree-stump legs. Both fully articulated arms ended in the wide-bore barrel of a Gauss rifle instead of hands. A pair of medium-class lasers protruded from large shoulder-mounted turrets on each side of the BattleMech's square-shaped head—for when combat got up close and personal.

One man and his wife stood nearby, gazing up at the *Gunslinger*'s head, where a bright red light glowed behind the cockpit viewscreen. It lent the 'Mech a menacing air, though Michael knew from experience that 'Mech cockpits were mostly dark, cramped spaces lit only by the muted glow of instrument panels, a few monitor screens, and various caution and warning lights that a 'Warrior never wanted to see. Theatrics, he decided about the red lighting. Just like the replica's metallic blue paint and the flashing sign dangling down from the ceiling. Flashing, the sign commanded: LET THE GAMES BEGIN.

"Wonder which 'Mech this is?" The wife was peering into the barrel of the left-arm Gauss rifle. She shuddered. "It certainly looks deadly enough."

"Don't know. *Crusader*, maybe?" her husband said. "Like the one in the match between Allard-Liao and Cox fighting those Skye Tigers a few years back . . ." He trailed off speculatively.

Michael wanted to laugh. If you shaved off twenty tons and reconfigured the offensive capability for missiles rather than direct-fire weaponry, then *maybe* by a wild stretch of imagination it might be a *Crusader*.

"It's a *Gunslinger*," he said quietly. "Designation is the Gun-One E-R-D. Eighty-five-ton assault class BattleMech. Twin Gauss rifles in the arms and quad lasers over the shoulders."

The couple looked at him with sudden interest, obviously noting his uniform. The white jacket and blue trousers piped with gold and red and sashed in dark blue were the dress of the Armed Forces of the Federated Commonwealth.

He had eschewed the cape, feeling out of place among steerage with such formal wear, but too proud to give up his uniform yet. Well, why not? He was allowed, as a reservist. His final discharge wouldn't be final for a few months yet. And his 'Mech *had* shut down from overheating, despite his former commander's charges of suspected pusilla-nimity—a fancy way of calling him a coward. He swallowed past the dryness the memory brought to his mouth.

"Lieutenant Michael Searcy," he said.

The man's wife obviously disliked what she saw and turned away with an audible sniff. "A Davion," she said.

That placed her and her husband as citizens of the Lyran Alliance. Despite the fact that both Inner Sphere states were ruled by a Steiner-Davion—Katrina leading the Alliance and Prince Victor the Commonwealth *née* Federated Suns—there was still bad blood between them. The Federated Suns half of the old Commonwealth resented the Alliance for letting Katrina pull out in a time of difficulty for Prince Victor. The Alliance, though, preferred Katrina and her more obvious embracing of her Steiner heritage. And then there was the resentment that the Lyrans had suffered during the Clan invasion while the Federated Suns had not, though of course there was no explaining that Prince Victor certainly was not to blame for *that*. And wasn't it Victor Steiner-Davion who even now was leading the Inner Sphere armies in a retaliatory strike against the Clans?

A fact that her husband had not forgotten, which bought Michael a small amount of grace. "AFFC, eh? You see any action against the Clans?"

Michael shrugged in a manner he hoped was self-effacing. "No, sir, I'm sorry to say. Just in the action during '57. I was"—he tried to keep his voice strong—"*let go* before the main offensive against Clan Smoke Jaguar began." Let go and lost his 'Mech—dispossessed—a fate worse than death for a MechWarrior.

But the man apparently did not want to hear about '57 and was even less interested in humility from a MechWarrior. Not here on Solaris VII. He grunted something noncommittal and allowed his wife to pull him around the *Gunslinger* replica to rejoin the crowd.

Leaning in to take a closer look at the 'Mech, Michael waited for the embarrassed flush to recede from his face. Lesson number one, he decided. People here *want* the flash and glamour. The theatrics. In a way that wasn't too different from the regular military. There, if you couldn't fit in with the unit, you had to show a strong performance that justified your actions. And Michael hadn't. Not enough time. One stroke of bad luck. Which is what had brought him to Solaris VII, the Game World. He glanced up again to the flashing sign.

LET THE GAMES BEGIN.

And they did, just the other side of the *Gunslinger* replica. A row of bank machines had been interspersed with betting terminals for the Solaris VII games, each terminal with a long line stretching away from it. Betting stubs littered the tiled floor, dashed hopes cast aside as people readied a new series of wagers. The custodians merely swept the stubs aside like so much dust, forming small drifts along the walls that young children took delight in kicking through.

Michael watched as the couple he'd tried to talk with joined a line at one computer to place their first bets. No care for the odds or even a review of the latest betting sheets. They were here to gamble and live the dark adventure that was supposedly life on Solaris VII. A place where the wars of the Inner Sphere were recreated for the pleasure of the viewing audience as BattleMechs were pitted against each other in the arenas. Michael shook his head, still unable to totally grasp the idea of a place where MechWarriors fought—and sometimes died—for *sport.* On no other planet in the Inner Sphere could this system work.

But then Solaris City itself was a microcosm of the entire Inner Sphere, each of its sections corresponding to one of the Great Houses. The spaceport was in the International Zone, which was the governmental center of the city. Most other duties changed hands at the sector borders. And even though the Great Houses had finally managed to resurrect the Star League in the face of the Clan invasion, here on Solaris VII the old rivalries and many new ones ran too deep to be so easily put aside.

Rivalries that were flaunted and exploited every night as the various House-affiliated stables fought each other in the arenas, each one clawing for position and prominence over the rest. And in the ratings.

Several monitors suspended over the bank of automated tellers and betting terminals showed clips from the latest bouts and promoted the evening's coming matches. Commentators talked over one another while the distant sounds of the battlefield added to the din.

Michael moved in toward one showing the latest box scores, fishing deep into a uniform pocket for his own betting receipts. The DropShip that brought him here had been fitted with impressive theaters for viewing the fights, even among steerage, and no one had been immune to the pull. Michael had hoped his four years in the AFFC might give him an edge. He crumpled up one ticket after another, missing the spreads by a few seconds with one fight, by a ton of armor on another. Finding a straight-up bet on the games wasn't easy; the simple win-lose wagers were reserved for long-odds upsets. It was how the entertainment commission kept a handle on the gambling, balancing out everything until only the savviest fight aficionados could hope to find the best wagers.

Michael knew this, but it hadn't kept him from trying. Nothing would ever keep him from _trying._ He found one winning bet among his tickets. He had taken the odds that Theodore Gross, the number-one ranked warrior on Solaris VII and this year's Champion, would successfully defend his title, but that the duel would run better than ten minutes. An eternity in one of Gross's matches, but it had paid off and recovered half of his initial stake.

And on the next monitor over, one of the screens

with louder accompanying sound, a Game World vidcaster was showing video footage and commenting on just that fight.

"Theodore Gross has never been put on the defensive so quickly, but that lucky shot found a flaw in his armor and managed to crack the shielding surrounding his fusion engine. The _Katana_ was bleeding waste heat. In the Jungle, that can often be a death sentence for a 'Mech."

Behind the 'caster, an outline of the huge, pyramidal Cathay arena was displayed onto a screen. Michael knew that it was filled with a lush tropical forest inside and maintained at temperatures that often ran a BattleMech at the edge of overheating. Yes, an engine hit would be bad in there. He also recognized the vidcaster as Julian Nero, one of the more popular commentators on Solaris VII. Nero usually commented fights at the Steiner Coliseum and was developing a reputation for infallible predictions. His "sure bets" often created immediate and rapid fluctuations from the odds-makers.

"Fortunately for the defending Champion, Stephen Neils got too eager. Once the younger warrior came within range of the _Katana_'s jump jets, allowing Gross to slip in behind him, it was all over." He winked at the screen. "Sorry, Stephen, I warned you." Back to business. "And now the Champion will be able to defend his title for the fourth time at the Steiner Stadium in two months. What can he expect from veteran Ervine Rebelke? We have this statement."

Nero's chiseled features were replaced with the rough visage of a battle-scarred veteran. Michael wondered what battle had caused the ugly scar running from upper brow down to the left ear—a real war, or an arena match. And was there really much difference between the two? Rebelke didn't think so as he sneered for the camera. "Theodore's good, but he's already past his prime. I'll bring the Drac down. In the Coliseum I'll *own* him."

So much smoke, Michael thought. Nero as well, who shook his head once as the camera cut back to him. "I certainly wish Mr. Rebelke luck. It promises to be a fast and brutal fight. That's for sure. The kind Theodore Gross enjoys, with his training in the Ishiyama Arena. A good evening's entertainment, for those of you with tickets for the live show.

"This from Julian Nero. Your man in the know."

The names and places were a buzz in the back of Michael Searcy's mind. Gross and Rebelke. Ishiyama and the Coliseum. Would he fight these men? In these arenas? It was why he was here, to try and recover some of his lost self-respect and prove to everyone his own skill. He knew he had it in him, if he got the chance to prove it.

Which meant first getting a dueling license, a sponsor, and a BattleMech. Even then he would have to fight his way up through the secondary arenas, before gaining equal footing with the likes of Gross and Rebelke in the Class Six Open Arenas of Solaris City. That could take years, and careers in the 'Mech games were too often measured in months. Months! Unless he could find a way to make himself a hot ticket. Coming to the Game World was no idle whim; Michael had researched it as thoroughly as possible. The ones who lasted in the games, in the ratings, were identifiable people—loved or loathed, that didn't matter. So long as people *remembered*.

Theatrics, yes. But on Solaris VII such details were important, and Michael had better get used to it.

Quickly.

Champion

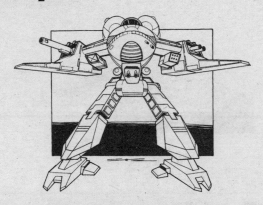

Wolf Trap

Cauldron-Born

Dervish

Thug

Cyclops

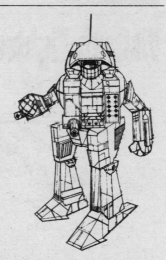

Overlord Class DropShip

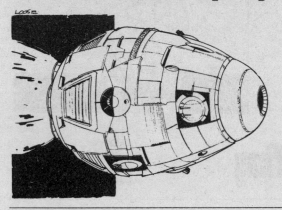

Visigoth Fighter

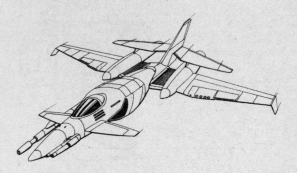

BATTLETECH®
Loren L. Coleman

❏**DOUBLE-BLIND** The Magistracy of Canopus has been the target of aggression by the Marian Hegemony, and in hiring Marcus and his gutsy band of can-do commandos, it hopes to retaliate. But the fact that the Canopians are armed with technology that is considered rare in the Periphery is the least of Marcus's problems. Marcus and his "Angels" will have to face the real force behind the hostilities—the religious cult known as Word of Blake. This fanatical group has a scheme deadly enough to trap even the amazing Avanti's Angels.... (0-451-45597-5—$5.99)

❏**BINDING FORCE** Aris Sung is a rising young star in House Hiritsu, noblest of the Warrior Houses that have sworn allegiance to the Capellan Confederation. The Sarna Supremacy, a newly formed power in the Chaos March, is giving the Confederation some trouble—and Aris and his Hiritsu comrades are chosen to give the Sarnans a harsh lesson in Capellan resolve. But there is far more to the mission than meets the eye—and unless Aris beats the odds in a race against time, all the ferro-fibrous armor in the galaxy won't be enough to save House Hiritsu from the high-explosive cross fire of intrigue and shifting loyalties.... (0-451-45604-1/$5.99)

Coming Next Month From Roc

Maggy Thomas

Broken Time

Kate Forsyth

The Cursed Towers

Book Three of the Witches of Eileanan

PENGUIN PUTNAM INC.
Online

Your Internet gateway to a virtual environment with hundreds of entertaining and enlightening books from Penguin Putnam Inc.

While you're there, get the latest buzz on the best authors and books around—

Tom Clancy, Patricia Cornwell, W.E.B. Griffin, Nora Roberts, William Gibson, Robin Cook, Brian Jacques, Catherine Coulter, Stephen King, Jacquelyn Mitchard, and many more!

**Penguin Putnam Online is located at
http://www.penguinputnam.com**

PENGUIN PUTNAM NEWS

Every month you'll get an inside look at our upcoming books and new features on our site. This is an ongoing effort to provide you with the most up-to-date information about our books and authors.

**Subscribe to Penguin Putnam News at
http://www.penguinputnam.com/ClubPPI**